The Chain
with
The Knowledge
and
Ready When You Are, Mr McGill

THE CHAIN

with
The Knowledge
and
Ready When You Are,
Mr McGill

JACK ROSENTHAL

faber and faber
LONDON · BOSTON

First published in 1986 by
Faber and Faber Limited
3 Queen Square London WC1N 3AU

Phototypeset by Wilmaset Birkenhead Wirral
Printed in Great Britain by
Redwood Burn Limited Trowbridge Wiltshire
All rights reserved

British Library Cataloguing in Publication Data

Rosenthal, Jack
The chain: three screenplays.
I. Title II. Rosenthal, Jack. Knowledge
III. Rosenthal, Jack. Ready when you are
Mr. McGill
822'.914   PR6068.07/
ISBN 0-571-14517-5

Library of Congress Cataloging-in-Publication Data

Rosenthal, Jack, 1931–
The chain with the knowledge and ready when you are,
Mr. McGill.
A play.
I. Title.
PR6068.078C46 1986   822'.914 86–10504
ISBN 0-571-14517-5 (pbk.)

CONTENTS

INTRODUCTION

It's not easy getting me out of the house. Come to that it almost takes an advanced course with the SAS to get me out of my *room*. It may be something to do with the childhood memory that going out to play usually meant getting home with fewer conkers than you went out with. But, personally, I blame Ernest Hemingway.

His 'Writing is the art of applying the seat of your pants to the seat of your chair' may be a touch smart-arse but, given a decent cushion, I suspect it's true.

For health reasons, I do risk one brisk walk a day. Roughly a hundred yards, to the fag shop and back. In pursuit of shameless, sensual pleasure, say once a fortnight, I take a leisurely limp to my local stationery shop. I lust after its computer keyboards, its inks and paints, paper-clips and Sellotape-dispensers, and ogle its reams of virgin A4. For the sake of respectability I buy a dozen ballpoints and go home again.

The rest of the time I'm at my desk, staring at the wall. Comforted in the belief that, even though I may not be writing anything, at least the seat of my pants is in the right place.

All this may (just) explain why I've grown increasingly interested in writing films not only to be shot on location, but with as many exteriors as possible, out on the streets: *they give me the only legitimate excuse I've got for going out to play without feeling guilty*. Once the shooting starts I can be out there, blinking in the daylight. Once it's over I can return to hibernation with an easy conscience and stare at the wall. There's only one occupational hazard – the temptation to start writing films about wallpaper.

The three screenplays in this collection all deal with people whose place of *work* is the streets. In the case of *The Knowledge*, which is about would-be London cab-drivers, the streets, themselves, are the work.

In all of them, the streets are intended to have a dramatic purpose beyond simply being settings for the action. They're supposed to complement the story and certainly to dictate the mood. A crowded street – or even a deserted one – is often worth a thousand close-ups. They should be as tangible as the characters who inhabit them. However eccentric or heightened those characters may be written, the job of the streets is to anchor them ankle-deep in reality.

Since home was where the scripts were born, and the streets was where they went out to play, I've divided my reflections on each of them accordingly.

Ready When You Are, Mr McGill

At Home

For a long time I'd pottered with the idea of writing a film about a day in the life of a film unit. Time and again, out on location with previous films I'd written, I'd watched different film crews share the same characteristics and the same incidents repeating themselves. The director's nonchalant smile of total command, while his eyeballs swivel in naked terror. The world-weary stoicism of the sound crew, treated by the camera crew as second-class citizens because 'this is a visual medium' (even though silent movies mimed their exit over half a century ago). The relentless ruination of take after take by passing house-wives, passing aircraft, passing clouds and resolutely immovable schoolkids. And the glorious day, usually about two-thirds of the way through the frenzied shooting schedule, when, as though by tradition, everybody's mind suddenly goes blank through raw exhaustion. No one knows what shot they're shooting, what film they're making, what their mother's name is or what the hell they're all doing in the middle of nowhere, in the rain.

The first hint that today's that day is when the director doesn't know whether to yell 'Action!' or 'Cut!' and yells both. Though not necessarily in that order.

Like most ideas, it was so far only *half* an idea. A framework. The second half had, in fact, been peeping back at me from behind a peeling seam of wallpaper for just as long. So obvious I just hadn't noticed. It was the thought of writing a screenplay about an 'extra' – one of the industry's part-time actors who may never have a line to speak but who appear in more films than John Wayne.

They, too, had kept me enthralled on my previous outings. They, too, shared common characteristics with the rest of their tribe. Their professional rivalry over who has how many lines to speak. The 'building' of their roles to include sneezing or coughing or simply 'reacting'. Quoting the Equity Rules better than the shop steward. Swapping starrier showbiz gossip than Louella Parsons. Sniffing the catering van on its way, like ageing Bisto Kids, before it had even set off. Being treated with irritated condescension by everybody else. And always, always, coming back for more.

It finally dawned on me that if a film director is half an idea, and a film extra is half an idea, perhaps if I put the two together. . . ?

The resulting story revolves around the two of them, dramatizing the inevitable backstage conflict that simmers in every show: which matters most – getting it right or sparing the feelings, and dignity, of anyone getting it wrong? And what's a show, anyway? Real Life getting on with it, or Art faffing about? The mongrel, in the last scene, has the last word. So to speak.

Granada TV producer Mike Dunlop commissioned the screenplay with Mike Newell to direct it. Newell read the script in my living room. I like to think I remember him licking his lips.

In the Streets

Mike Newell cast Jack Shepherd as the director – and then did the most heroic thing I've ever known a director do. Bravely assuming that the character was based (at least, in part) on himself, and since the film seemingly mattered more to him than his own feelings, he got Jack to study him at work on his current film. Warts, burgeoning hysteria, popping ulcers and all. Jack's performance was rewardingly superb; and Joe Black, as the extra, gave the performance of his life.

By its nature, each day's filming – of a film within a film –

wasn't just confusing. It was like a Chinese Box made of mirrors. When Mike barked at the lighting cameraman did he mean the real one (who looked like an actor) – or the pretend one (who looked like a cameraman)? When the First Assistant screamed at gawping housewives to shut up, did he mean the ones from the extras' coach or the ones on their way to Sainsbury's? When the wardrobe girl burst into tears was it because her boyfriend had upset her or because it said so in the script?

It all reached a climax when Mike asked the (actual) make-up girl to give the (fictional) sound recordist a dewdrop on the end of his nose. The real sound recordist heard the instruction and bitterly objected on the grounds of defamation of character, and convened a Sound Department meeting to discuss the withdrawal of labour. The real cameraman, who'd spent half his career trying to sniff dewdrops back up his nostril, had no such scruples, and it was *his* counterpart's nose that got the glycerine.

Somehow we got to the last shot in the schedule without either the unit or the actors going on strike, or even going mad. The last shot was to be of the dog cocking its leg. The lights were switched on, celluloid and tape began to roll, the clapperboard clapped, Mike whispered 'Action!' and the dog-handler let go of the dog. It ambled up to the whitewashed wall it was supposed to pee on, sniffed and stood there, all four legs rooted to the ground. After a couple of lifetimes, Mike sighed 'Cut!' The whole process was repeated over and over again, taking more takes than any other set-up in the film. And still the dog refused to pee in public. With dusk beginning to fall, he was fired for a less continent understudy, who gave his all for his Art.

The Knowledge

At Home

The phone rang. The voice at the other end introduced itself as Bob Brooks, an American director with an almost endless string of award-winning TV commercials to his name. He'd lived and worked in London for many years – and now wanted to make a TV film which would be his 'tribute' to his adopted city. And he had an idea: the Knowledge, which is the process by which every London cab-driver achieves his licence, and which is unique to London. Would I be interested?

We met, talked about it, and agreed it sounded a fascinating idea. Or – as usual – *half* a fascinating idea. I took a cab back home to sit and worry about it in comfort, and a few weeks later, the (once again, embarrassingly obvious) second half shyly suggested itself. It was simply to people the story with characters, who, in doing the Knowledge, would achieve some glimmering of *self*-knowledge.

Bob and I gathered a dozen cabbies around my kitchen table. They told us Knowledge-Boy anecdotes, some funny, some sad, but most of all they gave us a taste, a feel and an insight into their closed world. A few dozen cans of beer later, the idea felt more than fascinating, it felt irresistible. We were hooked. Round about midnight, we began to feel that the Knowledge was the Secret of Life. The Holy Grail had become a little shiny, oval Green Badge. I don't know what Bob's innermost ambition in life had been till then (mine was to have a fish-and-chip shop), but I've a suspicion that, starting that night, both of us began to silently nurse a new one. Writing *The Knowledge* was hard, but compared to *taking* it, it was child's play. I settled for that.

Producer Verity Lambert of Euston Films saw the gleam in our eyes, and hired us both.

On the Streets

A good location manager is vital to a film. He or she has to find locations that are not only dramatically precise and visually telling, as 'manageable' as possible from all the interference *Ready When You Are, Mr McGill* illustrates, but that are also convenient for car-parks, phones and . . . well, conveniences. It isn't easy. To find locations that satisfy all these requirements as well as being within 29,000 miles of the author's home seems somehow always out of the question.

The Knowledge was filmed in scores of streets all over London. None of them mine. This gave me the choice of leaving home in the rush hour, missing an hour's shooting, and arriving just in time to see some extra wolfing breakfast's last bacon butty from the catering van – or leaving home with the Dawn Chorus and getting there before anyone else. Usually to be moved along by a suspicious policeman telling me, 'They're going to be filming there in a minute.'

The filming itself went quite well, as Bob Brooks would say. ('Quite' is what Americans believe is the *really* English word for 'very'.) Bob and I, without the other knowing, had both been warned by people we'd worked with before to be wary of each other; that we'd both be implacably opinionated about every micro-detail in the film. We mutually confessed this when the film was finished – after the most harmonious working relationship imaginable. There was only one little thing on which we disagreed. Well, maybe two . . .

Nigel Hawthorne headed a superlative cast and gave what has proved to be an unforgettable performance as the Knowledge Boys' examiner, the Vampire.

The Chain

At Home

Everyone's got a horror story about moving house. And all of them make *Tess of the D'Urbevilles* read like *Bunty*. Statisticians tell us that, on average, we move house every seven years. Probably because it takes six years to stop gibbering.

The day I decided to make my most recent move, I began girding every loin I could lay hands on, even though the move itself was months away. It occurred to me that I should try to exorcize the whole nightmarish day by writing about it. I began collecting 'moving stories' (Benny Green told me the best one: the Mr Thorn of Hammersmith con-trick) and suggested to Quintet Films the idea of weaving seven of them into one screenplay, dramatizing the stupefying 'chain' system by which we all move into our next house just as the occupiers are leaving to move into theirs.

On the day of my move, a new – and, to me, even more

exciting – dimension strolled, tunelessly whistling, into the plot: the removal men themselves. Treading through our trauma. Chatting about Spurs or last night's telly or the Creation of the Universe while they hump Grandad's sideboard out of the door. And while we stand keening and palpitating and agonizing that if Grandad hadn't come to live with us, we wouldn't have had to move in the first place . . .

So there were the two halves of the idea: the movers sweating from exertion, and the moved sweating from panic. Both were interwoven in a complete circle of stories and streets to make the chain of removals a sort of London *La Ronde*.As the original *La Ronde* had linked each character in its chain by Love, I chose the Seven Deadly Sins as the (literally) motivating force behind each of the seven tales.

I now gathered half-a-dozen removal men round the kitchen table. Though half the number of the cabbies they saw off twice as many beers, but they were worth every burp. I did a couple of days' removals with them, ate dinners the size of houses in Greasy Spoons and learnt (and got) a few wrinkles. Quintet Films commissioned the screenplay. The producer was Victor Glynn and the director, Jack Gold.

In the Streets

The film was to travel from the bleak streets of the East End, step by step up-market till it reached the pampered ones of Knightsbridge, and back again. The most important streets of all, as far as I was concerned, were those the Homeless Woman plodded through in the City and West End . . . in search of newspapers to make her bed with. The streets themselves were to illustrate the class system of our society. The characters – at each stage older and wealthier than the stage before – were to humanize it.

When we were shooting *The Knowledge* one of my kitchen cabbies, John Thomas, became the official adviser. On *The Chain*, my kitchen removal men took it in turns to do the same. John had loved it. These lads got fed up with the glamour of show-business after about ten minutes. It was the heat-wave summer of 1984, and they spent it stretched out on prop settees in the middle of the streets, sunbathing while answering Jack Gold's queries. A bit (but, I suppose, only a little bit) like film stars being interviewed poolside in Bel Air. I think they were glad to get back to the real drama of their everyday lives.

Day One of the shooting shot me straight back to *Ready When You Are, Mr McGill*. We were setting up a scene, when the Third Assistant hurtled out of the Production Office caravan, calling, 'Urgent phone call for you, Jack!'

Jack Gold and I started towards the caravan.

'No, not *you*, Jack!' he hollered (respectfully) at Jack Gold, 'Jack *Rosenthal*.'

Jack stopped and I went on.

'No, not *you*, Jack!' yelled the Third Assistant. 'The *other* Jack Rosenthal!'

This time *I* stopped – and one of the extras shouldered his way out of the massed ranks of his colleagues stampeding the catering van, calling back, 'On my way, Sunshine!'

I could have stayed at home, after all, really.

The Chain

CHARACTERS

Sanders Removals Ltd
BAMBER
NICK
PAUL
TORNADO

Hackney to Tufnell Park
DES
DES'S MUM
STAN
MYRA
GARY
POLICEMAN
NEIGHBOURS

Tufnell Park to Willesden
KEITH
CARRIE
POSTMAN

Willesden to Hammersmith
ALISON
DUDLEY
GRANDPA
TASHA
OLD LADY
CARPET-LAYER
FOXX
BOZO
DINGY

Hammersmith to Hampstead
MR THORN
BETTY
NEIGHBOUR (EDGAR)
REMOVAL MEN

Hampstead to Holland Park
MRS ANDREOS

Holland Park to Knightsbridge
DEIRDRE WELDON
ALEX
MARK
ROSEMARY
REMOVAL MEN
POLICE CLAMPSMAN

Knightsbridge to Hackney
THOMAS
AMBROSE
HARRODS' MEN
CHAUFFEUR (ROBERT)

Central London
HOMELESS WOMAN
CAB-DRIVER
TEA-STALL PROPRIETOR
NEWS-VENDOR
RADIO ANNOUNCER
REVEREND

The Chain is a Rank Organisation, Quintet Productions, film made in association with County Bank and Film Four International. It was released in May 1985. The principal members of the cast were as follows:

BAMBER	Warren Mitchell
NICK	Bernard Hill
KEITH	Denis Lawson
ALISON	Phyllis Logan
GRANDPA	Maurice Denham
MR THORN	Nigel Hawthorne
BETTY	Anna Massey
MRS ANDREOS	Billie Whitelaw
DEIRDRE	Judy Parfitt
THOMAS	Leo McKern

Crew

Production Designer	Peter Murton
Director of Photography	Wolfgang Suschitzky BSc
Editor	Bill Blunden
Executive Producer	David Deutsch
Producer	Victor Glynn
Director	Jack Gold

EXT. PANORAMIC SHOTS OF CENTRAL LONDON. DAY

It's 7.30 am and the City is starting its day. Bustling pavements. Traffic building up. Over this fade up RADIO ANNOUNCER'S *voice* . . .

RADIO ANNOUNCER: (*Voice over*) And now – time for 'Sixty Second Sermon'. This morning, the Reverend Anthony Leonard of the Church of St Saviour-le-Strand, in the heart of London.

REVEREND: (*Voice over*) Good morning, Sodom and Gomorrah! Good morning, Sinners! No, that wasn't your radio sets on the blink again. 'Sinners' I meant – because sinners we are. All of us. 'Now, stroll on, Vicar!' I hear you cry. 'Sodom and Gomorrah? This is London, guv!' To which I say, 'Hang about, mate . . .'

INT. DES'S BEDROOM. DAY

DES is scrabbling clothes together from a chest of drawers and tossing them into an open suitcase on the bed.

REVEREND: (*Voice over*) . . . Is there no one in Hackney, for example, driven by the stirrings of Lust?

EXT. KEITH'S FLAT. DAY

Through the window, we see KEITH *leaning against the window frame, lethargically.* CARRIE *is bustling about enthusiastically in the background.*

REVEREND: (*Voice over*) . . . How about Tufnell Park? Nobody there, even as I speak, paralysed by Sloth?

EXT. BUS STOP. DAY

GRANDPA *makes his way to the end of the queue, brusquely shouldering his tight-lipped way past other commuters.*

REVEREND: (*Voice over*) . . . No one commuting to Willesden, perhaps, tortured by Envy?

EXT. MR THORN'S GARDEN. DAY

MR THORN, *in his dressing-gown, is uprooting rose bushes and placing*

them in a large cardboard box.
REVEREND: (*Voice over*) . . . And what about Hammersmith? Is no man there, I wonder, consumed by Avarice?

INT. MRS ANDREOS'S LIVING ROOM. DAY
Open on a framed picture of her late husband on the wall. MRS ANDREOS *is about to take it down. She stops. Looks sadly at the smiling face, shakes her head and replaces it.*
REVEREND: (*Voice over*) . . . Or, by the same token, is everyone in Happy Hampstead, for instance, innocent of Gluttony?

EXT. DEIRDRE'S DRIVEWAY. DAY
DEIRDRE *stands on her step watching her new Daimler being delivered. She glances coyly from side to side, hoping at least one neighbour has noticed it.*
REVEREND: (*Voice over*) . . . Or Holland Park, for argument's sake. Is no one there, at this very moment, stiff-necked with Pride?

INT. THOMAS'S FLAT. DAY
THOMAS *stands looking out of his window on to the street below. Reverse angle – so that we see his hands, clenching and unclenching fiercely behind his back.*
REVEREND: (*Voice over*) . . . And Knightsbridge, say. Is there not one benighted soul in Knightsbridge wracked with Wrath?

EXT. PANORAMIC SHOTS OF CENTRAL LONDON. DAY
The bustling City.
REVEREND: (*Voice over*) Citizens of Sodom and Gomorrah, we're embarking on a new day. Let's make it *different*. Let's make it – a day of *change*. A day without sin. For the sake of the loved ones around you, for *all* our sakes, and therefore your *own*, I pray you – *literally* for a change – have a nice day. *Please.*
(*During this the camera isolates one lonely figure . . . overtaken by purposeful office workers, dwarfed by imposing architecture . . . shambling slowly along. This is the* HOMELESS WOMAN. *She's old, but looks older. Like a bundle of incongruous rags,*

6

topped by a ridiculous, ancient (but prized) hat. Half mad, she
mutters incessantly to herself as she goes. Over the radio, a
brightly popped-up version of a hymn plays out the 'Sixty
Second Sermon' programme. Over this . . .)

RADIO ANNOUNCER: (*Voice over*)
That was the Reverend Anthony Leonard of the Church of
St Saviour-le-Strand, in central London. And now . . . the
traffic news.
(*His voice fades down under the welter of traffic sound. We*
watch the HOMELESS WOMAN *potter along. Busy people with*
lives to lead and work to do push roughly past her. Or carefully
avoid her. Or (as in most cases) are completely unaware of her.)

EXT. SANDERS REMOVALS LTD. YARD, NORTH LONDON. DAY
Three or four large Sanders lorries stand parked. It's 8 am and men
stroll separately in to start their day's work. Some are already
standing around chatting. Others stand around, or sit on their
haunches, reading the Sun – too sleepy to chat. All are waiting for
their team gaffers to come out of the office with the day's worksheet.
Two men are leaning against one of the lorries, rolling cigarettes.
These are PAUL *and* NICK. PAUL *is in his early twenties, foxy, full*
of beans (when fully awake, that is). NICK *is in his early thirties,*
muscular and tough, but more self-contained than PAUL. *Quiet,*
commonsensical – but only to be taken advantage of at the risk of
having your nose plastered over your face.
NICK *stands up properly (i.e. respectfully) as he sees an older man*
come out of the office, studying a worksheet. This is BAMBER, *the*
éminence grise *of the removal men. He's about fifty years old,*
strong (though nowadays he uses his strength sparingly), wise in
experience. Unlike the bulk of the workforce (young, transient) he's
been a removal man all his life. He likes it and takes pride in it.
Hearing the job denigrated is the one thing that ruffles his calm – and
he's got big fists to prove it. That apart, he's the most patient and (as
we shall see) most philosophical of men. He goes over to the lorry,
pondering over the worksheet.

NICK: What's the recipe today, Bamber?
BAMBER: (*Studying worksheet*) I wish she'd get a new typewriter
in there. Thirty years that *I* know of – and the Ys *still* come
out like Vs.

7

NICK: So what we got then? French Riviera to Bermuda?

BAMBER: Willesden to Hammersmith. Piece of pudding.

PAUL: Good. Bit of luck I'll be in the boozer by two.

BAMBER: I don't want to know.

> (*He hands* NICK *a folded, well-used exercise book from his inside pocket.*)
> Don't mind, do you, mate?

NICK: (*Sighs, wearily*) Oh, Christ . . . I thought the exam was *last* night.

BAMBER: Postponed till tonight. The classroom windows was vandalized. It was raining in.

> (*They climb into the cab of the lorry.*)

INT. SANDERS REMOVAL LORRY CAB. DAY

The three men sort themselves out on the seat – NICK *at the driving wheel,* BAMBER *in the middle of him and* PAUL.

PAUL: Anyway, there *is* no towns with a Y in them.

BAMBER: What?

PAUL: So it doesn't matter a toss if they come out like Vs.

BAMBER: York's got a Y.

PAUL: Oh. Yeah. That's right.

BAMBER: Yarmouth's got a Y.

PAUL: Yeah, all right! All right!

NICK: Yeovil's got a Y.

PAUL: I said all right! Jesus!

> (NICK *opens Bamber's exercise book.*)

NICK: Where do you want to start, then? The beginning again?

BAMBER: Socrates, please.

NICK: (*Flicking through pages*) Socrates . . . Socrates . . .

BAMBER: (*Consults worksheet*) First stop Flat 14, Verity Court, Station Gardens, Willesden. You want the *A to Z*?

NICK: (*Insulted*) Do me a favour.

> (*He starts the engine.*)

PAUL: There's nowhere in *London* with a Y. Nowhere *we* do.

BAMBER: Putney.

PAUL: Oh. Right.

NICK: Stepney.

PAUL: All right!!!

BAMBER: Finchley, Bromley, Camberley, Wembley, Osterley,

Sunbury . . .

NICK: Leyton . . .

> (NICK *drives off. Angle on gates as another man comes strolling, lethargically, in. This is* TORNADO, *whose aim in life is to get through a day's furniture removing without actually lifting anything. Permanently exhausted. Angle on lorry as it drives straight at him. He executes a well-practised side-step as it screams to a halt, then clambers aboard.*)

PAUL: (*Voice over*) We're not doing any of them, though! So where's she put a *V*?

> (*Angle on interior of cab as* TORNADO *scrambles into place behind the seat, with much sighing and moaning.*)

BAMBER: Morning, Tornado. Another day of challenge and opportunity.

TORNADO: (*Wearily*) That right? Feels more like Friday to me.

> (BAMBER *turns to* PAUL *and looks deep into his eyes.*)

BAMBER: Or Friday – according to her typewriter. That answer your question? Paul?

> (*Angle on yard as the lorry drives out and off into the street.*)

EXT. A DILAPIDATED STREET IN HACKNEY. DAY
People are going to work, to the shops, to school or just hanging around. About half of them are black.

> *Superimpose caption:* HACKNEY E9

A young black man, DES, *looking tense, is about to lower a huge bundle wrapped in threadbare blankets, by rope, from a bedroom window. (Passersby, used to such sights, ignore it.) Outside the house, an old battered Mini Estate is parked. The driver,* STAN, *middle-aged and white, is opening the rear doors.*

DES: (*Calling*) You ready, then, Stan?

> (STAN *jerks his eyes up to the window; clutches his heart.*)

STAN: Christ Almighty!

DES: What's up?

STAN: Don't pull tricks like that, Des, all right? Not to a sixty-a-day man. Only thought I was getting the bleedin' call, din't I?

DES: Well, you bloody *was*! (*Starts lowering the bundle.*) Three, two, one – zero. Here she comes.

STAN: Hang about. You got the kettle on?

9

DES: After we done the loading, all right?

STAN: *Before* we do the loading, Desmond. I think *before*'s the word you're looking for.

DES: Mind your big head.

(*He continues lowering the bundle down the side of the house.*)

STAN: (*Dismayed*) Are they all that size?

DES: There's only this and one more.

STAN: Oh, well, that's handy. Teabreak at half-time, then, all right?

(*He reaches up for the bundle and helps it to the ground. Unties the rope, which DES then hauls back up to the window. STAN starts dragging the bundle towards the rear of the Estate.*)

INT. DES'S BEDROOM. DAY

The room is dingily and sparsely furnished; all its personal clutter now removed. DES is at the window, now tying the rope round a huge, battered, disintegrating suitcase. DES'S MUM (black) stands at the door watching him. She's on the verge of tears. She holds a sweeping brush. DES turns to her, guiltily, tensely . . . almost in tears himself.

DES: Mum . . . don't.

DES'S MUM: Don't what?

DES: I'll come and visit. Every week. I told you that.

DES'S MUM: No one said nothing about visiting or not visiting. I can stand here if I want. 'S my house.

(*She turns away, martyred. He wrestles miserably with his torn emotions.*)

DES: Mum, leave off . . . How far am I going? Tufnell Park isn't Timbuctoo, is it? You can visit *me*! The Central Line or number 8 to Tottenham Court Road, then the 134. Or . . . you know, for the change of scenery and that, the 253 to Camden High Street, then the 27 to . . .

DES'S MUM: (*Stiffly*) There's sod all in Tufnell Park we ain't got in Hackney. Never will have.

DES: (*Helplessly*) Once a week. Definite.

DES'S MUM: Yeah. The minute she doesn't tip up her share of the rent and you think you can nick my bingo money . . .

DES: She's tipping up *all* the rent! She's the one with the bleedin' job, en't she!

STAN: (*Out of shot*) Oi, Des! That kettle singing yet, then?
(DES *secures the knot on the suitcase, frustratedly, and leans out over the window sill.*)

EXT. DES'S HOUSE. DAY
DES's *face appears at the window. He calls down.*
DES: Hang about! Last one.
(*He lugs the suitcase on to the sill.*)
STAN: It's throating time, you said! I'm coming up!
DES: I'm coming *down* now!
STAN: (*Hopefully*) What – you bringing the tea down *with* you, then, or what?
(*He has to break off to negotiate the suitcase, which is now dropping to head height. Suddenly, it's jerked upwards, out of reach. Then back down again. Then up again. One or two passersby slow down to watch, then walk discreetly on, having seen* DES *and* DES'S MUM's *tug-of-war at the window.* STAN *smiles at the passersby, embarrassedly.*)
(*To anyone passing*) Nothing to do with me, mate. I'm on wages.

INT. DES'S BEDROOM. DAY
DES *and* DES'S MUM *stand panting, facing each other, after their brief struggle.* DES *is now nearer tears than she is.*
DES: I mean, look on the good side . . . You're getting a lodger in here tonight, right? You couldn't do that if I wasn't going, could you? You'll be better off. Money coming in and that . . .
(*No reply. He sighs. Tentatively puts his arm round her.*)
Everybody leaves home *sometime*, Mum. It's human nature.
DES'S MUM: Doing what you and her do isn't human nature. It's sex.
(*For a moment, he looks as though he's going to explode, then turns and storms from the room.*)

EXT. DES'S HOUSE. DAY
STAN *shoves the suitcase into the Mini Estate and starts closing the rear doors. He calls up to the window.*
STAN: Two sugars for me, Des, all right? Good boy.

INT. DES'S HOUSE: STAIRCASE AND HALL. DAY

DES *is crashing down the stairs, angrily.* DES'S MUM *follows,
yelling after him.*

DES'S MUM: Well, I hope she feeds you like I do! She's never
   had a bleedin' elephant to feed!

DES: Ta, ta, Mum.

DES'S MUM: Half a bottle of tomato sauce on every meal.
   Tomato sauce bleedin' sandwiches . . .

   (*At the foot of the stairs,* DES *picks up a Sainsbury's carrier
   bag, crammed with the last of his belongings, and a pair of
   snazzy roller-skates, which he hangs round his neck.*)

   You won't get fat doing what you and her do every chance
   you get! You won't put no weight on getting what *she* gives
   you! *She* will! Bleedin' *pregnant!*

   (*He turns at the front door.*)

DES: She's in *love* with me, Mum!

DES'S MUM: Do me a favour!

DES: She is!

DES'S MUM: Just cos she gets you going behind the dog track
   after night school. . . ! That only means *you're* in love with
   her, you great wally! It doesn't even mean *that!* It means
   nothing.

   (*He opens the front door and steps out. She follows him.*)

EXT. STREET OUTSIDE DES'S HOUSE. DAY

DES *strides towards the Mini Estate.* DES'S MUM *calls after him.*

DES'S MUM: *Anything* with no bra on gets *you* going!

   (DES *struggles with the handle on the passenger door.*)

   You couldn't even watch *Miss World* without thinking
   things. *I* saw you.

DES: Stan!! This door ever open or what?

STAN: Special model, this, mate. Nothing opens. 'Cept when it's
   moving.

   (*He goes to Des's door and kicks it. It opens.*)

DES'S MUM: Mark my words. By Sunday you'll be kicking her
   out of bed to get you Kentucky Fried Chicken. Have they
   got one in Tufnell Park?

   (DES *gets into the Estate.* STAN *has meanwhile made his way to
   the driver's side and got in.* DES'S MUM *stands watching, tears*

now flowing, as STAN *tries to start the engine. Stay on her as we hear from inside the van . . .*)

DES: (*Out of shot*) Pull your finger out, Stan!

STAN: (*Out of shot*) I think I've pulled the bleedin' *starter* out! Where the hell is it?

DES: (*Out of shot*) Give it a kick or something!

STAN: (*Out of shot*) Ssshhh! Don't let it hear you! Once it gets offended, it'll *never* start . . .

(DES'S MUM *goes to Des's passenger-seat window. Puts her hand in her apron pocket and takes out a £5 note. She offers it to him.*)

DES'S MUM: (*Softly*) Little going-away present, sort of thing. Shove it in your pocket.

(DES *looks at her, heart and tear-ducts overflowing. Smiles at her, sadly. Shakes his head.*)

DES: Don't be barmy. Where you got five quid to chuck about?

DES'S MUM: It's not out of the gas or nothing . . .

DES: It's towards your draught excluders like sausage dogs, innit?

DES'S MUM: I'm not going in for the sausage-dog ones now.

DES: You *like* sausage-dog ones.

DES'S MUM: Buy her a bunch of flowers. New home, you have to have flowers.

(*They smile at each other, through their tears.* STAN *tries starting the engine again. With bone-rattling vibration, he finally succeeds.*)

DES: See you next week, then.

DES'S MUM: Thursday I'll be at the hospital with your Aunt Dorothy's gallstones.

DES: Right. Another night then, probably.

(*She bends forward to kiss him – and slips the fiver in his pocket.*)

I'll pay you back . . .

DES'S MUM: Go on with you. Not as though it's every day . . .

(*With a terrible grating and rattling, the Mini Estate drives off.* DES'S MUM *stands watching it go.*)

EXT. HACKNEY STREETS. DAY
Stan's Mini Estate driving along through the morning traffic.

STAN: (*Voice over*) You all right, then, mate?

DES: (*Voice over*) Don't half rattle, this thing, dunnit?

STAN: (*Voice over*) You know what they say, don't you?

DES: (*Voice over*) Who?

STAN: (*Voice over*) You can take the boy out of Hackney, but you can never take Hackney out of the boy.

DES: (*Voice over, not interested*) Oh. Who said that, then?

STAN: (*Voice over*) Dunno, really. Some smart-arse from Chelsea, I expect . . . (*Beat.*) I'll tell you something else . . .

DES: (*Voice over*) Yeah?

STAN: (*Voice over*) That fiver she gave you . . .

DES: (*Voice over, warily*) What about it?

STAN: (*Voice over*) You can pay me *today*, now. 'Stead of waiting for your dole money to come through.

EXT. LONDON STREETS. DAY
The Sanders Removals lorry driving through traffic. PAUL *eyeing the passing girls.*

INT. SANDERS REMOVALS LORRY CAB – TRAVELLING. DAY
NICK *driving, with Bamber's exercise book propped up in front of him.* PAUL *is hanging out of the window, whistling and cat-calling virtually everything in skirts.*

BAMBER: (*Grimacing in concentration*) . . . Which means that what he's saying, the point he's making, what his point is . . . is that virtue is knowledge, and that by whatsit, definition, wickedness is whatsit. Ignorance.

NICK: Um . . . yeah, near enough. Go on.

TORNADO: Just keep your good eye on the road, Nick, all right?

NICK: (*To* BAMBER) And Socratic Argument is. . . ?

BAMBER: Socratic argument is . . . um . . . arriving at the truth by eliminating the converse arguments which –

TORNADO: Any minute now we're going to arrive at the truth in a Socratic bleedin' pile-up through a shop window! How the hell can he drive while he's. . . !
(*He leans forward and grabs the exercise book away from* NICK.)

NICK: (*To* TORNADO) You're a right woman's plaything, aren't

14

you? Willesden, right? It could drive its-bloody-*self*!

TORNADO: (*To* BAMBER) *I*'ll test you.

BAMBER: I thought you couldn't read? (*To* NICK) Did *you* know he could read?

NICK: Only tealeaves.

TORNADO: (*Finding place in exercise book*) Right. Which one's after Socrates?

BAMBER: Descartes.

TORNADO: Who?

BAMBER: (*Turns, jabs finger on page.*) There! Underneath the Socrates gubbins.

TORNADO: (*Peers at it.*) Is that how you spell Socrates?

BAMBER: No! Descartes!

NICK: Told you.

BAMBER: Descartes's point, the point he's making, what he's saying is . . . is, 'I think, therefore I am.'

TORNADO: Am what?

BAMBER: Just am.

TORNADO: You can't be just am. You've got to be am *something*.

BAMBER: Am *right*. All right? Plato next, I think, innit? Or is it Kierkegaard?

TORNADO: (*Trying to find his place again*) Hang about, hang about . . .

NICK: Hang on to your breakfast, lads.

(*He hoots horn loudly.*)

EXT. STREET. DAY

NICK *swerves the lorry violently from the outside lane and overtakes a Rolls-Royce on its inside.*

INT. SANDERS REMOVAL LORRY CAB. DAY

BAMBER: Oi! Oi! That's out of order, Nick.

NICK: Yeah, I know, but it's a Rolls-Royce.

BAMBER: (*Honour satisfied.*) Ah.

EXT. A STREET IN TUFNELL PARK. DAY

It's fairly rough, though slightly more up-market than the street in Hackney. A POSTMAN *is meandering along, delivering mail in letterboxes.*

15

A self-drive hire van is parked outside a seedy Victorian house which has been converted into flats. The van's rear doors are open. A man in his late twenties comes out of the house carrying a tea-chest. This is KEITH. *He takes the tea-chest to the van and dumps it beside a few oddments of furniture . . . perhaps a bookshelf unit, a stool, some cushions. He's almost shaking with tension and worry. The* POSTMAN *approaches.*

KEITH: Anything for Hodges, 35C?

(*The* POSTMAN *holds out a registered buff envelope.*)

POSTMAN: One to sign for, that's all.

KEITH: (*Heart sinking*) Parking ticket?

POSTMAN: Eighteenth today. My record's twenty-seven.

KEITH: I only flogged the car on Monday. *Had* to – to hire *this* bugger. (*Beat.*) Can't you put 'Not known at this address'? We move to Willesden today.

POSTMAN: Willesden's not beyond the arm of the Law, you know.

KEITH: Give me a couple of day's grace, though, won't it? Ten quid.

(*The* POSTMAN *puts the envelope back in his postbag.*)

POSTMAN: 'S only money, innit?

KEITH: (*Smiles weakly.*) Right. Ta.

(*The* POSTMAN *goes on his way. Angle on front door as Keith's wife,* CARRIE, *emerges from it. She's Asian and pretty and bubbling with happy excitement. She squeezes out of the door, loaded up with two heavy suitcases, and a large transistor radio slung round her neck.*)

CARRIE: (*Singing out*) Can you give me a hand, Keith?

KEITH: I'm guarding this lot, en't I?

(*She lets it go and makes her way to the van.* KEITH *watches her, irritably. Particularly the radio.*)

Couldn't you have packed that with the rest of the clobber?

CARRIE: (*Cheerfully*) 'S my *music*, innit? Want my *music* with me, don't I?

KEITH: Bloody ton weight I know *that*.

CARRIE: It's *me* that's carrying it, Keith.

(*She's now reached him. She starts hauling the cases into the van.*)

16

Shall I switch it on, then?

KEITH: Why – will that make it lighter or something?

(*For the briefest of moments it looks as though his unshakeable decision to be miserable might finally burst her bubble – but she recovers, and smiles with brittle brightness.*)

CARRIE: Give us a send off, won't it? Music playing and that.

(*She hauls the second suitcase into the van.*)

'Scuse me, Keith. Men at work.

(*Angle on Stan's Mini Estate as it drives up towards the hired van. Angle on* KEITH *and* CARRIE *as they climb into the van –* CARRIE *at the driver's door,* KEITH *at the passenger's.*)

KEITH: You gave back the key, Carrie?

CARRIE: He was in the hall waiting for it.

KEITH: It's a wonder he didn't charge you wear and tear on it. Must be slipping.

CARRIE: He said we're still legally liable for the tiles around the Ascot.

KEITH: I'd have punched him in the mouth!

CARRIE: (*Gently, but pointedly*) You weren't there, Keith. You was busy guarding.

(*Angle on Stan's Mini Estate as it pulls up right behind the van, with a squeal of bare brake linings.* DES *gets out, clutching his carrier bag and wearing his roller-skates round his neck.* STAN *gets out, opens the rear doors and starts heaving out the disintegrating suitcase. Angle on* KEITH *as he climbs out of the hired van and approaches* DES. *During the following,* CARRIE *is doing a five-point turn to try and extricate the van.*)

KEITH: (*To* DES) Can you back up a bit? She might need another yard.

DES: How d'you mean?

KEITH: The wife. She's not driven one of these before.

DES: Yeah, well, we got gear to unload.

(KEITH *weighs up* DES, *the Estate and* STAN *unloading Des's luggage.*)

KEITH: You're not moving in, are you? 35C?

DES: 'S right.

KEITH: We're moving *out*.

DES: Oh.

KEITH: He's in there with the key if you want it. Mr Bridges.

Got a face like an ostrich's arse.

DES: (*Nervously*) No, 's all right . . . I'm waiting for the girlfriend and that . . . She did the deposit . . . You know, the signing and everything. It's hers, really. (*Beat. Looks around.*) Not here yet, I don't think.

KEITH: No. Ain't seen no birds about nor nothing . . . (*A pause.*)

DES: Where *you* off, then?

KEITH: Willesden, really. First-time buyers.

DES: You're *buyin'*??

KEITH: First time. That's why we're down as first-time buyers. That's the name it goes under, sort of style. Twenty-nine and a half grand, not counting solicitors.

DÉS: Jesus . . .

KEITH: (*Nervously*) 90 per cent mortgage. Million pounds a month for a million years. So that's me sorted out, innit? (STAN *is lugging the blanketed bundle from the Mini Estate. He calls.*)

STAN: Oi, Des! I've heard of the White Man's bleedin' Burden . . . Give us a hand to get them in, will you?

DES: We can't go in – she ain't here yet!

STAN: I don't want to charge you waiting time, do I? I mean, I got my window-cleaning in Dalston, half-ten. (DES *turns back to* KEITH, *worriedly.*)

DES: Decent flat, is it, then? 35C?

KEITH: 'S all right for rented. Mind you, *she*'d had it up to here. Wanted to go in for first-time buying . . .

DES: (*Vaguely*) Right.

KEITH: Watch the Ascot in the bathroom. Older than the bleedin' house. *I* reckon they built the house around it . . . Blows itself off the wall every time you unzip your fly.

STAN: (*Calling out to* KEITH) 'Scuse me, mate. Can't get a cuppa tea round here, can you?

KEITH: (*Pointing across the road*) Second on your left. The Olympic Kebab and Doner. Does tea, coffee, bacon sarnies and Durex Gossamer. (*Angle on* CARRIE *as she pops her head out of the driver's window of the van. She now needs only one hard pull on the wheel to manoeuvre out of the space.*)

CARRIE: OK, Keith!
    (KEITH *looks doubtfully at the tightness of the space.*)
KEITH: You sure you got room? They inspect for scratches and
    that when we take it back, you know . . . They *charge.*
CARRIE: Come on!
    (KEITH *smiles with indulgent wisdom at* DES.)
KEITH: Women . . .
    (*He gets back in the van.* CARRIE *drives them away.* STAN
    starts off towards the Olympic Kebab and Doner. DES *stands
    loitering in the street, his bundle and suitcase lying in the gutter.
    He looks one way, then the other. No girlfriend in sight. A
    neighbour in the flats peeps at him from behind a curtain.*)

EXT. TUFNELL PARK STREETS. DAY
The self-drive van driving along, through traffic.
CARRIE: (*Voice over*) Is it the mortgage?
KEITH: (*Voice over*) Is what the mortgage?
CARRIE: (*Voice over*) Why you're looking like that.
KEITH: (*Voice over*) Like what? I'm not looking like anything.
CARRIE: (*Voice over*) You're not smiling.
KEITH: (*Voice over*) No one's cracked a bleedin' joke yet.

EXT. WEST END STREET. DAY
The HOMELESS WOMAN *stops at a lamp-post litter bin. She roots
inside it for a moment. Rejects most of its contents. Finally takes out
a crumpled copy of the Sun. She tries to smooth it out. Then gives up
on realizing it's sodden and soiled. She folds it neatly into quarters,
puts it back in the bin and walks on.*

INT. HIRED VAN – TRAVELLING. DAY
CARRIE *driving, still putting up a bright front.* KEITH *is slumped
miserably in the passenger seat, staring twitchily ahead. Music
playing on the transistor radio on the shelf.*
CARRIE: Keith . . . We've worked it out a hundred times. So
much a week. Thirty-one pound fifty for –
KEITH: Yeah, well that was *theory*, wasn't it? Up till today.
CARRIE: We'll do it bit by bit. Room at a time. It'll be fun.
KEITH: Oh, that's all right, then.
CARRIE: Our own flat, Keith. Doing what we want. When we

want. (*Beat.*) It's supposed to be a happy day, Keith! We can start a family and that now.

(KEITH *swivels round and stares at her. Beat.*)

KEITH: What?

CARRIE: What?

KEITH: Can what?

CARRIE: Start a family.

KEITH: (*Incredulously*) Kids?

CARRIE: What?

KEITH: What d'you mean?

CARRIE: How d'you mean?

KEITH: We're buying a bloody twenty-nine and a half grand flat!!

CARRIE: Yeah, well, that's *why*, innit?

KEITH: Why what?

EXT. NORTH LONDON STREET. DAY

We see the Sanders Removals lorry (with PAUL *hanging out of the window whistling) overtaking Carrie's hired van, on its way to Willesden.*

EXT. STREET IN WILLESDEN. DAY

It's a street of blocks of mansion flats. A few FOR SALE *notices sprout from some of them. One of the notices has a* SOLD *sticker over it.*

Superimpose caption: WILLESDEN NW10

The Sanders Removals lorry rounds the corner into the street, and slows down opposite the sign. The street is lined with parked cars.

INT. SANDERS REMOVALS LORRY CAB. DAY

BAMBER, NICK, PAUL *and* TORNADO *in their seats.* TORNADO *is poring over the exercise book.* BAMBER *is screwing up his face in concentration.*

BAMBER: . . . So what he's saying, the point he's making, what his point is . . . is – the need for Man to act and choose don't come from philosophic thought, but – (*He breaks off and peers out of the window.*) You're double-parked; the natives'll never get out . . .

NICK: Should bloody drive helicopters then, shouldn't they?

TORNADO: You'll block the whole street stuck here. I think our best plan is to go back home to bed.

BAMBER: Break your heart, that, wouldn't it, darling?

TORNADO: (*Studying exercise book; to* BAMBER) Go on. 'The need for man to act and choose . . .'

BAMBER: '. . . is not from philosophic thought but from a spontaneous function of the will. Which is the basis of Existentialism.' Right, Paul?
(PAUL *turns to look at him.*)

PAUL: Eh?

BAMBER: *You* do things from a spontaneous function of the will, don't you, Paul?

PAUL: Do I?

BAMBER: 'Course you do. In which case, nip in and tell the customer we're here. Flat 14.

PAUL: Why me?

BAMBER: 'Cause you've got high cheek bones. Move!
(PAUL *starts clambering out of the cab, muttering.*)

PAUL: 'S always me, innit?
(*He drops down on to the road outside.*)

BAMBER: (*To* NICK) Is he having woman trouble again? Don't tell me. I don't want to know.

EXT. WILLESDEN STREET. DAY
From Nick's point of view, we see PAUL *strolling slowly towards the mansion flats.*

NICK: (*Calling*) Paul!
(PAUL *stops and turns.*)
It's *today* we're moving them. You never know, it might be a flatful of chorus girls.
(PAUL *grimaces at him, but nevertheless starts walking more quickly towards the flats.*)
(*To* BAMBER) Pathetic, isn't it . . .

EXT. ESTATE AGENTS' OFFICE, WILLESDEN HIGH STREET. DAY
CARRIE *slows the hired van to a stop outside the office.*

INT. HIRED VAN. DAY
CARRIE *switches off the engine.* KEITH *switches off the radio. A bleak pause.*

21

CARRIE: We used to *dream* of this day, Keith. We used to look
in estate agents' windows down the Holloway Road with
three fags between us till pay day and bloody *dream* of it.

KEITH: Yeah, well, we'll have to stop smoking *altogether*, now.
(*A trembling pause.*)

CARRIE: You said you'd get jobs on the side.

KEITH: No bleedin' option, have I?

CARRIE: All *other* firemen do jobs on the side. You said Les
could fix you up with decorating and a bit of garden
maintenance . . . and I'll do mornings at play-school, and
I've got my mail-order at night . . . and . . . and . . . (*Her
bubble is now burst beyond repair. She bites her lip, fighting
back tears.*) 'S what marriage *is*, innit? Home and kids, what
else? Nothing.

KEITH: I get round to everything in time, Carrie. First-time
buying, kids, you name it . . . (*Beat.*) In my own *time*,
right?
(CARRIE *looks at him, long and hard. She speaks gently but
firmly.*)

CARRIE: You never get round to nothing, Keith. You'd have
slobbed about in that dump all your life. You're a bone-idle
bastard, Keith. You need a kick up the arse.
(*A pause.*)

KEITH: There's a time and place for everything . . .

CARRIE: Well, it's Willesden. Today.

INT. MANSION FLATS, WILLESDEN. DAY

PAUL *mounts the stairs and knocks at the door of a flat.*

OLD LADY: (*Out of shot, inside*) Is that Mrs McGuire?

PAUL: Sanders Removals.

OLD LADY: (*Out of shot*) Not Mrs McGuire?

PAUL: No. I'd be telling a lie if I said I was Mrs McGuire,
madam. I couldn't live with myself.

OLD LADY: (*Out of shot*) I don't like opening the door.

PAUL: Well, it's either that or squeezing your furniture out the
letterbox, madam. I'm easy.
(*The door opens, warily. The* OLD LADY *peers at him from
inside the flat, across the tightened chain.*)
Morning.

OLD LADY: What do you want?

PAUL: Sanders Removals.

OLD LADY: In what way?

PAUL: Sorry?

OLD LADY: You can't come in. Even Mrs McGuire doesn't come in. And she *likes* the smell of cats.

PAUL: We've come to move your furniture.

OLD LADY: What for?

PAUL: You're going to Hammersmith!

OLD LADY: Hammersmith's south of the river.

PAUL: (*Mystified*) No, it ain't . . .

OLD LADY: Why would I want to go south of the river?

PAUL: You're not! You're going to Hammersmith!

OLD LADY: What for?

PAUL: 'Cause you're going to bleedin' *live* there, you stupid old sod!!
(*The* OLD LADY *begins to emit the short grunts of immediate palpitations. She slams the door in his face.*)

INT. HIRED VAN. DAY
Stationary outside the Estate Agents' office. CARRIE *is now openly weeping.* KEITH *is almost petrified with fear.*

KEITH: I thought deep down you wanted to move 'cause you liked their avocado bathroom suite. You said you'd always wanted an avocado bathroom suite.

CARRIE: (*Quietly, through her tears*) I wanted to move 'cause I didn't want you dying of old age before you're thirty, that's all. (*Beat.*) You can't bring up kids in an old folks' home, you know. Kids aren't allowed.
(*They sit for a moment, bleakly.*)

KEITH: (*Emptily*) Did you send out postcards with the change of address on?

CARRIE: Two weeks ago. I asked you to get the stamps. You didn't quite have the energy. I did it. (*Beat.*)

KEITH: That's it, then, innit? (*Sighs and opens his door.*) I'll go and complete or whatever it is . . . get the key and that . . .

CARRIE: I'll guard the van.
(*He stumbles out.* CARRIE *watches him in puzzled concern.*)
Are you all right?

EXT. ESTATE AGENTS' OFFICE, WILLESDEN HIGH STREET.
DAY

KEITH *emerges from the hired van, and walks into the office as though to his execution.*

CARRIE: What's the matter?

INT. WILLESDEN FLAT BEDROOM. DAY

DUDLEY *and* ALISON, *a couple in their early thirties, stand looking at the room. The bed has been stripped down to its mattress, all pictures and ornaments have been removed, two or three tea-chests stand in the middle of the floor. A wardrobe stands with its doors open.* ALISON *holds their toddler,* TASHA, *by the hand and smiles at the bare room through bitter-sweet tears.*

ALISON: Bye, bye, bedroom. Thank you for being such a nice bedroom. (*Tugs at Dudley's sleeve.*) Dudley . . .

DUDLEY: (*Obediently, to the room*) Bye, bye, bedroom.
(*They stand and smile wistfully at the room.*)

ALISON: You remember when that pigeon flew down the chimney when we were in bed . . . in the middle of . . . and you ran round and round with nothing on, chasing it with the Sunday newspaper . . .

DUDLEY: We weren't quite in the middle . . . We'd just started . . . Well, *I*'d just started. You were reading. Bang in the middle of Robert Cushman.

ALISON: (*To* TASHA) Say bye, bye, to Mummy and Daddy's bedroom, Tasha.

TASHA: (*Bored*) Bye, bye, Mummy and Daddy's bedroom.

ALISON: Good girl. (*Smiles tenderly at* DUDLEY.) It's more apt from her.
(*The doorbell rings.* DUDLEY *goes to the window and looks out. Angle on Sanders Removals lorry in the street from Dudley's point of view. Angle on* DUDLEY *as he turns from the window and smiles at* ALISON.)

DUDLEY: They're here.
(*The phone rings out of shot, in the living room.*)

ALISON: You let them in, I'll get the phone. (*Starts towards the door.*) Then I can say bye, bye to the phone at the same time.

DUDLEY: Good thinking.

(*He stands for a moment looking round the room, over this we hear . . .*)

ALISON: (*Out of shot, on phone*) Hello, Alison Metcalfe speaking . . . I'm afraid I've *unplugged* the answering machine.

INT. HIRED VAN. DAY

Still parked. CARRIE *looks bleakly at* KEITH *as he clambers back in from the Estate Agents'.*

KEITH: They haven't moved out yet. He rang them. The removal men have only just come. Be an hour or so yet. I knew it was too early.

CARRIE: Personally speaking, I think it's too late . . .

KEITH: How d'you mean?

EXT. WILLESDEN STREET. DAY

BAMBER, NICK, PAUL *and* TORNADO *are busy criss-crossing between the entrance to the flats and the lorry, carrying items of Dudley's and Alison's furniture (including the bed and mattress).* BAMBER *and* NICK *work hard and efficiently;* PAUL's *heart obviously isn't quite in it;* TORNADO *carries as little as possible, as slowly as possible.* NICK, *lugging a heavy piece of furniture on to the lorry, turns to* BAMBER.

NICK: I've left the big bookcase for *him.*

(*He indicates* PAUL, *on his way back to the flat.*)

BAMBER: It'll kill him.

NICK: In the interests of humanity.

BAMBER: Anyone can go to the wrong flat, Nick. It's a professional hazard.

NICK: Rest of her life, anyone happens to say Hammersmith, she'll have a bleedin' heart attack . . . If the big bookcase'd just ruin his sex life I'd be satisfied . . .

BAMBER: I don't want to know.

NICK: You've heard he's got four married women on the go? In shifts. Two a night.

BAMBER: I don't want to know.

(TORNADO *passes to (or from) the lorry.*)

TORNADO: I'll tell you who you don't hear much of these days.

NICK: You what?

TORNADO: Torvill and Dean.

25

(*They stare at him, blankly.*)

The papers used to be *full* of them, didn't they?

BAMBER: (*To* NICK) Say yes.

NICK: Yes.

TORNADO: Not now though. Shows you. Power of the Press.

(*He continues on his way. They carry on with their work.*)

INT. WILLESDEN FLAT LIVING ROOM. DAY

DUDLEY, ALISON *and* TASHA *are standing amid the tea-chests, furniture and rolled-up carpets in the denuded room. From the other rooms in the flat, we hear* BAMBER *and his team moving furniture.*

ALISON: (*Tenderly*) Bye, bye, living room.

DUDLEY: (*Nostalgically*) We never did get round to mirror-tiling the fireplace.

ALISON: No. Still.

(*There's a knock at the door.* BAMBER *enters.*)

BAMBER: Excuse me, guv. You've . . . er . . . you've said goodbye to the kitchen yet, have you?

ALISON: No, not yet . . .

DUDLEY: The bedroom and the bathroom, we have.

ALISON: Are we silly?

BAMBER: Not at all, madam. It's a very emotional time for you. Some houses I've done, it's worse than *Anna Karenina*.

ALISON: Did you want us to do the kitchen *next*?

DUDLEY: There's only the cooker and fridge and pots and pans. One tea-chest.

BAMBER: (*Delicately*) And a kettle?

ALISON: Kettle?

BAMBER: In the tea-chest?

DUDLEY: Well, yes . . . there's a kettle.

BAMBER: Long way down, will it be?

ALISON: Sorry?

BAMBER: Take a lot of fishing out, will it? Only the lads, you see, I find they work a lot quicker once they've had a squirt of rosy –

(*He's interrupted by an insistent ringing at the doorbell.* DUDLEY *and* ALISON *freeze.*)

DUDLEY: (*Apprehensively*) That him?

ALISON: (*Looks at watch.*) Oh, God . . . Must be.

DUDLEY: (*Sighs heavily, then to* TASHA) Come on, darling. *Grandpa*'s here.

BAMBER: So if the kettle's not too inconvenient . . .

(*But they've already left the room, as the doorbell resumes its ringing.* BAMBER *stands grimacing in frustration. Through the open door he sees* TORNADO *wandering out of the room, carrying nothing.*)

Where *you* crawling, then?

(TORNADO *peers in through the doorway.*)

TORNADO: Get a spanner for the kid's cot.

BAMBER: You can't carry a kid's cot in one piece?

TORNADO: I never thought.

BAMBER: Tornado, my love. You never go to the lorry empty-handed, all right? Never. Biggest sin in the book. An ashtray . . . anything . . .

TORNADO: Sorry, Bamber. I'm a bit off this morning. Bit of a lumber at home. The wife's brother's on leave from Northern Ireland and, last night he –

BAMBER: I don't want to know. Cop hold of that.

(*He slings Tasha's high-chair at him.*)

EXT. STREET IN WILLESDEN: ENTRANCE TO FLATS. DAY
DUDLEY, ALISON *and* GRANDPA (*Alison's father*). GRANDPA *is holding* TASHA *in his arms – while laying the law down.*

GRANDPA: And you've labelled all your *tea-chests* an' all?

ALISON: It was you that brought me the labels, Dad.

GRANDPA: Different colour for each door of the new house, same colour on whatever tea-chests go in what room, so's when you get there, you'll know what goes where and –

DUDLEY: (*Wearily*) They're labelled, they're labelled. Everything's labelled.

(TORNADO *struggles past them with the high-chair.*)

TORNADO: Sorry, guv. Mind your backs. Ta.

GRANDPA: Oi. What colour label you got on there?

ALISON: None, Dad! I *know* which room that –

GRANDPA: *They* don't, though, do they? (*To* TORNADO) All right, on your way. I'll sort you out at the other end.

(TORNADO *continues towards the lorry.* GRANDPA *turns back to* ALISON *and* DUDLEY.)

You go indoors. I'll organize this lot.

ALISON: I think you're a bit in the way, there, Dad . . .

(DUDLEY *tugs at her elbow to indicate they leave him to it.*
They go inside as BAMBER *is squeezing out, carrying an*
armchair. GRANDPA *watches him.*)

GRANDPA: You! Whoa!

(BAMBER *turns.*)

BAMBER: Am I having the pleasure of you addressing me, guv?

GRANDPA: You what?

BAMBER: Only I thought I heard you say, 'Whoa', you see. I
wasn't sure if you was talking to an horse.

GRANDPA: I'm just telling you – you'll want a blanket wrapped
around that, all right?

BAMBER: Why? Just won the Grand National, has it?

GRANDPA: What?

BAMBER: I'll just get on, shall I, guv?

(*He continues towards the lorry.* GRANDPA *calls after him.*)

GRANDPA: It needs a blanket for if you stand anything on top of
it, all right? And you shove it right at the back and tie the
castors to the van. I've seen enough chair legs broken with
you hooligans.

BAMBER: (*Still walking away from him*) Anything broken is
insured and claimable, guv. Paragraph 14, back of your
contract.

(*Angle on lorry as* BAMBER *starts loading the armchair.*
GRANDPA *comes trundling towards him.*)

GRANDPA: Don't come the verbals with me, mate. All I have to
do is ring your office, speak to your guv'nor . . .

(BAMBER *turns to face him. He smiles patiently, and delivers a*
little homily he's been delivering every weekday of his life for as
long as he can remember.)

BAMBER: Sir. Moving house is very upsetting. It's a big
upsetment. People get upset. According to medical opinion,
the loss of a loved one is the worst shock to the nervous
system there is. Divorce is the next worse. And the *third*
worse – is moving house. Well, 'course it is . . . On one
hand it's turning your *animal* instincts inside out – leaving
the cave, right? On the *other*, it's what your *human* instincts
want, innit? – Questing the Unknown and that. So –

28

wallop! (*Slaps his fist into his palm.*) What you got is the biggest emotional upheaval money can buy. So people get upset. (*Beat.*) Well, they've no need to. You leave the upsetment to us – and you won't even know it's even happened. Be a little holiday for you, all right? (*A little harder*) Fair's fair, it isn't even you that's bleedin' moving . . .

GRANDPA: 'Course I am. I'm having the granny flat in the new house, en't I? Even though I'm not a granny.

BAMBER: No?

GRANDPA: That's why they're *moving* to a big house. My daughter wants me *with* her.

BAMBER: Yes, she would. I can see that.

(*Angle on* BAMBER *as he starts back towards the entrance of the flats.* GRANDPA *trundles truculently behind him.*)

GRANDPA: All *my* stuff's in storage. Don't want your mob smashing up everything I've got. (*Taps his temple.*) Experience, you see. I've moved more times than you've had hot dinners . . .

(BAMBER *stops and turns. Sizes him up, dangerously.*)

BAMBER: *No*body's done *any*thing more times than I've had hot dinners. I have four a day at this game. And have done for twenty-seven years. And that doesn't include the Victory V's I suck in between. All right?

GRANDPA: What?

(*They've reached the door.* BAMBER *stands aside to let him pass.*)

BAMBER: After you, madam.

GRANDPA: (*Not quite hearing*) Eh?

INT. HALLWAY OF WILLESDEN FLATS. DAY

DUDLEY *is making his way to the entrance with* TASHA.

DUDLEY: Grandpa will play with you.

(BAMBER *approaches him from outside the flats.*)

BAMBER: Excuse me, guv, you're obviously an educated man. Can I ask you a question?

DUDLEY: Certainly.

BAMBER: What comes after 'S'?

DUDLEY: Sorry?

BAMBER: In the alphabet.

DUDLEY: (*Warily*) What comes after 'S'?

BAMBER: What comes after 'S'.

DUDLEY: 'T'.

BAMBER: Thank you. I'll have two sugars in mine, one of the lads takes one, and the other two take three. Ta very much.

DUDLEY: (*To himself*) Two in one – one in another – two in three.

(*He walks towards the flat.*)

EXT. TUFNELL PARK STREET. DAY

DES *is seated on his blanketed bundle on the pavement. His suitcase is beside him, his carrier bag in his arms and his roller-skates round his neck. He's very fed up. A neighbour peeps out from behind a curtain at one of the windows of the flats. A police patrol van drives slowly along the street, and comes to a stop beside where* DES *is camped out. The neighbour, mission accomplished, retreats behind the curtain again. A* POLICEMAN *gets out of the van and strolls up to* DES.

POLICEMAN: Morning.

DES: (*Warily defiant*) Morning.

POLICEMAN: I like your skates.

DES: Ta.

POLICEMAN: Yours, are they?

DES: Yeah.

POLICEMAN: You got a name, have you?

DES: Desmond.

POLICEMAN: And where do you live, Desmond?

(DES *nods towards the flats.*)

DES: There. Well, Hackney, in a way. But *there*, now, sort of.

POLICEMAN: I see. (*Beat.*) This isn't Hackney, Desmond.

DES: No, I know.

POLICEMAN: Oh, good. (*Nods at bundle.*) Taking in washing, are you?

DES: No.

POLICEMAN: What are you doing, then?

DES: Sitting here.

POLICEMAN: (*Sighs heavily.*) Of course. Open it up, sunshine.

(*Angle on neighbour's window as the neighbour peeps from*

behind the curtain again – now joined by another neighbour.)

INT. HALLWAY OF WILLESDEN FLATS. DAY
As the team passes to and fro, in and out of the flat or in and out of different rooms with furniture, GRANDPA *stands hovering, keeping his eye on things and generally getting in the way of things – seen from the bottom of the staircase. From somewhere in the flat, we hear . . .*

PAUL: (*Out of shot*) I've screwed the legs off the TV.

BAMBER: (*Out of shot*) I don't want to know.

PAUL: (*Out of shot*) For loading!

BAMBER: (*Out of shot*) Oh, I see what you mean. Good lad.
    (*From two different rooms in the flat, we hear . . .*)

ALISON: (*Out of shot*) Dudley! Have you seen my Carmen
    Rollers?

DUDLEY: (Out of shot) They're under miscellaneous.

ALISON: (*Out of shot*) Were they switched on?
    (*Meanwhile,* TORNADO *and* NICK *are carrying a tallboy down the stairs.*)

TORNADO: (*Out of the blue*) It's every page you turn to, innit?

NICK: What is?

TORNADO: Computer adverts. Which computer to buy. Bleedin'
    thousands of them. You need a bleedin' computer to read
    them.

NICK: What you supposed to do with it when you've got one,
    anyway?

TORNADO: Oh, they do everything, computers.

NICK: Like what?

TORNADO: Everything.

NICK: *What*, though?

TORNADO: You name it.

NICK: You bleedin' name it.

TORNADO: Well, it's progress, innit . . . They've given us this
    fuller, richer life, en't they?
    (GRANDPA *grabs them as they try to carry the tallboy past him.*)

GRANDPA: (*Calling upstairs*) Dudley! You've got a yellow label
    on this tallboy! I thought I was copping for the tallboy? . . .
    Alison said. (*To* NICK) Put it down.

INT. WILLESDEN FLAT KITCHEN. DAY

It's now almost totally denuded. DUDLEY *is filling a black plastic bag with rubbish.* ALISON *is pouring mugs of tea from a kettle.*

DUDLEY *and* ALISON *freeze on hearing* GRANDPA's *shouts.*

GRANDPA: (*Out of shot*) If it's granny flat, it should be a blue label. So I'm telling this geezer – for yellow read blue, all right? Granny flat. Get a grip, Dudley!

DUDLEY: (*Tensely*) Jesus . . .

ALISON: (*Unhappily*) I know.

DUDLEY: And this is *before* he's moved in with us.

ALISON: Don't.

> (*They look at each other. Smile sadly. From down the hall, we hear . . .*)

PAUL: (*Out of shot*) Hold it! Hold it! Back up a bit!

BAMBER: (*Out of shot*) What's happened?

PAUL: (*Out of shot*) I've no clearance this side.

BAMBER: (*Out of shot*) Tip it! You're not tipping it. Put it down. I can take a hint.

ALISON: It was a happy flat, wasn't it, Dudley?

DUDLEY: We'll be all right.

> (*There's a knock at the door.* BAMBER *enters, hoping tea's ready.*)

BAMBER: Everything in order, madam? You didn't want me for anything?

ALISON: No . . .

BAMBER: Oh, dear, the lads said you wanted to see me. They must be winding me up. They said you wanted to see me – urgent.

ALISON: I could make you a cup of tea, if you'd like . . .

BAMBER: (*Hammily surprised*) Oh, really? Well, that's very nice of you, madam. The lads *will* be surprised.

DUDLEY: I'm afraid we couldn't find the sugar.

BAMBER: In the other plastic bag, sir. (*Nods towards it.*) Four inches down under the bag of self-raising flour.

DUDLEY: Oh, right.

ALISON: Do you like it strong or weak?

BAMBER: Anyway it comes, madam. We was all in the army or Girl Guides.

DUDLEY: I'm afraid we didn't order milk today, what with us moving . . .

BAMBER: The lady in Flat 25 tells me she'd be more than happy to oblige, sir.

ALISON: (*Smiles.*) In that case – tea up!

(BAMBER *goes to the door and calls out.*)

BAMBER: Tidings of comfort and joy, lads! Comfort and joy!

INT. BACK OF SANDERS REMOVALS LORRY. DAY

It's now almost completely (and beautifully) stacked with furniture.
BAMBER, NICK, PAUL *and* TORNADO *are either standing, or
sitting on the floor, or leaning against furniture, drinking tea and
smoking.* NICK *is consulting Bamber's exercise book.* GRANDPA *is
standing some way off checking the length of their tea-break on his
pocket watch.* TASHA *holds his other hand, counting the seconds.*

NICK: Be fair, though, Bamber . . . That's barmy, innit?

BAMBER: (*Defensively*) It's a point of view, innit? It's just the philosophical point he's making . . .

NICK: He can't say nothing's *real*!

BAMBER: He's *not* . . .

NICK: I'm real. You're real. Missiles is real. (*Indicates* PAUL.) What he's got in his Y-fronts is real. He's got 127 kids from here to Potters Bar to prove it.

PAUL: 128.

BAMBER: No, no . . . what Plato's saying . . . is that there's what's real to *us*, sort of thing . . . and what's sort of what's really real . . . in a sort of ideal state . . . and that's *realler* . . . really. Look – I'll give you a similar – once we've shifted this lot to Hammersmith, them flats aren't really real.

TORNADO: Like them flats en't real, once we've shifted this lot to Hammersmith?

NICK: There's an echo in this van.

TORNADO: Is that what you're saying?

BAMBER: Somebody was.

TORNADO: The old lady he (*Indicating* PAUL) nearly finished off . . . Them flats are real to her en't they. It's bleedin' *Hammersmith* that ain't real. To *her*.

BAMBER: I am not Plato, all right?

TORNADO: You're bloody cocoa, mate.

PAUL: Plato wants to work on *this* job for a week. He'd know what's real. My back ache's real.

TORNADO: *No* one wants to work on *this* job, mate.

PAUL: No way.

(BAMBER *looks from one to the other, furiously. They've
touched his raw nerve.* NICK *knows this of old – looks at the
other two, tensely.*)

NICK: Careful, lads . . .

BAMBER: (*Ominously quietly*) This ain't any old job. This is a
public service.

PAUL: That's true. I got more on the dole.

BAMBER: (*Exploding*) Get back on the bleeder, then! *Think* what
we do! Think what *midwives* do!

(PAUL *and* TORNADO *stare at him, stunned. Even* NICK *is
thrown.*)

PAUL: What??

NICK: Eh?

TORNADO: 'S he on about?

BAMBER: It's a long time since we crawled out the primeval
swamps. On our bellies. You don't *know* what we do.

TORNADO: *I* do. Break my back humping ten-ton wardrobes.

NICK: You – you what?

PAUL: When?

NICK: Where was I at the time? You fall *asleep* in them, mate!

TORNADO: No union. Subs off the gaffer every week. *I* pay *him*
every Friday!

BAMBER: Albert Einstein said that chopping wood is more use
and satisfaction than any –

PAUL: When did Albert Einstein ever chop wood?

NICK: When *he* was humping ten-ton wardrobes.

PAUL: Listen, the only satisfaction in this job is like last week,
the Crouch End to Clapham job. The feller's missus
stripping off in the bedroom when I walk in to get the
dressing table, and –

BAMBER: I don't want to know.

PAUL: And she says to me, 'Before you move the bed, darling,
do you think you might just see your way to – '

BAMBER: That's it! Tea-break over! Back in! Move!

PAUL: And she's lying there, pulling down her –

BAMBER: Take your cups with you! No slopping on the ramp!

No fag-ends in the van! Mush!
(*He ushers them out. They throw fag-ends and tea-slops in the gutter as they go.*)

INT. WILLESDEN FLAT. HALLWAY AND LIVING ROOM. DAY
DUDLEY *and* ALISON *stand looking at the bareness all around.*
ALISON *is holding a large rubber plant. An air of sadness.*
DUDLEY: (*Indicates plant.*) That can go in the lorry if you want.
ALISON: No. (*Hugs it closer to her.*) It's been with us ever since we
    moved in.
DUDLEY: (*Nods.*) Right.
ALISON: Flourishing.
DUDLEY: New leaves every year.
ALISON: (*Looks at him, sadly.*) There'll be sunlight in
    Hammersmith, as well, won't there? (*Beat.*) Same sun, isn't
    it?
    (*They stand in silence for a moment, then* ALISON *suddenly
    explodes.*)
    He didn't even *want* to live with us till he heard old Sam Foley
    was getting a granny flat! Sam Foley went to Fuengirola with
    his daughter, we had to take *him* to Fuengirola! Sam Foley got
    a pocket calculator for Christmas, *he* had to have one! (*Beat.*)
    He doesn't *need* a pocket calculator – he *is* a pocket bloody
    calculator! He doesn't even *like* us, Dudley, the old –
DUDLEY: (*Uncomfortably*) Alison . . . he's your father . . .
ALISON: Oh, mother, come back . . . we've lumbered ourselves
    with a bloody mausoleum with a granny flat . . . just 'cause
    he's eating his heart out, 'cause Sam Foley's got one.
    (TASHA *starts crying, out of shot. An empty pause.*)
DUDLEY: Bye, bye, flat.
ALISON: (*Through tears*) Bye, bye, flat. (*Beat.*) And thank you.
    (*They turn to the front door.*)

EXT. WILLESDEN STREET. DAY
DUDLEY *and* ALISON, *and the rubber plant, emerge from the front
door.* DUDLEY *slams it closed. Angle on* GRANDPA *seated in the
passenger seat of Dudley's car (parked next to the Sanders Removals
lorry), with* TASHA. *As they approach the car, he opens the door for*
ALISON *and* DUDLEY.

GRANDPA: (*Grins happily.*) One door closes, another one opens, eh?

INT. BACK OF SANDERS REMOVALS LORRY. DAY
BAMBER, NICK, PAUL *and* TORNADO *are finishing loading the tea-chests.*
TORNADO: (*Abruptly*) Floppy discs!
NICK: What?
TORNADO: (*Triumphantly*) To name but *one*!

EXT. WILLESDEN STREET. DAY
DUDLEY *and family drive off.*

EXT. ESTATE AGENTS' OFFICE, WILLESDEN HIGH STREET. DAY
CARRIE *is at the wheel of the parked hire van, staring sightlessly ahead.* KEITH *is looking at his watch.*
KEITH: That's an hour. Should be ready for us now . . .
(*Silence.*)
Go and sign my life away, then. Collect the keys to heaven . . .
(*She ignores him. He sighs heavily, gets out of the van and goes into the estate agents' office. As soon as he's in,* CARRIE *starts the engine and drives off down the street.*)

EXT. CABBIES' TEA STALL, CENTRAL LONDON. DAY
The HOMELESS WOMAN *is clutching an empty cup, as she has been for half an hour or so. Her eyes never leave a* CAB-DRIVER *who is reading a newspaper while drinking his tea. The* PROPRIETOR *watches her, irritatedly. Glances at his watch. Exchanges wry glances with other* CABBY CUSTOMERS, *and nods towards the displayed sign, reading:* NO LOITERING. *They follow his glance and nod their sympathy with him.*
The CAB-DRIVER *goes – and leaves his paper on the counter. The* HOMELESS WOMAN *immediately returns her cup, and scuttles over to the newspaper. She grabs it, folds it, and is about to stuff it in one of her carrier bags, when the* CAB-DRIVER *returns, takes it from her and goes. She wanders off in the opposite direction.*

EXT. WILLESDEN STREET. DAY

NICK *and* BAMBER *are securing the load in the lorry and locking the doors, ready for departure.* PAUL *and* TORNADO *sit on a wall outside the flats, dragging on fags. Now parked behind the lorry is* CARRIE *in the hired van. She sits, staring at the flats, tears in her eyes.* PAUL *watches her, turns to* TORNADO.

PAUL: Why's she just sitting there like that?

TORNADO: Might be tired.

PAUL: I think I might be in here . . .

> (*He gives his hair a quick comb and goes over to her. Angle on* CARRIE *in van as* PAUL *approaches and leans down to her window.*)

You lost, miss?

CARRIE: Yes.

PAUL: Where are you going?

CARRIE: Round in circles. Up the spout. No – not up the spout. Nowhere. What's it matter?

PAUL: (*Baffled*) Right.

> (*He wanders away towards the removal lorry, glancing back from time to time, warily. Angle on the cab of the lorry as* BAMBER, NICK *and* TORNADO *pile in. Angle on Nick's driving mirror. In it, he sees* KEITH *racing, white-faced, down the street towards Carrie's van. Angle on the van as* KEITH *reaches it, flings open Carrie's door and starts dragging her out. She fights back – having the effect of half-pulling him in with her. Angle on* PAUL *as he's about to get in the lorry, and he turns to see what the commotion's about. He stares at the two struggling figures.*)

Hang about, lads . . . She's got a bloke in with her now . . . Having it off. Half-past ten in the morning. You never see that in Chiswick, hardly. Do you think she's on the game?

> (*Angle on* NICK *looking in his driving mirror.*)

NICK: They're not having it off – they're having a domestic! They're bleedin' killing each other!

> (*He jumps out of the cab. Angle on van as* NICK *races over to it, followed by* PAUL, TORNADO *and* BAMBER. *By now,* KEITH *has dragged* CARRIE *half out of the van again.* NICK *and* PAUL *grapple with him, and finally separate them. They*

all stand panting, beside the van.)

BAMBER: Now I don't want to know what it's about . . .
Whatever it's about . . . All I'm suggesting is you discuss it
like reasonable human beings . . .

KEITH: (*Bitterly to* BAMBER) The Halifax doesn't give 90 per
cent on *kids*, you know! You can't get mortgages on kids!

NICK: You what?

BAMBER: Leave them! Don't ask!

CARRIE: (*Angrily to* BAMBER) I didn't mean start a family *today*!
I didn't mean open the door, walk in, lie down and start a
family before the cooker's even been connected!

BAMBER: (*To his team*) I said *come on*!
(*He starts trying to usher them away. They stand, fascinated.*)

KEITH: It's all right for her. All her lot work like there's no
bleedin' tomorrow.

CARRIE: Like there *is* tomorrow! Working *for* tomorrow!

KEITH: It's in their blood.

CARRIE: What's in your blood? *Your* lot? You ain't *got* no blood!

BAMBER: (*To his team*) Move! Hammersmith!
(*He now physically pulls the lads away and towards the lorry.*)

CARRIE: If starting a family's too much like hard work you just
lie there . . . have a nice rest . . . *I'*ll do the bouncing up
and down . . .

PAUL: (*To* BAMBER, *looking over his shoulder*) What's she say?
(BAMBER *hustles him aboard.* KEITH *and* CARRIE *stand for a
moment, in exhausted silence.*)

KEITH: You want to start unloading, then?
(*No reply.*)
I'll help you in a minute. My muscles have seized up or
something. I know it sounds barmy, Carrie . . . I don't
think I can move.
(*A pause.*)

CARRIE: (*Quite calm*) Well, it won't be for long, Keith . . .

KEITH: (*Puzzled*) What? I mean *move*. My arms and that.

CARRIE: Then we'll sell it. And you go back to your mum's.
And I'll go back to my sister's. And we'll pack it in.
(*Pause.*) Not as though there's kids, is it?
(*She picks up the keys, which have dropped on the pavement in
the skirmish, switches on her radio, and to a musical*)

accompaniment, she makes her way, with as much dignity as she can muster, to the entrance of the flats. By now, NEIGHBOURS *are at windows and doorways, watching. KEITH stands paralysed at the van. He calls after her.*)

KEITH: P'rhaps if I got a sedative or something from Dr Wardle (*Beat.*) Perhaps I need a sedative . . . (*Beat.*) Or maybe hypnosis.
(*She goes into the flats and slams the door behind her.*)

EXT. STREET BETWEEN WILLESDEN AND HAMMERSMITH. DAY

The Sanders Removals lorry driving through traffic.

NICK: (*Voice over*) Where in Hammersmith?

BAMBER: (*Voice over*) Burlington Road.

INT. CAB OF REMOVAL LORRY – TRAVELLING. DAY

BAMBER, NICK, PAUL *and* TORNADO.

PAUL: I know the quickest way to Shepherd's Bush. Round the Shepherd's goolies. Get it?
(*BAMBER looks at him in weary disgust.*)

BAMBER: Does your missus know you're running around with four married women?

PAUL: She hasn't said.

BAMBER: (*To* NICK) *Do* him!
(*BAMBER grabs PAUL and levers him towards NICK. NICK grabs PAUL's neck (while still driving) and gives him a long, savage kiss.*)

PAUL: (*Struggling*) Get off, you kinky bastard! He's giving me a love-bite!

BAMBER: See if she says anything *tonight!* (*Nods.*) OK, Nick.
(*NICK releases him. They drive on.*)

EXT. AN AVENUE IN HAMMERSMITH. DAY

A more up-market street than the one in Willesden. Outside a house (with a granny flat) is an estate agent's sign reading: SOLD. *Parked at the kerb is a removal van, which bears no name or address.*

THREE MEN *are loading a settee into the back of it.*

Superimpose caption: HAMMERSMITH W6

FIRST MAN: That the lot?

SECOND MAN: Must be. All that's left in there's floorboards.

FIRST MAN: Right. Let's get started.

> (*A man of about forty emerges from the front door of the house. He's pink and plump and ex-public school. This is* MR THORN.)

MR THORN: (*Calling*) I say! Are you there?

SECOND MAN: (*Calling back*) Just on our way, guv!

MR THORN: Beg to differ, old mate. You haven't finished.

THIRD MAN: (*To the other two*) What's he talking about? It's as bare as a baby's bum in there.

MR THORN: (*Calling*) Let's be having you.

> (*He goes back indoors. The* THREE MEN *look at each other, puzzled.*)

SECOND MAN: (*To the other two*) Hang on.

> (*He sets off towards the front door. Angle on three punks strolling down the street: a boy called* FOXX, *and two girls, called* BOZO *and* DINGY. DINGY *carries an ex-navy kitbag. Passersby give them a wide berth.*)

INT. HAMMERSMITH HOUSE DINING ROOM. DAY

MR THORN *is unscrewing a doorknob from the door leading to the kitchen. His wife,* BETTY, *is sweeping ashes from the firegrate into a plastic bag. The* SECOND MAN *enters.*

SECOND MAN: Yes, guv?

MR THORN: Do you know how much I'm paying your people? (*Beat.*)

SECOND MAN: Um . . . you fixed it up with the office, didn't you? When you phoned acceptance of the estimate . . .

MR THORN: *I* know how much, old mate. I know precisely how much.

SECOND MAN: I don't think you could get cheaper, guv. The boss undercuts every single –

MR THORN: All I'm saying is you haven't *finished*. All right? Let's just finish the job, and off we go, and everybody's –

SECOND MAN: We *have*, though, guv. All loaded. Ready for the off.

MR THORN: (*Sighs impatiently.*) There's the ashes from three fireplaces, the doorknobs from every door, the fingerplates from every door –

40

SECOND MAN: (*Bewildered*) Ashes?

MR THORN: What?

SECOND MAN: You're taking the ashes?

>   (MR THORN *sighs indulgently; smiles wryly at* BETTY. *She seems embarrassed.*)

MR THORN: (*To* BETTY) Evidently not a rose man. (*To* SECOND MAN) You don't grow roses, I take it?

SECOND MAN: En't got a garden, have I?

MR THORN: No, well, there you go. That's your prerogative. To each his own. *Here*, you see, we've twelve rose-bushes and – (*To* BETTY) – how many where we're going?

BETTY: (*Embarrassed*) Thirty-one.

MR THORN: (*To* SECOND MAN) Thirty-one. You follow? Now – (*Resumes his earlier list*) – there's also the light switches from every room, and the light bulbs from all the ceilings, all right?

BETTY: (*Tentatively*) I honestly think light bulbs are fixtures and fittings, dear. *And* switches and fingerplates . . . *And* doorknobs.

MR THORN: Yes, dear. *Ours*. (*To* SECOND MAN) So. Back to your van. Return with a screwdriver. Lightbulbs, doorknobs, fingerplates and switches in one plastic bag, the ashes in another, and away we go. Make sense?

SECOND MAN: Right, guv.

>   (*He exits.* MR THORN *continues unscrewing the doorknob. He glances from time to time at* BETTY, *busy with the ashes, then . . .*)

MR THORN: You're a bit of a pain, at times, Betty. Not always.

BETTY: We've *no* rose-bushes here now, anyway. You uprooted five to take with us. (*Beat.*) And killed the other seven in the attempt.

MR THORN: (*An irritated pause, then reasonably*) Everything costs money, Betty. Nothing's free.

BETTY: (*A little scared of provoking him further*) Not being greedy. Being satisfied with what you've got. That's free.

MR THORN: Most expensive thing in the world, dear. (*Peers at her swept ashes.*) You've missed a bit. In the corner.

EXT. SHEPHERD'S BUSH STREET. DAY

The Sanders Removals lorry travelling through heavy traffic towards

Hammersmith. PAUL *is, once again, half out of his window whistling passing talent.*

BAMBER: (*Voice over*) . . . No, no, what his point is, the point he's making, what he's saying is . . . is that Nature Abhors a Vacuum . . .

NICK: (*Voice over*) Yeah, well, you was saying the opposite, wasn't you?

BAMBER: (*Voice over*) I was using Socratic Argument . . .

NICK: (*Voice over*) We *done* Socrates. I thought we was doing Spinoza now.

BAMBER: (*Voice over*) We *are!*

PAUL: (*Voice over*) What's 'abhors' mean, anyway?

BAMBER: (*Voice over*) Not what you *think* it means. All I'm trying to prove is that nothing isn't something.

TORNADO: (*Voice over*) Well, that's bloody obvious, mate.

BAMBER: (*Voice over*) *Nothing*'s obvious, my lad. That's the *beauty* of Socrates.

PAUL: (*In shot, peering at passing* WOMAN) That bird's *tits* are obvious. That's the beauty of *tits.*

BAMBER: (*Voice over*) I don't want to know.

EXT. AN AVENUE IN HAMMERSMITH. DAY

The FIRST MAN *and* SECOND MAN *are each carrying a plastic bag towards the rear of their removal van. The* THIRD MAN *is watching them from the driver's seat.*

BAMBER: (*Voice over*) According to Socrates, the only thing in this world that's obvious – is that *nothing* is . . .
(*The* FIRST MAN *slings in his bag. It's the light bulbs and doorknobs bag. There's the crash of shattering glass. He shrugs.*)

THIRD MAN: I thought you said you had the *ashes*?

FIRST MAN: Easy come, easy go.
(*Angle on* MR THORN *and* BETTY *as they emerge from the house.* MR THORN *locks the door behind them. He's carrying five uprooted rose-bushes and a bag of golf clubs.*)

BETTY: I'm sure they could have taken your golf clubs in the lorry.

MR THORN: No, no, not the golf clubs, dear. Oh, no.
(*As they make their way down the garden path to their parked Volvo, he suddenly stops, looks at an enormous stone lion in the*

garden, then turns and calls to the MEN.)
I say! Are you there?
(*They turn, irritably. He points to the stone lion.*)
You can't manage this chap, can you?
FIRST MAN: (*To* SECOND MAN) Jesus . . .
BETTY: (*Embarrassed*) You can't take that, Ralph! It was a
selling point when we advertised the house. . . !
MR THORN: Estate agents' blurbs do not constitute a contract,
dear, and are therefore not binding. Worth a few bob, that
. . . (*Calls to* MEN) Well?
FIRST MAN: We're running a bit late, guv.
MR THORN: It won't take two minutes. It's probably lighter
than it looks.
BETTY: I thought you always say time's money, dear?
MR THORN: (*Torn*) Um . . . all right, forget it. (*Calls to* MEN)
On your way. 55A, Christchurch Hill, Hampstead, OK?
FIRST MAN: See you there.
(*He and his mate lock the doors of their van. As Mr Thorn and
Betty approach the Volvo . . . Angle on next-door*
NEIGHBOUR *as he walks quickly* (*trying not to give the
impression of running*) *from his house towards* MR THORN.)
NEIGHBOUR: Um . . . Ralph!
(*Angle on* MR THORN *and* BETTY *at their Volvo. The*
NEIGHBOUR *approaches them.*)
MR THORN: (*Muttering to* BETTY) I thought you'd *done* all the
fond farewells . . .
(BETTY *smiles and offers her hand to be shaken.*)
BETTY: Bye, bye, Edgar. If you're ever passing through
Hampstead . . .
(*The* NEIGHBOUR *shakes her hand, absently. That isn't what
he's come trotting out for.*)
NEIGHBOUR: (*To* MR THORN) My battery charger.
MR THORN: Sorry?
NEIGHBOUR: You've still got my battery charger. From last
winter. (*Beat.*) The winter *before*, Marjorie thinks . . .
MR THORN: Oh, hell, it's somewhere in there. (*Nods towards
removal van.*) Look. The minute we've unpacked. OK?
NEIGHBOUR: You'll bring it?
MR THORN: Absolutely. Or post it.

NEIGHBOUR: You won't forget?

MR THORN: Betty. Edgar's battery charger. Top priority, OK?
(*Smiles, shakes his hand.*) All the best.
(*He gets into the Volvo, followed by* BETTY. *The* NEIGHBOUR
*watches, stony-faced, as the removal van drives off with his
battery charger, followed by the Volvo.*)

EXT. ANOTHER HAMMERSMITH STREET. DAY
*The removal van is driving along; the Volvo right behind it. After a
moment, the Volvo overtakes the van and accelerates away, straight
ahead. The removal van promptly turns left down a side street, and
disappears from view. The Volvo continues straight ahead. As it does
so, the Sanders Removals lorry (with the whistling* PAUL *hanging
out of the window) crosses it in the opposite direction.*

EXT. POLICE STATION, TUFNELL PARK. DAY
STAN, DES'S MUM *and* DES (*with his skates still round his neck) are
dragging Des's blanketed bundle and suitcase out of the station, and
across the pavement towards Stan's parked Mini Estate. A
POLICEMAN suddenly emerges from the doorway.*

POLICEMAN: Oi! Hold it right there!

STAN: (*Stiffens guiltily; mutters to* DES) Play mutt and jeff. . . !

DES'S MUM: (*Whispering*) What is it?

STAN: Bleedin' vehicle. Tax, insurance, MOT and three bald
tyres.
(DES'S MUM *turns. She (and we) now see that the*
POLICEMAN *is carrying Des's carrier bag. He walks up to
them and hands it to* DES.)

POLICEMAN: Just watch your step, all right?
(*He goes back into the station.* DES, DES'S MUM *and* STAN
(*much relieved) resume lugging Des's gear into the Estate.*)

DES: Thanks for helping out, Mum. And getting Stan. Thanks,
Stan.

DES'S MUM: You did very well, Desmond. Left home nearly
two and a half hours before you got into trouble.

DES: D'you want to come back to the flat with me? 'S only a
couple of streets. Myra's bound to be there by now.

DES'S MUM: If I know Myra, she'll *never* turn up.

DES: Bound to.

DES'S MUM: I want to stand in the street all day, I can do it in Hackney. (*To* STAN) When you've dumped his stuff back, can you give me a lift home?

STAN: I'll need petrol money again, Des. I've my bricklaying in Bethnal Green, half twelve.

(DES *looks at his* MUM, *hopefully. She looks pointedly away.*)

DES: (*To* STAN) When my dole money comes through, eh?

STAN: I mean, what with my overheads and that. It's all cash-flow, innit?

(*They continue loading the luggage.*)

EXT. THE AVENUE IN HAMMERSMITH. DAY

The Sanders Removals lorry is now parked outside what used to be the Thorns' house. In front of it is Dudley's car. In front of that is a carpet firm's van. BAMBER, NICK, PAUL *and* TORNADO *jump from their cab on to the pavement.* NICK *sees the carpet van and freezes.*

NICK: I don't believe it!

BAMBER: What?

NICK/PAUL/TORNADO: Carpet layer.

(*They all grimace in irritation.*)

BAMBER: When will they ever learn!

NICK: Never.

BAMBER: (*Sighs, irritatedly.*) Come on. Chucking-off time.

(*He goes back to the lorry and unlocks it.*)

INT. HAMMERSMITH HOUSE LIVING ROOM. DAY

A CARPET-LAYER *is nailing down rods for a fitted carpet (or part-way through fitting the carpet itself).* TASHA *is playing with his hammer in the middle of the floor – which the* CARPET-LAYER *isn't at all pleased about. There's a chaos of sound –* DUDLEY *and* ALISON *in different rooms of the house.* ALISON *calls out to him –*

ALISON: (*Out of shot*) Dudley! The pilot light's gone out!

DUDLEY: (*Out of shot*) I haven't lit it yet! Your Dad's pinched my matches.

ALISON: (*Out of shot*) I mean the electric one!

DUDLEY: (*Out of shot*) That's the immersion heater!

ALISON: (*Out of shot*) I *said* the immersion heater!

DUDLEY: (*Out of shot*) No, you didn't!

(BAMBER, NICK, PAUL *and* TORNADO *hump furniture up the*

45

stairs or in the hall, out of shot.)

BAMBER: (*Out of shot*) Where you crawling with that?

TORNADO: (*Out of shot*) Obeying your instructions, en't I? Ours not to reason why . . .

BAMBER: (*Out of shot*) You winding me up or something? (*During all this,* GRANDPA *is seated like King Canute on a tea-chest in the middle of the room.*)

DUDLEY: (*Out of shot*) Alison!

ALISON: (*Out of shot*) Coming!

DUDLEY: (*Out of shot*) I can't find Tasha!

ALISON: (*Out of shot*) Who?

DUDLEY: (*Out of shot*) What?

ALISON: (*Out of shot*) It's all right, it's all right! Everybody keeps . . . Everything's all right!

GRANDPA: (*Calling*) Tell them anything with a white label comes in here. And watch the banisters going upstairs. I've seen more scratched paintwork than they've had – (*Checks himself*) – than anybody.
(ALISON *runs in, carrying clothes or an item of furniture in her hands, very flustered.*)

ALISON: Dad. If you must sit on a tea-chest, I'll empty that one, and you can take it down to your granny flat and sit on it in there.

GRANDPA: I'll go when I've sorted these cowboys out, love, not before.
(NICK *enters, carrying a table.*)

NICK: 'Scuse me, madam . . . Two things . . . One, is *this* joker . . .

GRANDPA: (*Angrily*) Me?

NICK: Not you, sir, you're customer. We never complain about customers. Specially little uns. (*Nods towards the* CARPET-LAYER.) We can't unload in here while *he's* here, madam. Either *before* he's here, or *after* he's here. It buggers us up, madam. We have nightmares about carpet-layers. (*Nods grimly at the* CARPET-LAYER.) Nothing personal.

ALISON: Oh, dear. He was booked, you see . . . I thought . . .

NICK: So we'll just have to stick this room's stuff in the basement till he's out of the way, all right?

GRANDPA: No, it bloody *isn't* all right!

NICK: (*To* CARPET-LAYER) How long will you be, then, squire? Fortnight?

CARPET-LAYER: (*Through clenched teeth*) The more I'm left alone, the quicker I can get on, all right?

NICK: (*Sighs, then to* ALISON) Don't worry. We'll try a touch of the Mary Poppins. We'll manage.

(*He turns to go.*)

ALISON: What was the other thing? You said there were two.

NICK: (*Beams at her.*) I thought you'd never ask, madam.

ALISON: Sorry?

NICK: That's very nice of you. I take one, one takes two, and the other two take three. Doesn't matter about biscuits.

ALISON: Oh, tea! Sorry! Um . . . now I don't know if the kettle's in a tea-chest labelled green or –

NICK: Don't you worry, madam, *we* do.

(*He exits.*)

CARPET-LAYER: Excuse me, missus. I can't get my hammer off your little boy.

ALISON: He's a little girl.

EXT. AVENUE IN HAMMERSMITH. DAY

Mr Thorn's Volvo appears, driving back down the street towards his old house. It pulls up near the Sanders Removals lorry. MR THORN *gets out and calls to* BAMBER *and* PAUL *who are carrying furniture into the house.*

MR THORN: I say! Are you there?

(*Angle on* BAMBER *and* PAUL *as they turn.*)

BAMBER: (*To* MR THORN) Is this a conversation, sir? In which case you'll notice I'm balancing a ten-ton lump.

(MR THORN *approaches.*)

MR THORN: Are the new people in? The new occupiers?

PAUL: You're not a French polisher, I hope?

MR THORN: Beg pardon?

BAMBER: French polishers and carpet-layers. They come in pairs.

MR THORN: I see.

BAMBER: Mind your back.

(*He squeezes past with the furniture and continues towards the*

47

house. MR THORN *has to follow behind.*)

INT. HAMMERSMITH HOUSE KITCHEN. DAY
It's in half-unpacked tea-chest chaos. ALISON – *by now in a state of
frantic Remover's Tension, is pouring tea from the kettle into a
trayful of cups and mugs. Much to her annoyance and disgust,* MR
THORN *is rooting through the kitchen drawers.*
MR THORN: Very nice of you to let me do this, Mrs
    Metcalfe . . .
ALISON: I don't believe I *am* letting you do it! I can't believe
    you're *doing* it! Elastic *bands*??
MR THORN: In one of these somewhere . . . I'm sure . . .
ALISON: You drop your wife off in the middle of Hampstead
    while you come chasing back to Hammersmith for elastic
    bands??
MR THORN: A whole pile of them, actually . . . Forty or fifty in
    a little plastic . . . Ah!
    (*He takes a small plastic bag of elastic bands from a drawer.
    He beams at her.*)
    Seek and ye shall find.
ALISON: Well, I'm sorry, I think the whole thing's absolutely –
    I don't think the kettle'll squeeze to a cup for you,
    unfortunately. Not one window opens in this kitchen.
    Gunged up with twenty-year-old paint – Excuse me.
    (*She exits with the tray, in high dudgeon.*)

EXT. HAMPSTEAD HOUSE. DAY
BETTY THORN, *in almost hysterical agitation, comes racing down
the street, with the rose-bushes, and hauls herself into a telephone
kiosk. After a moment, she flings herself out again, and lunges into
the next one, spilling money from her handbag on to the floor as she
does so . . .*

INT. HAMMERSMITH HOUSE LIVING ROOM. DAY
Seated on tea-chests, sipping tea, are BAMBER, NICK, PAUL *and*
TORNADO. *The* CARPET-LAYER *is still laying the carpet. To do so,
he has to lift* TASHA *out of the way and plonk her down again.*
ALISON *puts her on her knee.* DUDLEY, *with an armful of books, is
standing beside* BAMBER, *who's riffling through a big volume.*

CARPET-LAYER: Is there one for *me*?

NICK: I think *I*'ve got yours – I thought the more you was left alone, the quicker you'd be.

(*The* CARPET-LAYER *goes out to make his own cup of tea*.)

BAMBER: (*In his element*) Ah, now, you see . . . there's a lot of these we don't *do* . . . We just have the set books . . . I mean, Haringey's very good for background courses and that . . . but this is more your *in-depth* and that, innit?

DUDLEY: I don't think I've ever looked at it, really . . .

BAMBER: Ah, son, you don't know what you're missing – I mean, we're just one night a week at Haringey . . . We done him – Aristotle, Daddy of them all – (*Jabs finger at page*) – but I don't think we touch . . . (*Flicks through pages and glances at names*.) Bertrand Russell . . . there's a name to conjure with.

ALISON: Where's my Dad got to?

DUDLEY: Wandering about finding fault. He said he'll come when these lads have gone.

(MR THORN *enters from the kitchen with his bag of elastic bands and a hot-water bottle*.)

MR THORN: Found this as well, fallen down the side . . . Well, I'll say thank you, Mr and Mrs Metcalfe, and I hope you'll be very happy in your new –

DUDLEY: If you'd have left one lousy light bulb, I'd have been a sight happier, Mr Thorn!

(*As* MR THORN *starts to leave, the phone rings*.)

You forgot to rip the phone out, Mr Thorn.

MR THORN: Sorry?

(*The* CARPET-LAYER *re-enters with tea.* MR THORN *is about to leave*.)

DUDLEY: (*Into phone*) Hello?

MR THORN: Hello.

DUDLEY: (*Into phone*) Who? Hang on, Mrs Thorn.

MR THORN: (*Stops*.) Sorry . . . Did you. . . ?

DUDLEY: Your wife.

(*He hands the phone to* MR THORN.)

MR THORN: Gratias. (*Into phone*) Sorry I've been so long, dear, I'll be with you in – (*Beat, then stunned*) What??!! (*Beat*.) Good God Almighty! (*Beat*.) What do you . . . What the hell are you . . . (*Beat*.) Hang on, hang on! One thing at a time!

EXT. STREET IN HAMPSTEAD. DAY

BETTY THORN *is seated on the garden wall of a house, holding the rose-bushes and the golf clubs.* NEIGHBOURS, *passing by with their shopping, skirt her warily, nudge each other and go into their own houses, peeping back at her before they close their doors.*

Superimpose caption: HAMPSTEAD NW3

The Volvo comes racing down the street and screams to a halt outside the house. A white-faced MR THORN *leaps out from the driver's door.* BAMBER — *carrying Mr Thorn's hot-water bottle — comes out of the passenger door. They go over to* BETTY, *who becomes more and more hysterical at the sight of her husband.*

BETTY: What are we going to do?? Ralph . . . what are we . . . She won't budge . . . And our removal men have vanished off the face of the earth and *hers* say she just cancelled them on the spot . . . so they drove off to another job in Paddington . . . And, when I rang the solicitor to tell him, he said if the keys aren't handed over it's not ours, anyway . . . and everything's gone insane, Ralph . . . We've got no home . . . we've got no furniture . . .

BAMBER: (*Homily time.*) All right, madam . . . now don't you upset yourself . . . Moving house is very upsetting. It's an upsetment. People get upset. According to medical opinion, the loss of –

(BETTY *stares at him, blankly, then turns to her husband.*)

BETTY: Who's he?

MR THORN: The *other* removal tribe.

BETTY: (*Boggling*) He isn't! I've already spoken to *her* men. They're on their way to Paddington . . . And he's not one of *ours* . . . I *know* ours . . .

MR THORN: No, no, he's moving the Metcalfes into *our* house . . . *old* house . . .

BETTY: Well, what the hell's it got to do with *him*!?

BAMBER: (*Placidly*) I've been in this game twenty-seven years, madam. I've seen it all. (*Beat.*) Now, first things first. Your furniture. How late are they?

MR THORN: They left Hammersmith with us. Fully loaded. An hour ago.

BETTY: An hour and a half ago. Over.

BAMBER: And they weren't stopping off for dinner?

MR THORN: Coming straight here. They ate sandwiches while they were loading. Cheese and tomato.

(BAMBER *winces at such unprofessionalism*.)

BAMBER: What's the name of the firm?

MR THORN: There's their leaflet.

(*He gets out his wallet, removes a leaflet and hands it to* BAMBER.)

Wandsworth number, I think . . .

(BAMBER *looks dully at the leaflet, both sides. It confirms his suspicions*.)

BAMBER: They *have* no name. Or address.

MR THORN: There *is* a phone number.

BETTY: Discontinued. I rang.

BAMBER: (*Reads from leaflet:*) 'Cheap removals. We will move your furniture anywhere, any time, cheaper than anyone else, guaranteed. Phone for free estimate.'

BETTY: The operator said there's no such number now. I rang.

MR THORN: There *was* though! When I rang for the estimate and fixed up the entire –

BAMBER: They were probably borrowing a knocking shop. Did you sign an official contract?

MR THORN: (*Uncomfortable glance at* BETTY.) Well . . . not in so many words . . .

BETTY: He rang to tell them to come and give him an estimate. They did. He said yes. And that was it. (*Beat.*) Till today.

BAMBER: (*Sighs*) How much *was* the estimate?

MR THORN: Two fifty.

BAMBER: And what was *real* firms quoting? Five? Six?

MR THORN: (*Guiltily*) Between the two.

BAMBER: (*Grins.*) Well, it's cost you nothing in the end – that's one consolation. Apart from all your furniture, of course.

BETTY: (*Helplessly*) Oh, God!

(*Wheels round hysterically on her husband.*) 'Cheap removals'!! Cheaper than anyone else! Everything we own! Everything! You stripped the whole house – down to the doorknobs.

BAMBER: (*To* MR THORN) By the way, sir, that's not strictly legal . . .

BETTY: It's everything he does! His whole life! We're only moving because he knew we'd get over the odds for our house and this one's going cheap because her husband's died! (*Yells*) I wish *mine* would!

MR THORN: (*Embarrassed*) Betty . . . We're in a strange street . . .

BETTY: (*At the top of her voice*) All to save 250 lousy pounds! The cocktail cabinet alone was worth twice that! (*She withdraws into a quietly-sobbing helplessness and sits down again on the wall.* BAMBER *turns to the white-faced* MR THORN, *still holding the hot-water bottle.*)

BAMBER: You go and report the theft, sir. I'll go and see the lady in here. What's her name?

MR THORN: Andreos. Mrs bloody Andreos.

BETTY: (*Dully, beyond caring*) She's just sitting there. She says she's not leaving. Ever. (BAMBER *indicates to* MR THORN *that he should go to the phone kiosk.*)

MR THORN: Right. (*Takes a few coins from his pocket, examines them, then turns to* BETTY.) Have you got a 10p for two fives?

EXT. HAMMERSMITH HOUSE. DAY

GRANDPA *makes his way from the front door, carrying some small item of furniture, stuck liberally with blue labels, towards his basement granny flat. He's muttering to himself, as he goes. He looks with disdain at a labelled key he's carrying.*

GRANDPA: Bloody Yale. Sam Foley got a Yale and a *Chubb* for *his* granny flat. I'm not bloody good enough for a Chubb. (*As he nears the door of the flat, he becomes aware of heavy rock music coming from it. The nearer he gets, the louder it becomes. Puzzled, he puts the key in the door and turns it. It's locked. Bewildered, he bends down and calls through the letterbox.*) Hello? Is some bugger in there?

EXT. STREET CORNER, CENTRAL LONDON. DAY

The HOMELESS WOMAN *watches wistfully as a van drops a bundle of the latest editions of the* London Standard *on to the pavement*

52

beside a news-stand. The NEWSVENDOR *picks them up and places them on the stand. He sees her staring at them. He holds up a copy of* Vogue *with mock-elegance, as though offering it to her as a more apposite purchase. She turns and shuffles away down the street.*

INT. HAMPSTEAD HOUSE LOUNGE. DAY
The room is furnished in a mixture of cheap, English modern and traditional Greek. There's a lady of about fifty years of age, seated at a table, looking slowly and seemingly emotionlessly through a huge autograph album. There's a knock at the door. BAMBER *enters.*
BAMBER: Mrs Andreos, I presume? Good morning, madam.
　　(*She pays him no attention whatsoever. He respectfully walks towards her, and sits down opposite her. A pause.*)
　　Madam. Moving house is very upsetting. It's an upsetment.
　　People get upset. Well, they've no need . . .
MRS ANDREOS: (*Calmly, Cypriot accent*) I certainly have no
　　need. (*Smiles.*) I no moving one inch.

EXT. HAMMERSMITH HOUSE GRANNY FLAT. DAY
GRANDPA, *in a panic, now has* NICK *and* DUDLEY *with him at the door of the flat.* NICK *hammers on it, and calls out loudly –*
NICK: This is the SAS speaking. Whoever you are, you have ten
　　seconds to get out, all right? Ten, nine, eight, seven,
　　six . . .
　　(*He catches a glimpse of a sudden movement in the small window. He looks. So do* GRANDPA *and* DUDLEY. *Angle on window as a sign is wriggled into place on the inside. It's a beautifully coloured, artistically lettered sheet of cardboard, reading:* THIS IS AN OFFICIAL SQUAT. KINDLY PISS OFF.)

INT. BASEMENT FLAT, HAMMERSMITH. DAY
It's occupied by FOXX, BOZO *and* DINGY *– the three punks we saw earlier in the street. The rock music is coming from a small cassette player standing on the floor next to the navy kitbag, in the otherwise totally denuded room.* FOXX *is sterilizing a pin with a lighted match, and then tattooing his arm with the pin, dipped in drawing ink.* BOZO *is lying on the floor, spaced out.* DINGY *returns from placing her sign in the window, and resumes writing artistically-designed slogans with a marker pen on the bare walls.* NICK *continues*

53

hammering on the door, out of shot.

FOXX: If they must bang, the least they could do is bang on the
beat, right?

BOZO: Right.

NICK: (*Out of shot*) Right then. It's tear gas and stun grenades.
Ten, nine, eight, seven, six . . .

FOXX: (*To* DINGY) How do you spell 'Beelzebub'?

DINGY: (*Middle-class accent*) With the utmost difficulty, given
your education. Your arm's not long enough anway, Satan's
just as good. Do Satan. (*Takes a sip from a dirty mug – then
spits it out.*) This your mug, Bozo?
(BOZO *peers at it, blearily.*)

BOZO: 'Tis now. Nicked it from Fat Harry's in Luton.

DINGY: Well, next time you nick anything, get them to wash
out the curry sauce first, all right?

GRANDPA: (*Out of shot*) We'll get the Law on you! Bleedin'
parasites! I fought a bleedin' war for you lot! Monte
Cassino!

BOZO: Foxx? Turn up the volume, will you?
(FOXX *does so. They resume their activities in the welter of
sound.*)

INT. HAMPSTEAD HOUSE LOUNGE. DAY

A silence. MRS ANDREOS *and* BAMBER *are still at the table.*

MRS ANDREOS: (*Slowly, gently, matter of fact*) Eleven different
house in twenty year. Twenty year since we come from
Cyprus. Each time we move, he say me, '*This* one I make
like a Mediterranean villa. Limassol.' And he knock this
wall away, and that wall and take staircase away and put in
new and knock more wall away . . . And each time, I say
him, 'Darling, the picture window very nice. But I look out
of it. I no see Mediterranean. I see Tesco's. We want like
home, please we go *home*.'
(*A pause.*)

BAMBER: Understandable.

MRS ANDREOS: But, no. That for him is the happiness. The
bricks are knocking out and the plaster fly everywhere . . .
in my hair, in my bra – I take off at night, I got falsies
made out of plaster – in my kleftiko . . . everywhere . . .

And *him*, he *sings*. He take all old house and try to make
new. This . . . this was slum. He make it palace, yes?

BAMBER: Beautiful.

MRS ANDREOS: It nearly kill him. As soon as he is finished, he
see house in Holland Park, he start sing again. He say me,
'We buy, knock many wall away, it be like Limassol.'
(*Shrugs*.) I say him, 'Darling, even in Limassol a villa has
walls, you not young man no more. I no want
Mediterranean villa. I want nice *English* house. I got one. I
had *ten* nice one before this one. All you do is make youself
ill.' (*Confidentially*) He had a plastic in his hip for the
arthritis.

BAMBER: It's tetanium, madam. They use tetanium now. I got a
brother-in-law with one.

MRS ANDREOS: But it's like I talk to a wall. The wall before he
knock away. I say him, 'You know what you are? A glutton
for punishment.' Of course, he no listen. A glutton always
want more. (*Pause*.) He go to builder's merchant. Pick up
tiles. 'These', he say merchant, 'for new floor in hall.' He
pick up RSJ. 'This', he say him, 'for new kitchen ceiling.'
And then . . . and then his *heart* say him back, 'Enough,
I've had enough.' (*Beat*.) Three months ago last Tuesday,
twenty-five past nine in the morning, in builder's merchant.
(*A pause*. BAMBER *nods towards the man's wristwatch on her
wrist*.)

BAMBER: That his watch, was it?

MRS ANDREOS: Swiss made. Incabloc. (*Beat*.) Everyone fly me
from Cyprus. Family I never even seen. (*Beat*.) They all say
me, 'What a beautiful home you got. Is like Limassol.'
(*A silence*. BAMBER *shuffles uncomfortably for a moment*.)

BAMBER: Mrs Andreos . . . the couple outside. They've bought
this house now. You have to get your stuff out.

MRS ANDREOS: (*Firmly*) No.

BAMBER: You've got to go to Holland Park.

MRS ANDREOS: No.
(*A pause*.)

BAMBER: Holland Park's lovely. Be nice and cosy I bet . . . now
you're on your own.

MRS ANDREOS: I cosy here. I always was.

55

BAMBER: If it's still got its walls standing, the rooms'll be smaller, won't they? Be even cosier.

MRS ANDREOS: I no moving one inch.

(BAMBER *takes a deep breath, then speaks a little more firmly.*)

BAMBER: Mrs Andreos . . . You mustn't break the chain.

MRS ANDREOS: (*Blankly, a statement*) Chain.

BAMBER: If you don't go, them out there have no home, the people in Holland Park can't move to where *they're* moving to, the people where *they're* moving to can't move to where *they're* moving to. Everything stops. Everyone loses thousands in deposits . . . Everything in chaos. Standstill. End of civilization, innit?

MRS ANDREOS: Good. Teach them to be as happy as they are.

BAMBER: Ah, now that's a *different* chain, dear. Now you're on to human nature. That's more in the realm of philosophical observation you're into there . . . which, coincidentally enough, you Greeks started in the *first* place.

MRS ANDREOS: Eh?

(BAMBER *concentrates; then rubs his chin; racks his brain . . .*)

BAMBER: Um . . . you'll excuse me intruding in your grief, madam . . . You were very close, were you? You and the late Mr Andreos?

MRS ANDREOS: (*A fond little smile*) Oh. Once maybe. Sometimes. In our younger days. Maybe six or seven houses ago. (*Shrugs.*) My heart said 'Enough' back in Battersea. That's when I used to go to sleep, thinking, 'One day I get my own back for all this . . .'

(BAMBER *stares at her. Light at the end of the tunnel.*)

BAMBER: Today, Mrs Andreos.

MRS ANDREOS: (*Doesn't understand*) Please?

BAMBER: (*Excitedly*) *Today's* that day! That's how you get your own back!

MRS ANDREOS: How?

BAMBER: Go to Holland Park, my love; move in; and, once you're in, *don't change a blind thing!*

MRS ANDREOS: Eh?

BAMBER: Change nothing. Just sit in a nice English house, like you've always wanted. (*Smiles.*) That'd show him.

INT. HAMMERSMITH HOUSE HALLWAY. DAY

PAUL *and* TORNADO, *the last items of furniture now unloaded into the house, make their way from different rooms.* NICK *is standing with* GRANDPA *and* DUDLEY.

GRANDPA: (*To* NICK, *desperately*) What d'you mean, I can't do nothing??

NICK: Sod all, guv, legally. That half-hour between that bloke moving out and you lot turning up, no legal occupier, was there? In they go, boo–boom!

DUDLEY: What about the Law?

NICK: That *is* the law, guv.

GRANDPA: He means the police!

TORNADO: Two weeks it'll take *them*, guv. I know. I done it myself.

GRANDPA: Got rid of squatters?

TORNADO: No. Squatted. Elgin Avenue, Maida Vale. Nice place an' all. Lovely cornices . . .

(*He and* PAUL *exit into the street.* NICK *turns awkwardly to* DUDLEY.)

NICK: Well, we'll be off, then, guv.

DUDLEY: Right . . . well, thanks very much for everything.

(*The phone starts ringing out of shot, in the living room.*)

NICK: (*Awkwardly*) Um . . . the gaffer, usually, um . . . when a job's finished, sort of thing and that . . . he . . . um . . . you know, if you're satisfied with the move and that . . . he . . . um . . .

ALISON: (*Out of shot, calling*) It's all right, I'll get it! Where did we put it? Oh, I know!

(*The phone stops ringing, answered by* ALISON.)

(*Out of shot, into phone*) Alison Metcalfe here. I'm afraid the answering machine isn't plugged in yet.

NICK: . . . only with him not being here at the moment . . . I mean, if everything's been to your satisfaction . . .

(DUDLEY *finally cottons on.*)

DUDLEY: Oh, sorry!

(*He gets out his wallet, takes a £10 note out, and hands it to him.*)

NICK: (*Attempting surprise*) Oh, thank you, guv . . . Very nice. Good luck, then.

(*He starts to go.*)

ALISON: (*Out of shot, calling*) Dudley!

INT. HAMMERSMITH HOUSE LIVING ROOM. DAY

ALISON *stands holding the phone. She calls out to the hallway.*

ALISON: Can one of the removal men come to the phone? It's
the other one. (*Into the phone*) Hang on . . . one of your
colleagues is coming.

(NICK *enters.*)

(*To* NICK) It's your *other* colleague . . . The older one.

NICK: (*Takes phone.*) Ta. (*Into phone*) Hello, precious.

INT. HAMPSTEAD HOUSE LIVING ROOM. DAY

MRS ANDREOS *is now dressed in her outdoor clothes. She's taking
pictures off the wall and stacking them. One of them is an
ornamental, embroidered map of Cyprus.* BAMBER *is speaking into
the phone.*

BAMBER: Now, listen. We're doing a dodgy. Hampstead to
Holland Park. I've fixed up a price with the customer. Nice
bit of bunce for us. Tell the lads, all right? It's all in readies
– (*Pause.*) 55 Christchurch Hill. (*Pause.*) No, I've phoned
the gaffer and told him we're taking a trip to Friern Barnet
to reccy Tuesday's storage job. (*Pause.*) Nah, *course* he
didn't believe me. Now, listen . . . no rush, it's not a big
job, hour at the most. Anyway, contracts can't be
exchanged for hours yet . . . the solicitors won't be
finishing their egg and chips till half-three . . . so you and
the lads go and have a bit of beef bourguignon, all right?
(*Pause.*) No, I'm fixed up. Shish-kebab on toast.
Everything all right your end? (*Pause.*) Don't tell me, I
don't want to know.

(*He replaces the phone and turns to* MRS ANDREOS.)

Right, dear. We have lift-off.

EXT. HAMMERSMITH HOUSE. DAY

NICK, PAUL *and* TORNADO *are in the cab of the Sanders Removals
lorry, the engine running.* GRANDPA *is pleading with* PAUL *at the
window.*

GRANDPA: What happens if we smash the door down, smash

their faces in, and *kick* them out?

PAUL: You get done for assault.

(*The lorry drives off. Angle on bedroom window of the house where* DUDLEY *and* ALISON (*holding* TASHA) *stand watching the lorry drive off . . . Angle on* GRANDPA *as he wanders aimlessly and disconsolately back towards the house.*)

INT. HAMMERSMITH HOUSE BEDROOM. DAY

DUDLEY *and* ALISON *turn away from the window.*

DUDLEY: (*Slow realization*) Oh, God . . . Oh, my God . . .

ALISON: Mmm?

DUDLEY: If it's two weeks before we get them out . . . You realize what that means?

ALISON: (*Smiles.*) Don't worry . . .

DUDLEY: Don't worry?? For two weeks he'll have to move in with us! *Really* with us . . . in here.

ALISON: (*Grins.*) No, darling.

DUDLEY: What?

ALISON: He won't. I just rang Sam Foley. He's offered to put him up in his granny flat. (*Beat.*) Where he can really eat his heart out.

(*She links her arm into* DUDLEY'*s, surveys the room, and beams happily.*)

Hello, bedroom.

DUDLEY: Hello, bedroom.

EXT. STREET IN HOLLAND PARK. DAY

Very fashionable indeed. Outside a house bearing the name THE VILLA, *a team of* REMOVAL MEN *load up a last item of furniture, lock up, climb in the cab and drive off.*

Superimpose caption: HOLLAND PARK WI I

In the driveway stand two cars: a brand-new Daimler and a five-year-old Vauxhall. DEIRDRE WELDON, *her eighteen-year-old son,* MARK, *and her sixteen-year-old daughter,* ROSEMARY, *are carrying their personal treasures from the house to the cars.* DEIRDRE *has a large framed photograph of herself (other people in the background);* MARK *has a home computer and* ROSEMARY *has a cat in a cat basket.* DEIRDRE'*s husband,* ALEX, *comes out of the house and slams the door behind him. He's carrying a silver model of a yacht.*

*The rest of his family are about to load their objects into the
Daimler's boot, when* DEIRDRE *catches sight of the cat basket.*

DEIRDRE: Rosemary!

ROSEMARY: What?

DEIRDRE: (*Indicates cat.*) Not Lady Diana, surely!

ROSEMARY: She's coming with us, isn't she?

DEIRDRE: In a brand-new Daimler? Real-hide interior? She's
hardly one day old yet . . .

ROSEMARY: Lady Di? She'll be four at Christmas.

DEIRDRE: The Daimler, dear, don't be moronic, I've a busy
day.

(*Slightly niggled,* ROSEMARY *starts to put the cat basket in the
Vauxhall instead.*)

MARK: Quite honestly, Mum, I do think you could have waited
one more day before you got it. A new car and a new house
on the same day *is* a bit OTT.

ALEX: (*Arriving at his Vauxhall*) Proposed and seconded.

(DEIRDRE *turns to him with smiling irritation.*)

DEIRDRE: It *is* Knightsbridge we're going to, dear . . .

ALEX: There's no by-law you have to have a brand-new car.
Even in Knightsbridge. They won't deport you . . .

(DEIRDRE *surveys the three of them.*)

DEIRDRE: Anyone anything else to add to ruin the day? Street
demonstration over? Good. Can we get on?

(*She watches* ALEX *loading the ship.*)

Alex, all the silver's well insured. That could have gone
with the removal men.

ALEX: (*Loading it, nevertheless*) It isn't silver. It's EPNS.

DEIRDRE: Then why does it need a personal chauffeur, at all?

ALEX: It was a wedding present.

DEIRDRE: The *piano* was a wedding present. *That*'s gone with
the removal men.

ALEX: The piano wasn't from the chaps. (*Indicates her picture.*)
If anything could have gone with the men, it's that. No one
knows it's Placido Domingo behind you. It's only his back.

DEIRDRE: I thought we were getting on?

(*She loads the photograph, closes the boot, gets in the driver's
seat of the Daimler.* MARK *gets in the passenger seat. During
this,* ALEX *and* ROSEMARY *get in the Vauxhall.* DEIRDRE

60

opens her car door and calls across to ALEX.)
I'll take the Residents' Parking place at the new house, yes?
You can bob that around a corner somewhere.
(*She closes the door. Both cars move off out of the drive.*)

EXT. SAME STREET: VAUXHALL – TRAVELLING. DAY
ROSEMARY: (*Voice over*) What's she calling the new car?
ALEX: (*Voice over*) Maggie.
ROSEMARY: (*Voice over*) After. . . ?
ALEX: (*Voice over*) I expect so.

INT. SAME STREET: DAIMLER – TRAVELLING. DAY
DEIRDRE: Looking ever-so-slightly shabby down here, these
    days, isn't it?
    (MARK *looks out in puzzlement, at the beautiful, pristine
    houses.*)

INT. SAME STREET: VAUXHALL – TRAVELLING. DAY
ROSEMARY: Gets high on all this, doesn't she?
ALEX: (*Sighs.*) Let's face it. She's never really got over not being
    in the Queen's Honours List at birth. She's always thought
    she was too good for everyone. Now she's proving it.
    Knightsbridge.
    (*They drive in silence for a moment.*)
ROSEMARY: Can we *afford* Knightsbridge?
ALEX: Darling, we can't afford the *Daimler.*
ROSEMARY: Does she know?
ALEX: She doesn't believe in accountants.
    (*A pause.*)
ROSEMARY: What *does* she believe in?
ALEX: If you haven't got it, flaunt it.

EXT. STREET IN HOLLAND PARK. DAY
*The two cars motoring along. We see another removal van parked
down the street.* MEN *are loading furniture into the lorry.*

INT. THE DAIMLER – MOTORING. DAY
DEIRDRE *stares, stiffening, at the lorry, then at* MARK.
DEIRDRE: Who lives at 36?

61

MARK: The allergy specialist.
DEIRDRE: They seem to be moving too . . . (*Brakes to a stop.*) How
do I open the window?
(*MARK presses a button. The window lowers. DEIRDRE pops her
head out.*)

EXT. STREET IN HOLLAND PARK. DAY
DEIRDRE *addresses one of the removal men, from her seat.*
DEIRDRE: Excuse me. Young man?
(*The MAN stops work, turns to her. She beams at him.*)
Where are these people moving to?
REMOVAL MAN: Belgravia.
(*DEIRDRE's face very slowly drops.*)
DEIRDRE: Sorry?
REMOVAL MAN: Belgrave Square, Belgravia.
(*To DEIRDRE, it's a death sentence.*)
DEIRDRE: (*Smiling*) Oh. Nice.

INT. DAIMLER – STATIONARY. DAY
MARK: Mind your nose, Ma.
DEIRDRE: The allergy specialist.
(*She turns away from the window, and stares unseeingly ahead.
MARK presses a button. The window closes again.*)
MARK: Belgrave Square, eh? The good part or the bad part, I
wonder?
(*No response.*)
Mother. Release the handbrake. Mother!
(*She releases the handbrake like a zombie.*)
Now put it in drive.
(*She does so. The car starts off towards what has now become the
shanty-town of Knightsbridge.*)

EXT. STREET BETWEEN HAMPSTEAD AND HOLLAND PARK. DAY
The Sanders Removals lorry driving along. NICK *at the wheel.*

INT. SANDERS REMOVAL LORRY – TRAVELLING. DAY
MRS ANDREOS *is seated between* NICK *and* BAMBER. PAUL *and*
TORNADO *squashed behind the seats. Wedged in* MRS ANDREOS's
arms is the embroidered map of Cyprus.

MRS ANDREOS: Maybe it because they slow eaters, these solicitor
people. I like slow eaters. It show they want to taste the food
for ever . . . Savouring. Like love . . . like love passion.
(BAMBER, NICK *and* TORNADO *all throw* PAUL *a quick,
apprehensive glance.*)
Maybe that's it.
BAMBER: Nah. Not in the case of solicitors I shouldn't think,
madam. It's 'cause it's Friday. Busiest day for
house-removing. It's their way of showing you who's boss.
Trick of the trade. Keep every bugger waiting. They learn it at
college.
NICK: (*To* MRS ANDREOS) You ought to see the state of *their*
houses . . . when *they* move . . .
MRS ANDREOS: (*Puzzled*) 'State'?
NICK: Muck.
MRS ANDREOS: Solicitor people have mucky houses?
PAUL: Solicitors, doctors and teachers. We had one last Tuesday,
Balham . . .
TORNADO: Wednesday.
NICK: Cooker was so greasy it damn-near slid out on its own . . .
TORNADO: (*Indicating* PAUL) He got flea-bites, didn't he?
NICK: Always has had – number of beds he's been in and out of.
(*A pause.*)
MRS ANDREOS: Shall we sing?
(*They all look at her.*)
BAMBER: Sing?
MRS ANDREOS: It's nice on a drive. A nice sing-song.
(*Now* that's *something they've never come across before* . . .)
Maybe we sing a little Boy George. You like Boy George?

EXT. LITTLE VENICE. DAY
The Sanders Removals lorry travelling. BAMBER, NICK, PAUL,
TORNADO *and* MRS ANDREOS *singing, voice over.*

EXT. HOUSE IN KNIGHTSBRIDGE. DAY
*Extremely opulent apartment house. Among the swanky cars parked
outside (including a Rolls-Royce) in the Residents' Parking Zones, is a
Harrods' Depository van.*
Superimpose caption: KNIGHTSBRIDGE SW1

HARROD'S EMPLOYEES, *in uniform and bowler hats, emerge from the apartment block, carrying items of antique furniture, or re-enter after loading.*

INT. KNIGHTSBRIDGE APARTMENT. DAY
An elderly man, THOMAS, *is seated on a leather, button-back Chesterfield, talking to his solicitor,* AMBROSE, *across a coffee table with drinks on it. From time to time, during the scene, the* HARRODS' MEN, *with discreet and subservient silence, enter and take out items of furniture.*

AMBROSE: I'm sorry, Thomas, I think you're raving mad. I've said so all along. I say it again.

THOMAS: (*A trace of submerged Cockney accent*) Good thing I've no respect for your opinion, then, isn't it?

AMBROSE: One word and you could stop this whole charade . . .

THOMAS: 'Charade,' he says. The only real thing I've done in forty-two years. You understand nothing. No wonder you're such a good lawyer.
(*A pause.* AMBROSE *sighs, helplessly.* THOMAS *smiles.*)
What would you do in my place, Ambrose?
(AMBROSE *fidgets uncomfortably.*)
Go on a binge for six months, a year – whatever it is? What would you binge it on? What *is* there?
(AMBROSE *sighs. He shrugs, defeated.*)
I haven't lost my senses, old man. I've just *come* to the buggers, that's all.
(*He suddenly picks up a vase of flowers from the coffee table and hurls it through the air. It smashes in small pieces against the wall.*)

AMBROSE: Christ Almighty!
(*The* HARRODS' MEN *sweep up the mess during the following*:)

THOMAS: (*Calmly*) You ever been angry, Ambrose? So bloody angry you want to kill? (*Beat.*) Now, in that sense, yes, I *am* raving mad. Mad at God, at me, everything. I'd quite like to kill. Have another brandy – rots your liver.
(*A pause.*)

AMBROSE: I don't blame you for being angry, Thomas . . . You've every right . . .

THOMAS: Agreed.

AMBROSE: (*Quietly*) It's just so pig-headed, though, it's –

THOMAS: (*Shouting*) Of course it's bloody pig-headed!! That's the whole bloody idea!

(*A silence.* AMBROSE *pours himself another brandy.*)

AMBROSE: (*Gently*) Look . . . all I'm saying . . .

THOMAS: I know what you're saying. I don't know why you bother.

AMBROSE: . . . is that for the next six months, a year, or – who knows? – *two* years –

THOMAS: (*Quietly*) Not as much as that. I'll be lucky if it's one.

AMBROSE: (*Uncomfortably*) Well, whatever. Even if it's only a *week*. Why do it? When you could stay here . . . or the Savoy . . . or the Bahamas and . . . and . . .

(*He peters out embarrassedly.* THOMAS *smiles, and finishes his sentence for him.*)

THOMAS: And die in peace?

AMBROSE: (*Sighs.*) Well . . .

('*Yes*' *is what he leaves unsaid.*)

THOMAS: (*Briskly*) Look, just sort out the money side . . . get this lot into Sotheby's or Christie's, whatever . . . You know where to reach me.

AMBROSE: (*Wryly*) I'm afraid I do.

THOMAS: (*Explaining, indulgently, as though to a child*) If I've got to die, I'd like to go back home to do it. To the warmth and quiet. I'd like to go back home.

AMBROSE: (*Exploding*) *This* is your bloody home!

(THOMAS *smiles genuinely.*)

THOMAS: Did you enjoy that? Good isn't it? There's a couple of Mings in the hall. Have a go at *them*. (*Gets up briskly.*) Come on. I think we're in these lads' way. If you fancy watching Leyton Orient with me next season, let me know . . . (*Beat, corrects himself.*) Not Leyton Orient now, is it? Just Orient. Same thing.

(*He goes to a bureau and takes out a cheap ashtray, bearing the legend* A PRESENT FROM SOUTHEND, *and stuffs it in his pocket. He then goes to the door, picks up a suitcase which is standing beside it, and goes out.* AMBROSE *stands up, downs the rest of his brandy and follows him.*)

EXT. KNIGHTSBRIDGE STREET. DAY

THOMAS *and* AMBROSE *come out of the front door. Thomas's*
CHAUFFEUR *opens the door of the Rolls-Royce, takes his suitcase.*
AMBROSE *goes up to one of the* HARRODS' MEN.

AMBROSE: The house-keeper has instructions to look after you.

HARRODS' MAN: Thank you, sir.

THOMAS: (*To* CHAUFFEUR) Home, James. It's all right – I know
    your name's Robert . . . but home.
    (*He and* AMBROSE *get in the Rolls-Royce. The* CHAUFFEUR
    drives off.)

INT. HOLLAND PARK HOUSE KITCHEN. DAY

MRS ANDREOS *is paying* BAMBER *in £5 notes.* NICK *is finishing
unpacking a tea-chest of crockery and pans which he has stacked in
cupboards.*

NICK: Your frying pan's down here, madam, all right?

MRS ANDREOS: Anywhere for now, thank you . . . You
    shouldn't be doing this for me.

BAMBER: Every couple of months we get a special case, madam.
    You're a special case.

MRS ANDREOS: (*Grins.*) Maybe I move again . . . every couple of
    months . . . I let you know.
    (PAUL *and* TORNADO *enter, looking pretty exhausted.*)

PAUL: All shipshape everywhere. Everything unpacked and put
    away. I've put all your long dresses on one hanger.

MRS ANDREOS: You very, very kind.
    (PAUL *and* NICK *pick up the last remaining empty tea-chests
    and start for the door.* BAMBER *puts the wad of fivers in his
    inside pocket and pats it.*)

BAMBER: Right, then, we'll be on our way, madam. Get these
    out of your way at the same time.

MRS ANDREOS: Wait! That's for the boss man. Now, a little
    something for the boys.
    (PAUL, NICK *and* TORNADO, *taking tea-chests out, call
    reciprocated 'Good luck, then's', 'All the best's', etc.*)
    Now . . .

BAMBER: (*Guiltily*) Er . . . no, no . . . um . . . we'll be getting
    quite a chunk of this . . . (*Pats pocket again.*) Really.

MRS ANDREOS: Listen, I've moved enough times to know better

. . . Always a little something for the boys.

EXT. HOLLAND PARK HOUSE. DAY
NICK, PAUL *and* TORNADO *are lifting the ramp back into the lorry,
prior to locking the doors.*
TORNADO: Think we're going to do all right out of her . . .
    Bunce on top of bunce, innit?
PAUL: Well, she must be loaded, mustn't she?
NICK: 'S more than that, innit? She loves us.
    (*They turn on hearing the front door bang. They (and we) see*
    BAMBER *somewhat sheepishly and uncomprehendingly coming
    from the house, carrying the embroidered map of Cyprus. They
    watch him blankly till he gets to them.*)
BAMBER: She said she wanted us to have something more
    valuable than money.
NICK: (*Blankly*) And what did *you* say?
BAMBER: I remember opening my mouth . . . but I don't think
    nothing came out.

INT. HALLWAY OF KNIGHTSBRIDGE APARTMENT. DAY
With a face like sulking granite, DEIRDRE *is directing* REMOVAL
MEN *to different rooms with her furniture.* ROSEMARY *appears from
down the hallway, holding a cat-litter tray.*
ROSEMARY: Ma? Lady Di's tray?
DEIRDRE: (*Irritably, preoccupied*) What?
ROSEMARY: Where should it go? There's no back porch.
    (MARK *passes, with an armful of books, from a tea-chest.*)
MARK: Well, she can't do it outside. Not in Knightsbridge.
    She'll have to tinkle in her knickers like everyone else.
DEIRDRE: (*Petulantly*) Anyway, we're not really Knightsbridge
    here.
MARK: (*Puzzled*) What?
DEIRDRE: We're virtually Belgravia . . . more or less.
ROSEMARY: (*Mystified*) Come again?
DEIRDRE: (*Floundering*) Well, Belgravia *Borders*, anyway . . .
    (*They stare at her.*)
    . . . *Abutting* Belgravia Borders . . .
    (MARK *and* ROSEMARY *exchange a look, and* MARK *exits.
    We go with him to . . .*)

INT. KNIGHTSBRIDGE APARTMENT 'LIBRARY'. DAY

ALEX *is sorting out books from tea-chests.* MARK *enters.*

MARK: I think her mind's crumbling.

ALEX: Only one thing can save her now – moving to
Buckingham Palace.

MARK: Can we *do* that on BUPA?

> (*We suddenly hear* DEIRDRE *scream, out of shot. Both men
> freeze, then run from the room.*)

INT. KNIGHTSBRIDGE APARTMENT LIVING ROOM. DAY

DEIRDRE *is standing at the window, horrified at what she can see
outside.* ALEX *and* MARK *race in, followed by* ROSEMARY, *still
holding the cat-litter tray.*

ALEX: What's happened?

> (*She points outside. They all look where she's pointing.*)

EXT. STREET IN KNIGHTSBRIDGE. DAY

From ALEX's *point of view, we see the wheels of the Daimler being
clamped by a* POLICE CLAMPSMAN. *The windows and windscreen
are plastered with stickers. The police vehicle stands beside it.*

INT. KNIGHTSBRIDGE APARTMENT LIVING ROOM. DAY

DEIRDRE, ALEX, MARK *and* ROSEMARY *at the window.* ALEX *is
biting the inside of his mouth to stop himself laughing.*

DEIRDRE: Tell them, Alex! We're residents! We're allowed!
Tell them!

> (*She takes her Resident's Parking Permit from her handbag
> and thrusts it at him. He exits with it.*)

EXT. STREET IN KNIGHTSBRIDGE. DAY

From DEIRDRE's *point of view, we see* ALEX *stroll slowly to the*
CLAMPSMAN *and talk to him for a moment. He produces the permit.
The* CLAMPSMAN *looks at it, and shakes his head. Angle on* ALEX
and CLAMPSMAN.

CLAMPSMAN: Not for this *car*, is it, squire?

ALEX: Sorry?

CLAMPSMAN: Different registration number.

ALEX: (*Slow realization*) Oh, hell . . . we applied when we had
the old . . . *this* is now our . . . We're the ones who live

here, though. It's our space . . .

CLAMPSMAN: Case of right resident, wrong motor, mate. Discrimination, really. They never get this trouble in Brixton. Nice banger. Bet it eats petrol, dunnit? Company car, is it?

EXT. STREET IN HACKNEY. DAY
Local pedestrians and traffic. Amid the traffic, we see the Rolls-Royce bearing THOMAS *and* AMBROSE *along. It turns a corner into . . .*

EXT. THE DILAPIDATED STREET IN HACKNEY. DAY
The same street that Des moved from. The Rolls sweeps along, ROBERT *driving,* THOMAS *and* AMBROSE *in the rear seats.*

THOMAS: (*Voice over*) A lot of sharp kids came from these streets in those days. Mickey Lomax lived down there . . . on the right. Owns half the container fleet in Hong Kong now . . .

INT. ROLLS-ROYCE – TRAVELLING. DAY

THOMAS: Little Jewish kid lived at the backs there. (*Points.*) Used to crack on he was a Catholic so's he could get a tanner every Friday night for lighting the rabbi's fire. You weren't supposed to light your own in those days, not on the Sabbath. I don't know if it applies today. He got a medal at Saint-Nazaire. Posthumous.

EXT. THE DILAPIDATED STREET IN HACKNEY. DAY
THOMAS *and* AMBROSE *being driven along.*

THOMAS: (*Voice over*) Used to have a pal down there. Maurice Blackstone. Underpresser. He had a kid – Don – real little comic, pants at half-mast. Writes songs now. West End hits . . . Broadway. (*Pause.*) Couple of kids at my school had trials with Leyton Orient. Don't know what happened to them. This is it.
(*The Rolls stops outside Des's Mum's house. Angle on* THOMAS *as he gets out and hauls his suitcase with him.*)
Thanks, old chap. Letters to number 94. The fewer the better.

AMBROSE: Stark, raving mad. They'll get you on that. The family. Unsound mind.

THOMAS: Love to Natalie. (*To* CHAUFFEUR) Thanks for
everything, Bob. Mind how you go.
(*He goes to the house and rings the bell. The Rolls drives off down
the street, and away. Angle on number 94 as* THOMAS *rings the
bell again. He stands watching some* BLACK KIDS *kicking a ball
about. Then knocks loudly at the door. After a moment or two,*
DES'S MUM *opens the door.*)
DES'S MUM: (*Warily*) Yes?
THOMAS: Mr Jackson.
DES'S MUM: (*Mentally curtsying*) Oh. Right. (*Looks at suitcase.*)
That all you got with you?
THOMAS: That's all.
DES'S MUM: Come in, then.
(*He starts to go in with her.*)
Did you ring the doorbell?
THOMAS: Yes.
DES'S MUM: It doesn't work.
THOMAS: I don't think it ever did.
(*She throws him a slightly puzzled glance, then closes the door after
them.*)

EXT. SANDERS REMOVALS YARD, NORTH LONDON. DAY
The removal lorries are all parked again after their day's work. NICK,
PAUL *and* TORNADO *are sitting on their haunches, rolling cigarettes. A
couple of* MEN *are cleaning another lorry.*
PAUL: What did the doctor say?
NICK: Nothing wrong with her.
PAUL: What about the dizzy spells?
NICK: He said it's worry that does that.
PAUL: Oh. And *is* there anything worrying her?
NICK: Yeah. The dizzy spells.
(BAMBER *comes out of the office (carrying the embroidered map of
Cyprus) and scanning Saturday's worksheet.* NICK *gets to his feet
again as* BAMBER *approaches.*)
PAUL: What's tomorrow look like?
BAMBER: (*Consults worksheet.*) Two-man packing job, Palmer's
Green – (*Nods at* PAUL *and* TORNADO.) – so you two get a lie-
in – ready for four-man move to Bermondsey, Monday. Or
Monday, according to her typewriter . . . in Bermondsev.

(*They start to walk towards the gates.* BAMBER *gets the exercise book from his pocket. Opens it. Hands it to* NICK.)
Where was we?

NICK: It's going-home time!

BAMBER: Last one, innit? The exam's in two hours. Weather permitting.
(NICK *sighs and pores over the page. They all walk along, during the following* . . .)

NICK: I can't pronounce him.

BAMBER: Vico. Giambattista Vico.

NICK: Irishman, is he?

BAMBER: Now what he's saying, the point he's making, his point is . . . is there's birth and growing, then decaying, then rebirth and regrowing again . . .

PAUL: Well, that's cobblers, innit?

BAMBER: What is?

PAUL: Who gets reborn? Who that *we* know?

NICK: (*To* BAMBER) Come on, head down. He sums it up, how?

BAMBER: (*Concentrating*) He sums it up . . . like if you leave your doorstep and travel as far as you can, well, all you do is wind up on your own doorstep again, what you started from.

TORNADO: What – even if you travel right round the world?

BAMBER: Well, of course. Bound to, en't you? World's round, innit? What he's getting at, really, is that it takes the whole journey . . . all your life and that . . . to get to know *yourself*, what you're about . . .

PAUL: I know what *I*'ll be about *tonight*, darling. Few Guinness down the pub till leg-over time, then trousers down and –

BAMBER: I don't want to know.
(*He takes the exercise book from* NICK *and stuffs it in his pocket.*)
Ta.
(*A pause. They walk along.*)

TORNADO: And the funny thing is – I once *knew* a bloke called Torvill.

NICK: What?

TORNADO: Vic Torvill. No relation, I don't think. He had all Rosemary Clooney's records and a drooping eyelid.

PAUL: Who's Rosemary Clooney?

TORNADO: I don't know if he could skate, though. He never said.

(*They walk out of the gates.*)

INT. DES'S – NOW THOMAS'S BEDROOM, HACKNEY. DAY
Thomas's present-from-Southend ashtray is now on the bedside table.
THOMAS *is packing clothes from his suitcase into a leaning chest of*
MFI drawers. There's a knock at the door. DES'S MUM *comes in*
holding a cup of tea.

DES'S MUM: No sugar, right?

THOMAS: Ta.

DES'S MUM: My Des used to take four. They do at that age, don't they? Settling in all right, then?

(THOMAS *takes the mug and sits on the bed.*)

THOMAS: It's changed. It's all changed. It's the same, but it's changed. Long as it's warm and quiet . . .

DES'S MUM: (*Defensively*) I told the man it'd be better if you saw it first yourself . . . but he said . . . (*Beat.*) I mean it's only a room . . . I'm the first to admit . . .

THOMAS: Fireplace has gone. Used to be a proper fireplace over there. Big mirror over it. And the bed was across that way. Me on that side, my brother on that.

DES'S MUM: (*Defensively*) They had it modernized before we came.

THOMAS: My dad used to hide his pay packets up that chimney, so's my mum wouldn't know what he was earning. Then one day my brother and me . . . playing sticking our heads up the chimney – who could get it the highest – and we found them. Gave them to my mum. He was earning twice what he was tipping up. They nearly got a divorce over it. (*Beat.*) Except in those days people didn't.

DES'S MUM: I didn't know it used to be *your* house . . . the man never said . . .

THOMAS: (*Shivers.*) Getting a bit nippy, isn't it? Does the fire work?

DES'S MUM: I have to get the element seen to. It may be the wiring in the walls . . . but Des thought it was the element. (*We hear reggae music through the wall from next door.*

Growing louder and louder. THOMAS *jerks his head towards the
wall, worriedly.* DES'S MUM *panics slightly.*)
Sometimes if you just knock on the wall . . .
(*She knocks on the wall. The music gets louder.*)
The other side's usually quite quiet.
(*She starts to go, anxiously.*)
I told the man it was only a room.
(THOMAS *sits, cold and bleak, as the music hammers his
eardrums.*)

EXT. STREET IN CENTRAL LONDON. DAY
The HOMELESS WOMAN *stops at a Christian Science office. In the
window is a mounted display copy of the* Christian Science Monitor
newspaper. She looks at it, and goes in.

EXT. STREET IN TUFNELL PARK. EVENING
It's now about 6 pm. DES *is seated on his blanketed bundle, his
roller-skates round his neck, eating Kentucky Fried Chicken and
chips. Along the street comes a dilapidated motorbike and sidecar. A
young black man is riding, and a young black girl is riding pillion,
her arms around his waist. This is* MYRA. *Around her neck are a
pair of roller-skates identical to Des's. The sidecar is jammed with
luggage.* DES *watches them, almost disinterestedly, still eating his
chips, as the bike stops at the kerb beside him.* MYRA *dismounts, and
starts lugging her belongings from the sidecar and on to the pavement.*
MYRA: Thanks, Gary. What do I owe you?
GARY: (*Grins.*) Leave off. I'll think of some way to pay me back.
    (*She laughs.* DES *is puzzled.*)
MYRA: Hi, Des. This is Gary from work. (*To* GARY) This is
    Des.
GARY: (*To* DES) All right?
DES: All right?
GARY: (*To* MYRA) See you tomorrow, then, darling.
    (*He rides off.*)
DES: Where you been, then?
MYRA: Work. Where d'you think?
DES: Oh.
MYRA: You been here long?
DES: All bleedin' day, en't I?

MYRA: (*Laughs.*) If you'd sometimes think with your brains instead of your balls . . . Why didn't you go in?

DES: It's your flat. He has to give you the key. He's gone now. Went hours ago.

MYRA: I just seen him. Picked up the key from his office on the way. What's he care who has the key? You should've just gone in.

(*They start hauling their luggage towards the front door of the flats. Then* MYRA *turns towards him and smiles enchantingly.*) Still. Goin' in now, en't we? *Together.* (*Tenderly*) Gi's a kiss, then.

(*He kisses her perfunctorily. She smiles, promisingly.*) You feeling randy?

(*It's been a long day. The longest of his life. He tries to think of an answer. Tries to feel. He's too numb to do either. A long, long, pause.*)

DES: (*Emptily*) I think I did this *morning* . . .

(*A beat, then, zombie-like, almost unaware of each other's presence, they continue hauling their luggage across the threshold.*)

INT. WILLESDEN FLAT. NIGHT

KEITH *is lying exhausted on the settee.* CARRIE *is arranging the few pieces of furniture they have round the room. Then stops. Surveys the effect. Then rearranges them. Finally, she lugs the settee (with* KEITH *still on it) into a better position.*

INT. HAMMERSMITH HOUSE BEDROOM. NIGHT

DUDLEY *and* ALISON *are in bed, with* TASHA *in between them, asleep. Now satisfied that she's in dreamland,* ALISON *gently climbs out of bed, picks up* TASHA *and pops her in her cot. She then returns to bed . . . and* DUDLEY's *waiting arms.*

EXT. STREET. NIGHT

GRANDPA, *with an overnight bag, approaches a basement flat. He presses the bell, which is labelled* BASEMENT FLAT: MR S. FOLEY, *and looks, bitterly, at the Yale lock and the Chubb lock. We hear them being unlocked. He manages a pathetic attempt at a friendly smile as the door opens.*

INT. HAMPSTEAD HOUSE LIVING ROOM. NIGHT
In the totally bare room, MR THORN *is seated on the floor counting his rubber bands.* MRS THORN *is seated on the floor at the other end of the room. The golf clubs are nearby. Cut to her hand as it reaches towards one of them . . . and slowly tightens its grip . . .*

INT. HOLLAND PACK HOUSE. NIGHT
MRS ANDREOS *hangs up the picture of her late husband on the wall. Looks at his face. Smiles. And, forgivingly, kisses his lips.*

INT. KNIGHTSBRIDGE APARTMENT BEDROOM. NIGHT
DEIRDRE *and* ALEX *are in bed.* ALEX *is fast asleep.* DEIRDRE *lies looking at the Placido Domingo photograph propped up on her dressing table. Water starts dripping on it. She looks up in horror at the ceiling. Cut to the ceiling. There's a deep crack in the plaster. Through it comes a steady trickle of water.*

INT. BAMBER'S BEDROOM. NIGHT
On the wall is the embroidered map of Cyprus. BAMBER *is in bed, finishing his notes in his exercise book. He closes it, puts it down on his bedside table, and turns out the light. Blackness.*

EXT. CENTRAL LONDON. NIGHT
The HOMELESS WOMAN *finds a doorway, or bench, and very carefully wraps around herself (under her coat) about a dozen copies of the* Christian Science Monitor. *And settles down for the night.*

EXT. PANORAMIC SHOTS OF CENTRAL LONDON. NIGHT

The Knowledge

CHARACTERS

CHRIS
JANET
GORDON WELLER
BRENDA WELLER
TED MARGOLIES
VAL MARGOLIES
TITANIC WALTERS
LILIAN WALTERS
MISS STAVELY
MR BURGESS
CONSTANTINE
O'REILLY
CAMPION
HARRY
CLIFF
STAN
CAFÉ PROPRIETOR
RECEPTIONIST
EDDIE HAIRSTYLE
MARGARET LOUISE (Janet's sister)
JOANNA (Ted's daughter)
CAFÉ OWNER
ARAB
ARAB'S WIFE
GINGER

Cabbies, Knowledge boys, Applicants at the Carriage Office, Policemen, Drivers, Passengers, Passers-by, Salesmen, Factory Workers, Members of Ted's family, Gordon's girlfriends, People in the Social Security Office.

The Knowledge was produced by Euston Films and first shown on Thames Television in December 1979. The principal members of the cast were as follows:

CHRIS	Mick Ford
JANET	Kim Taylforth
GORDON WELLER	Michael Elphick
BRENDA WELLER	Maureen Lipman
TED MARGOLIES	Jonathan Lynn
VAL MARGOLIES	Lesley Joseph
TITANIC WALTERS	David Ryall
MR BURGESS	Nigel Hawthorne

Crew

Art Director	Brian Morris
Director of Photography	David MacDonald
Editor	Ben Rayner
Producer	Christopher Neame
Executive Producer	Verity Lambert
Executive in Charge of Production	Johnny Goodman
Director	Bob Brooks

INT. KNOWLEDGE BOYS' CAFE, PENTON STREET. DAY
It's small, a bit crummy, its clientèle almost exclusively
KNOWLEDGE BOYS *of various ages. A group of them is seated at*
two of the tables, toying with mugs of tea and bacon sandwiches.
they all seem tired and strained. They're clutching call-over sheets.
One of them – HARRY *– is flicking searchingly through his Blue*
Book – which is coloured pinky-beige. Another – CLIFF *– sits*
opposite, watching the flicking, waiting for it to stop. He moistens his
lips, nervously. It stops.

HARRY: French Embassy to Fulham Cemetery.

CLIFF: (*His mind blank with fear*) What?

HARRY: What do you mean, 'What'?

CLIFF: French where?

HARRY: Embassy.

CLIFF: Oh. (*Tortured pause.*) *Which* cemetery?

HARRY: You idle sod! You haven't learned it!

> (*Jeers and catcalls from the others.* CLIFF *shifts guiltily in his*
> *chair.*)

CLIFF: Um . . . hang about . . . hang about . . .

> (CHRIS *and* JANET *enter. He's twenty-one, and she's twenty,*
> *dressed in worn, working clothes.* JANET *carries a battered*
> *skateboard. They've never been here before. They look round for*
> *a second to get their bearings – then* CHRIS *sits at a table, while*
> JANET *goes to the counter to order.* HARRY *holds up the Blue Book*
> *an inch from* CLIFF's *face to show him that both the French*
> *Embassy and Fulham Cemetery exist in black and white.*)

HARRY: Page 10, right? Run Number 8.

CLIFF: Hang about . . .

> (*Another Knowledge boy –* STAN *– at the next table, sits back,*
> *arms folded behind his head, and starts reciting effortlessly,*
> *rapidly and nonchalantly.*)

STAN: Leave on the right Albert Gate, left the Carriage Road,
left Alexandra Gate, forward Exhibition Road, right
Thurloe Street, comply South Kensington Junction, leave
by Old Brompton Road –

CLIFF: (*Lamely*) Oh, the French *Embassy*!
    (HARRY *closes the book in mock disgust.*)
HARRY: Jesus. . . !
    (JANET, *at the counter, and* CHRIS *in his chair, exchange a mildly baffled glance.*)
CHRIS: What are they on about?
JANET: (*Nodding towards the* PROPRIETOR) Shall I ask the feller?
CHRIS: It doesn't matter.
JANET: (*Angry loud whisper*) If you want to know!!
CHRIS: I don't.
    (*An irritated sigh from* JANET. *She turns to the* PROPRIETOR.)
JANET: Excuse me –
PROPRIETOR: Knowledge boys.
JANET: What?
PROPRIETOR: On the Knowledge. Poor buggers.
    (*Cut to the* KNOWLEDGE BOYS.)
CLIFF: (*Very tentatively*) Er . . . leave by Old Brompton Road, like Stan said, correct. Then . . . um . . . forward where-d'you-call-it . . . um . . . right Fulham Palace Road –
STAN: *Left*, you numb berk! *And* you missed out Lillie Road!
    (*Cut to* CHRIS, JANET *and* PROPRIETOR.)
CHRIS: And what's the Knowledge, then?
JANET: (*Suddenly, a little excited*) 'S all right, *I* know –
PROPRIETOR: It's a form of euthanasia.
CHRIS: What do they have to do?
PROPRIETOR: Be half-mental, far as I can see. (*Pause.*) If you've got a death wish, I believe that helps.
    (*Cut to the* KNOWLEDGE BOYS.)
CLIFF: (*To* HARRY) Tell you what. Try me on Woburn Square to Northern Polytechnic, instead.
HARRY: What the hell for??
CLIFF: I know that one.
    (HARRY *gently slaps* CLIFF's *face with Eric Morecambe reproach.*)
HARRY: Clifford. Darling. It's your *mother* that asks you the ones you know. The sadists up the road ask you the ones you *don't*. That's how they become sadists in the first place, know what I mean?

JANET: (*To* HARRY) Excuse me!
(*The* KNOWLEDGE BOYS *turn to her.*)
CHRIS: (*Uneasy*) Janet!
JANET: (*To the* KNOWLEDGE BOYS) This Knowledge. How do
you get on it?
HARRY: Metropolitan Police Public Carriage Office. Just down
the road. Twenty, twenty-five yards.
STAN: Twenty-two.
CHRIS: (*To* JANET) Hang on. We don't know what it entails or
nothing! (*To the others*) I mean it'll entail things, won't it?
CLIFF: Blood, sweat and tears, that's all.
JANET: (*To* HARRY) Ta. (*To* CHRIS) Right, that's it.
CHRIS: (*Baffled*) What's *what*? I don't know what the hell
you're –
JANET: Tempting, innit?
CHRIS: What is?
(JANET *offers him a spoonful of apple pie, brought from the
counter.*)
JANET: Have a bit of apple pie.
CHRIS: No, thanks. I just want to know what –
JANET: Go on. Half each.
CHRIS: What are you all worked up about?
(*She thrusts the spoonful of pie towards his mouth. He leans
forward and starts feeding from it.*)
(*Voice over*) So that was it. How it all started. I applied to
go on the Knowledge – and I didn't even know what it *was*.
(Pause.) I found out, though. By hell, I found out.

INT. APPOINTMENTS WINDOW, CARRIAGE OFFICE. DAY
Some months later. The GIRL RECEPTIONIST *is attending to a*
MAN *at the window.*
RECEPTIONIST: Applying for the Knowledge?
MAN: 'S right. (*Hands her his Driving Licence.*) Driving Licence.
RECEPTIONIST: Thank you. Birth certificate?
(*He hands her his birth certificate.*)
MAN: All go, innit?
RECEPTIONIST: Thank you. (*Hands him documents.*) Now that's
your application form. You fill it in. And that's your
medical form – your doctor fills that in. And that's your slip

83

for the photographer in Upper Street. For your photo. Six copies.

MAN: I've already got a photo. From when I won Wimbledon.

(*The briefest of suspicious glances from the* RECEPTIONIST.)

Wimbledon and District Snooker Contest. I always just say Wimbledon. Well, you have to be barmy, haven't you? Keeps you sane. (*Beat.*) I always say *that*, an' all.

RECEPTIONIST: (*Drily*) It has to be the official six photos from Upper Street.

(*The* MAN *takes his forms, as* CHRIS *passes by, having climbed the stairs from the street entrance. He's dressed in his shabby best. Nervous, ill-at-ease, looking a bit lost.*)

Applying for the Knowledge?

CHRIS: Me? No. I've done the applying.

RECEPTIONIST: Fair enough.

CHRIS: Already.

RECEPTIONIST: Yeah. OK.

CHRIS: (*Shows her a form he's clutching.*) I'm here for my acceptance interview to, you know, go on it, sort of thing . . .

RECEPTIONIST: Room 12.

CHRIS: That's what it says on here.

RECEPTIONIST: Well, that's where you go.

CHRIS: Well, that's what I thought, innit, really . . .

(*He continues on his way down the corridor, confident he knows the way . . . then stops, turns . . . just to make sure.*)

Which way is room 12?

RECEPTIONIST: The way you're going.

CHRIS: Right. No problem. Right.

(*He continues on his way. Stay on him as . . .*)

(*Voice over*) At the time I started on the Knowledge, I was on the payroll of the biggest firm in England – the Department of Social Security.

INT. DEPARTMENT OF SOCIAL SECURITY. DAY

Hands doling out money to other hands across a counter. The hands are CHRIS's. *He's at the head of a doleful dole queue. Wearing a shabby jerkin and jeans – and the blank defeated face of the unemployed.*

CHRIS: (*Voice over*) I'd been with them ever since I left school nearly. With my six 'O' levels.

    (*Counting his money, he wanders to the exit. He stops, out of habit, at the* JOBS VACANT *notice board. Already standing scanning it, is a* MIDDLE-AGED MAN. *Throughout the following exchange, they don't look at each other, but simply stare at the notice board.*)

MAN: Makes you laugh, dunnit? Never-sodding-never-land.

CHRIS: I get a bit sick of laughing. (*Beat.*) Makes your face ache.

INT. CORRIDOR, CARRIAGE OFFICE. DAY

CHRIS *approaches room 12. Looks at the number clearly labelled on the door, then checks with the number on his form, then tentatively knocks and opens the door. The other* APPLICANTS *all turn to look at him. The sea of faces throws him even more.*

CHRIS: Is this the Room 12 for starting the Knowledge?

GORDON: You what?

CHRIS: It says Room 12. (*Beat.*) I expect there's only the one . . .

    (*He goes in.*)

INT. WAITING ROOM, CARRIAGE OFFICE. DAY

CHRIS *enters. Seated on straight-backed chairs lined round three of the walls are seven men and one woman. Two of the men are black. Ages vary from twenty-one to forty-eight. All of them are working class, dressed in their best – however humble that may be. The atmosphere is as tense and nerve-racked as any dentist's waiting room. The applicants include* GORDON WELLER (*about thirty-five*), TED MARGOLIES (*about twenty-six*) *and* TITANIC WALTERS (*about forty-eight*). GORDON *leans across to the others, in turn, for a light for his cigarette. No one seems able to help. Finally, the young woman* (MISS STAVELY) *gives him a light. He takes a deep drag.*

GORDON: Cheers.

    (*He winks at her. She looks away. She smiles at* CHRIS. *He looks away. The silence is broken by the door crashing open – and* MR BURGESS *swings briskly, noisily in. He's in his late forties, an ex-policeman. Big and very intimidating. Although, in this scene, he's at his friendliest, that's nothing like as friendly as anyone else's.*)

BURGESS: Afternoon!

> (*One or two almost inaudible replies. Everyone tenses even more. He strides over to the vacant fourth wall.*)

And no smoking if you don't mind. Except in the case of expectant fathers who shouldn't be here in the first place.

> (GORDON *dumps out his cigarette and turns to his neighbour.*)

GORDON: (*Drily*) Soon as you're enjoying your-bleeding-self. Subject normal.

BURGESS: Not that I mind you choking *yourselves* to death, but I'm only halfway through decorating the old lady's kitchen – washable vinyl.

> (*No one's amused.* BURGESS *takes a sheaf of files from under his arm.*)

Now if you cast your minds back a few months, you may have fond memories of filling these in. Your completed application forms – tea rings and all. Just sing out when I call your name – then I can put a face to each of you.

> (*He calls out the name attached to each file, in turn.*)

Walters, Kennington Oval.

TITANIC: Here.

BURGESS: If any of you wish to call me 'sir', I shall try not to be offended. Stavely, Dulwich.

MISS STAVELY: Yes, sir.

BURGESS: Constantine, Notting Hill.

CONSTANTINE: Yes, sir.

BURGESS: O'Reilly, Kilburn.

O'REILLY: Here, sir.

BURGESS: Campion, Kentish Town.

CAMPION: Here, sir.

BURGESS: Matthews, Stepney.

CHRIS: Sir.

BURGESS: Weller, Gunnersbury Park.

GORDON: Present and correct.

> (BURGESS *raises his eyes very briefly to see if there's a 'sir' to come. There isn't. He resumes.*)

BURGESS: Margolies, Clapham.

TED: Here, sir.

BURGESS: (*Putting the files on a small table*) Terrific. You all know your own names. My living shall not be in vain. Now . . .

(*He takes a deep breath and launches into his speech. He's given it a hundred times before: every word, every pause, every expression is now second nature.*)

. . . my name is Mr Burgess – no applause, please – and this little chat is called your Acceptance Interview. It means you're now – starting today – officially on the Knowledge. Which by a remarkable twist of logic, brings us to Question Number One: namely, what exactly *is* the Knowledge?

GORDON: Well, all it is really is boning up in your head all the macaroni about –

BURGESS: Thank you, Mr Weller. That was known as a rhetorical question. I *know* what the Knowledge is. In other words, *I* tell *you*. In other words, you keep your mouth shut and listen. You might learn something.

(GORDON *glances at the others and grins. No one grins back. He catches* BURGESS's *eye – and stops grinning.*)

Namely, what exactly *is* the Knowledge?

(*He steps across to a huge wall map of London. Drawn on it is a circle, indicating a six-mile radius from Charing Cross. Cut to close-up* GORDON.)

GORDON: (*Voice over*) I knew what it was all right. The next greasy step on the treadmill. Like everything else. With a bunch of greens dangled in front of your hooter. Well . . . I'd tried everything else in my time, hadn't I? Gordon Weller, the cowboy of Wild West Three. Cowboy plumber, then cowboy electrician, then cowboy carpenter . . .

INT. TRENDY MIDDLE-CLASS KITCHEN. DAY

GORDON, *in overalls, is vainly trying to fit a fitted kitchen. The trendy, middle-class* LADY *of the house watches, in growing horror, as he cack-handedly ruins the fitments.*

GORDON: (*Voice over*) Then, since April, cowboy kitchen-installer. (*Beat.*) And I made a right cow out of all of them.

(*He beams confidently through his panic at the appalled* LADY *as he continues ruining her £4,000 kitchen.*)

(*Voice over*) Three cocked-up kitchens later, I thought, 'Hang up your boots, Cowboy. Let's find a cushier number, shall we? E.g. charging Arabs fifteen quid from London Airport.'

INT. WAITING ROOM, CARRIAGE OFFICE. DAY
BURGESS *at the wall map.*
BURGESS: As laid down by the London Hackney Carriage Act
of 1843, all the Knowledge means . . . (*Pause*) . . . is that
you commit to memory . . . (*Pause*) . . . every street within
a six-mile radius of Charing Cross. (*Circles the radius on the
map.*) Every street – and what's *on* every street. Every
hotel, every club, every hospital, every department store,
every shop, government building, theatre, cinema,
restaurant, art gallery, park, church, synagogue, mosque,
etcetera, etcetera, etcetera. And etcetera. Every building or
amenity in public use. You name it, you've got to know it.
Or, in the words of the poet, John Keats, 'That is all you
know on earth, and all you need to know.'
(*A bleak smile.*)
Keats *House*, for the uninitiated, is halfway down on the
right-hand side of Keats Grove, leaving on right Devonshire
Hill, leaving on right Hampstead High Street, NW3.
(*Everyone looks as though they're in a state of shock.* MISS
STAVELY, *alone, tries a small smile.* BURGESS, *picks up a
small pinky-beige booklet.*)
Now *this* . . . is your Bible. It's called the Blue Book . . .
probably because it's coloured pink. Don't ask me why
pink is called blue. A bit like Life in a way. Try not to
worry about it. (*Pause.*) Now, in the same way that pink is
blue, when I say this is your Bible – it *isn't.*
(*He smiles. No one's amused.*)
It's more your little Sermon on the Mount: it tells you what
you've got to know – not how to get to know it.
(*He turns to page 1.*)
One page 1, you'll find a list – which we call a page – of
routes – which we call runs. Run number 1 on page number
1 is Manor House Station to Gibson Square. Manor House
is the starting point, Gibson Square the finishing point. Not
that anyone has ever *wanted* to go from Manor House to
Gibson Square. But *you*'ve got to know *how* to. All the
one-way systems, traffic lights, roundabouts, streets – and
what's *on* every street. Right?
(*Everyone stares at him, blank and bemused.*)

88

So far – piece of pudding. Except for one little thing. There's not one page – there's twenty-six. And there's not one list on each page – there's eighteen. So that's four hundred and sixty runs altogether, with say fifteen streets on each one, which means, at a nice round figure, that the macaroni you have to bone up in your head, Mr Weller, is a grand total of five and a half thousand streets . . . and the few thousand buildings on those streets. (*Pause.*) By heart. (*Pause.*) And *that*, gentlemen, *lady* and gentlemen, is – (*Pause for effect*) – *not* the Knowledge but the *first* part of the Knowledge.
(*Everyone's heart – except* TED's *– is in his boots.*)
Now, don't blame me. The Knowledge goes back three hundred and fifty years. Slightly before my time. It was started in 1644 by decree of the Lord Protector, one Oliver Cromwell.

O'REILLY: (*Muttering to his neighbour*) Trust that bastard to have something to do with it . . .

BURGESS: (*Demonstrating on wall map*) The *second* part of the Knowledge is the streets of *Outer* London . . . we've got a nice few hundred of them for you. And the *third* part is the Driving Test. In a *cab*. You don't have to be *brilliant*. Perfect will do fine.
(*Cut to* TED, *close-up*.)

TED: (*Voice over*) Fair enough. No danger. If it was perfection he wanted, perfection he'd get. Only better.

EXT. TED'S HOUSE. EVENING
Four taxis drive up and stop outside the house. From one of them emerges TED'S FATHER *and* GRANDFATHER, *from the second his* FATHER-IN-LAW, *and from the other two his two* BROTHERS. *They all greet each other briefly and ring the bell of the door.*

TED: (*Voice over*) Better than my grandad when he was a cabby. Better than my old man now. And my father-in-law. And my two brothers. I was going to be the best Margolies that ever pushed a cab. Better than the lot of them.
(TED *opens the door and greets them as he lets them in.*)

INT. TED'S LIVING ROOM. EVENING
TED, *his* FATHER, GRANDFATHER, FATHER-IN-LAW, *and*

BROTHERS *are seated round the table playing poker. During the following,* VAL *(Ted's wife) places cans of beer and sandwiches in front of them.* (TED *has a cup of tea instead of beer). She gives* TED *an affectionate kiss on the head as she passes.*

TED: *(Voice over)* I mean, granted, not even Val was exactly over the moon, me grafting at a laundry. I worked the Hoffman press at the time. I mean, like she said, it's not skilled but it's not rubbish. But *they* all reckoned it was. Like I was breaking a family tradition. Like I'd married out or something. Val said I should punch them in the mouth – treating me like rubbish. So that was it . . . I'm not a violent man . . . I came on the Knowledge instead.

INT. WAITING ROOM, CARRIAGE OFFICE. DAY

BURGESS: Now, if you fondly imagine you can master the Knowledge, sat in your front parlour, with your Blue Book in one hand and your girlfriend in the other – *(To* MISS STAVELY) excepting your presence, Miss Stavely – watching Liverpool win one–nil in the last three seconds of *Match of the Day*, thank you, goodnight and God bless. Because you *can't*. There *are* Knowledge schools that can guide you . . . but, in the end, you only learn the Knowledge by *doing* the bugger. Every single street of it. There is no other way. And I'll tell you a little secret, seven out of the ten of you sitting here today will *never* make it. *(Beams at them.)* Everybody happy?
(Cut to close-up TITANIC)

TITANIC: *(Voice over)* Happy? Always have been, mate. I could write a bloody book on happiness. Cheapest book on the market. Bound to be. There'd be no bleeding pages in it.

INT. CAR WASH. DAY

Sodden and drenched, TITANIC *is sloshing about in floods of water, washing down a car. There's a queue of cars waiting to be attended to. The* DRIVER *of the next in line leans out of his window.*

DRIVER: Get your finger out, Noddy! Cars depreciate in the wet!

TITANIC: *(Muttering to himself)* I've been depreciating since I was born, mate. And I was worth sod-all *then.* *(Aloud to the*

DRIVER) Shan't be a minute, sir. (*Then, muttering to himself*)
That put *him* in his place!
(*He continues sloshing – but more quickly.*)
(*Voice over*) Happy in my work. Happy at home.

INT. TITANIC'S LIVING ROOM. NIGHT
Titanic's wife, LILIAN, *is seated at the table doing a crossword
puzzle.* TITANIC *enters from the kitchen, with his meagre supper,
and sits down at the table to eat it. He's wet and weary.* LILIAN
completely ignores him.
TITANIC: (*Voice over*) Lilian did competitions. Spot-the-Ball;
place in order the best features of the latest Ford Fiesta;
crosswords by the thousands. And she hadn't a clue. Never
won nothing. (*Sighs.*) And *she* reckoned *I* was a disaster.
That's how I got my nickname, wasn't it? Titanic. (*Sighs.*)
She hadn't spoken to me since our honeymoon. Seventeen
years previous. (*Beat.*) She never said why.

INT. WAITING ROOM, CARRIAGE OFFICE. DAY
BURGESS: Now, just in case you're all having too good a time –
one last thought. (*Holds up an application form.*) On page 2
of your forms, you answered the following two questions –
which are deliberately in heavy, black type. 11.a. 'Have you
ever been convicted of any offence or been bound over?'
And 11.b. 'Are you the subject of any outstanding charge or
summons?' (*Puts the form down again.*) All of you answered,
'No.' And all of you told the truth. Because we've checked.
With the Police. As we always continue to do right through
your career as a cabby – if you ever *have* one, that is.
Consequently, if your hobby is mugging old ladies, or
driving a vehicle with a gallon of Martinis inside you and a
cherry on your head, go into politics not cab-driving.
Because, one conviction *ever* – and you're back in the bus
queue. Right.
(*A pause. He and his voice soften, confidentially.*)
Now, the Knowledge sounds impossible. It isn't. Otherwise
there'd be no such phenomenon as the London cabby. It's
true that no taxi-driver in no other city in no other country
in the world has to know a *fraction* of what you have to

know. And not many brain surgeons, neither. But there we are. That's how we built an Empire – and, no doubt, how we knocked the bugger down again. We live, we learn . . . What we, in our ignorance, call Knowledge . . .

(*Cut to close-up* CHRIS.)

CHRIS: (*Voice over*) If I'd only known then what I know now, eh? By hell. I mean, I was only doing it for Janet, wasn't I? She'd got this mental attitude, sort of thing – no job, no nothing. Not even living together. (*Pause.*) I mean the acrobatics fellers go through just to, you know, get their end away and that . . . Now, *that*'s Knowledge. (*Beat.*) We live, we *never* bloody learn.

EXT. FACTORY, STEPNEY. DAY

CHRIS *is hovering at the gates. Looks at his watch.*

CHRIS: (*Voice over*) Till then the highlight of my day had been meeting Janet for her lunch-break. Well, *edited* highlight really – she didn't get long. Five o'clock I'd do an action replay and meet her again.

(WORKERS *start filtering out of the factory, including lines of girls, their arms linked, chatting.*)

(*Voice over*) All morning with nothing to do but wait for half-twelve. And all afternoon waiting for five o'clock. Like I was a baby, still on the breast, waiting for my next feed. (*Pause.*) All I had was Janet. All I wanted. *She* loved *me* an' all.

(JANET *emerges.* CHRIS's *face immediately lights up.* JANET *smiles back. It seems to take quite an effort. He moves towards her.*)

(*Effusively*) Hi!

JANET: (*Restrained*) Hello, mate.

(*He moves to take her arm. She pulls back irritatedly. Then smiles quickly to cover up.*)

Well, let me get out of the bloody gates.

(*He smiles back, hurt, disconcerted. They walk off.*)

INT. GARAGE/JUNK SHED. EVENING

CHRIS *and* JANET *are irritatedly straightening their dishevelled clothing. Standing watching them, deadpan, is Janet's sister,*

MARGARET LOUISE, *who's just interrupted their fumbling love-making. She's about seven years old.*

CHRIS: (*Voice over*) Three nights before I applied to go on the Knowledge, Janet's sister, Margaret Louise, had caught us in their dad's garage discussing the American involvement in Cambodia. We'd nowhere else we could go. We was banned from her mum and dad's flat – they didn't want her getting serious with a dead-leg on the dole. And the only time my mum saw her, she slung a bucket of water on her head. In case Janet just wanted me for my dole money. She had a decent Afro till then.

JANET: All right, Miss Bloody Piggy, what's it take to keep your mouth shut?

MARGARET LOUISE: A skateboard.

INT. WAITING ROOM, CARRIAGE OFFICE. DAY
Close-up CHRIS.

CHRIS: (*Voice over*) There was one advertised, second-hand, in the evening paper. House up Pentonville way. Which is how we came to wander in that café in the first place. So here I was. (*Pause.*) Wasn't I?
(BURGESS *is handing the appropriate application forms to each applicant.*)

BURGESS: Now take these back to the young lady at the Appointments Window. She'll book your first appointment. Which means your first *test* – so it isn't called an Appointment. Come to that, it isn't called a test either. It's called an Appearance. (*Bleak smile.*) Funny old world we live in. (*Resumes.*) Now that first appearance will be in fifty-six days' time. Your next one will be fifty-six days after that. And so on. Eventually – if you're still with us – it'll be every twenty-eight days, finally every fourteen. How long it takes you before you get your licence and your pretty Green Badge is up to you. And, no doubt, God. If you're a genius it could be a year. On the other hand it might take two. Or seven. Or ten. If it looks as though it's taking longer than that, I should pack it in and have a go at ballet dancing. Any questions?
(*They all sit in miserable silence. A pause.*)

No? In that case, thank you and good luck.

(*Everyone starts to leave, numbly, except* TED, *who stands hovering at one side.* BURGESS *hands* GORDON *his application form.*)

(*Quietly*) I notice you're not averse to standing on your accelerator, Mr Weller?

GORDON: (*Puzzled*) Sorry?

BURGESS: November 18, 1966, Brixton Road, 45 miles per hour.

(GORDON *stares at him, trying to remember.*)

GORDON: 1966? I wasn't even bloody born!!

BURGESS: I told you we check with the Police. (*Smiles.*) Watch it.

(GORDON *takes his form and exits with the others.* TED *stands smiling, somewhat ingratiatingly, at* BURGESS.)

Yes, Mr Margolies?

TED: I just wanted to say how, well . . . my father's a cabby, sort of thing, and his father before him, and the wife's, like, and two of my brothers . . . and how, you know, being in the blood really, I expect . . . I feel I'm already, you know . . . Anyway, they all wish to be remembered to you . . . well, not my grandad, of course, and to pass on their very best wishes . . .

BURGESS: (*Calmly*) Mr Margolies. Passing the Knowledge is different from anything else in the world. It's unique. It's not *who* you know; it's *what* you know. (*Bleak, chilling smile.*) Know what I mean?

(TED *swallows, chagrined.* BURGESS *strides out of the room.*)

EXT. CRUMMY MOTOR-BIKE SHOWROOM. DAY

CHRIS *stands admiring a beautiful gleaming new motor-bike, on the forecourt. At the doors of the showroom,* JANET *is fishing pound notes out of her handbag. The* SALESMAN *wheels out to her an ancient, dilapidated moped. She pays him.* CHRIS *looks at the moped, heart sinking.*

CHRIS: (*Voice over*) I don't know what I'd have done without Janet. Sod-all, knowing me. It meant everything to her, the Knowledge. Well, it meant a *future*, didn't it? It was like buying her own engagement ring in a way.

INT. GORDON'S LIVING ROOM. EVENING

With some difficulty and impatient exasperation, GORDON *is zipping himself into brand-new oilskins and leggings. His wife,* BRENDA, *stands watching in shocked disbelief.*

BRENDA: *What* Knowledge?

GORDON: I've just informed you what Knowledge, darlin'. Pity you missed it – I've got a lovely speaking voice.

BRENDA: What about your kitchen-installing?

GORDON: That's daytime, innit?

BRENDA: And what's this?

GORDON: Evenings, innit?

BRENDA: *Mine* an' all??

GORDON: What?

BRENDA: My wrestling! And my drag acts at the White Lion! And my mail-order! And my odd chicken-in-the-bleedin'-basket! We like a ride out of a sodding evening.

GORDON: (*Still zipping up*) Yeah, well, that's gone the way of all flesh an' *all* now. The Viva turned into a moped at three o'clock this afternoon.

BRENDA: (*Horrified*) Gordon!!

GORDON: (*Peremptorily*) Oi!!
(*She quietens down, petulant but chastened.*)
This is *me* under this lot! It's not anybody! It's Gordon Weller. All right?
(*She sighs submissively. He frowns in sudden – and urgent – discomfort.*)
Oh, hell.

BRENDA: What?

GORDON: (*Sighs wearily.*) Well, that's life, innit?

BRENDA: What is it?

GORDON: (*Starts unzipping everything he's zipped.*) Only want a Jimmy Riddle, don't I? (*Tugging irritatedly at a zip*) It'll take me half an hour to find it – let alone get it out!

BRENDA: (*Curtly*) I know the feeling!
(*She turns on her heel. He gives her a dirty look, then continues unzipping.*)

INT. TITANIC'S LIVING ROOM. EVENING

TITANIC *is finishing oiling an old rusty pushbike.* LILIAN, *dressed*

*in old ill-fitting clothes, is doing a fashion competition in a
newspaper.* TITANIC *gets up, picks up an* A-to-Z, *puts scarf and
raincoat over his arm and starts pushing the bike out of the room. He
glances at* LILIAN.

TITANIC: Cheerio, love.

> (LILIAN *ignores him. He puts the scarf round his neck and exits
> with his bike.*)

EXT. BACK STREET. EARLY EVENING

Behind the block of flats where Janet lives. JANET *is fixing a
clipboard of lists of streets on to the moped. Excited.* CHRIS, *in
second-hand oilskins, sits astride the moped. Despondent.*

JANET: All organized, then? Do we have lift-off?

CHRIS: I think I'll pack it in.

JANET: Oh, nice. Nothing like starting off on the right foot.

CHRIS: I'll never *learn* it all, Janet.

JANET: You haven't *tried* yet!

CHRIS: I can't do nothing, me.

JANET: Here we go again. Thanks. That's what a girl likes to
    hear.

CHRIS: What if it takes me seven years!

JANET: Why, what else have you got to do? (*Realizes her* faux
    pas. *Apologizes wearily.*) Sorry.

CHRIS: I'll be past it!

JANET: Some blokes take a *year*, you said!

CHRIS: I'm me, though, ent I? I'm not other blokes. Never have
    been.

JANET: Chris! It's your first run! You've four hundred and sixty
    to learn! They're not coming riding past *you*! Half my
    bottom sodding drawer's gone on this!
    (*An angry pause.*)

CHRIS: You're at work all day. *After* work's the only chance we
    get for a quick –

JANET: That's why you're doing it, innit, you berk! The quicker
    you get the Knowledge, the quicker we can have a quick
    everything. Now, get lost – and mind the roads.

CHRIS: I *will* get lost. (*Looks at the papers in his clipboard.*) Page
    1, number 1: Manor House Station to Gibson Square.
    Where the hell's Manor House Station for a kick-off?

JANET: What's your *A-to*-bloody-*Z* for?
(*He starts the engine and wobbles a few yards down the alley. Then stops and turns round in his seat to look at her.*)
CHRIS: You don't fancy coming with me, do you?
JANET: (*Exploding*) Chris! There's a great big world out there!
CHRIS: (*Meaning that that's frightening*) I know!
JANET: (*Meaning that it's exciting*) Well, then!
(*He rides off unhappily.* JANET *watches him – equally unhappily.*)

EXT. TITANIC'S STREET. EARLY EVENING
TITANIC *is wobbling shakily down the street on his pushbike. He passes a church. Its wayside pulpit reads:* THE FEAR OF THE LORD IS THE BEGINNING OF KNOWLEDGE (PROVERBS 1.7). *He falls off his bike.*

EXT. NORTH LONDON STREETS. EARLY EVENING
In the midst of the traffic, we see CHRIS *riding unsteadily along on his moped, scanning the street names and buildings, stopping occasionally to check with the list on his clipboard – or pencil a note on it.*
CHRIS: (*Voice over*) From Manor House Station leave on left Green Lanes, right Highbury New Park –
JANET: (*Voice over*) Hang on. Hang on. What's the building on the left?
CHRIS: (*Voice over*) Um . . . Islington Town Hall.
JANET: (*Voice over*) Well, if it is, some slimy bastard's moved it.
CHRIS: (*Voice over*) Thames Water Authority. Stoke Newington Pumping Station.
JANET: (*Voice over*) Thank you.
CHRIS: (*Voice over*) Right Highbury New Park, and left Highbury Grove, right St Paul's Road . . .

INT. JANET'S PARENTS' FLAT. EVENING
MARGARET LOUISE *is standing on look-out duty on the balcony peering down at the bus stop, in case her parents approach.* CHRIS *and* JANET *are on the settee. She is holding a reporter's notebook listing runs and the clipboard.*
CHRIS: Um . . . right St Paul's Road . . .

JANET: You've said that once.

(*His inability to concentrate may have something to do with him nuzzling her neck and trying to unbutton her blouse.*)

CHRIS: Um . . . comply Highbury Corner . . .

(*He's stuck again. A long pause.*)

JANET: (*Prompting*) Comply Highbury Corner . . .

CHRIS: My head won't concentrate . . .

JANET: I've noticed.

(MARGARET LOUISE *bursts in from the balcony.*)

MARGARET LOUISE: Mum and dad! Getting off the bus!

(JANET *and* CHRIS *leap up.* CHRIS *grabs crash helmet, notebook and clipboard.* MARGARET LOUISE *stands with her hand held out for payment.* JANET *pays her from her purse, as she and* CHRIS *race out of the door.*)

INT. TED MARGOLIES'S KITCHEN. LATE

The same night. Tired, but elated, TED *is at the table eating home-made fish and chips. His helmet is on the table.* VAL *is sitting opposite him with his clipboard and notebook of runs. He recites the run with speedy assurance.*

TED: Forward Highbury Park, forward Highbury Grove, right St Paul's Road. Comply Highbury Corner, right Theberton Street – which leads to Liverpool Road and Liverpool Road Hospital – then right Gibson Square. (*Grins.*) Bingo!

VAL: Another chopped and fried?

TED: I couldn't honest.

VAL: For my being proud of you, doll.

TED: I couldn't, doll.

(*She nevertheless puts another piece of chopped fried fish on his plate. He grins at her.*)

Ta.

INT. TITANIC'S LIVING ROOM. NIGHT

TITANIC *is huddled before a lukewarm paraffin heater, holding his list of runs – his eyes closed in concentration.* LILIAN *noisily crosses from the kitchen on her way to bed. She wears a tattered dressing-gown, her hair is in curlers, and she carries a cup of cocoa and a book of crosswords.*

TITANIC: (*Struggling to remember*) Forward Highbury Park . . .

um . . . forward Highbury Grove . . . er left, no *right*, no
left St Paul's Road . . . (*He glances at the run.*) No, *right*.
(*Quietly desperate, he glances up at* LILIAN *as she passes. She
ignores him and noisily barges off to bed. He slumps slightly,
then resumes.*)
Comply Highbury what's-it . . . doodah . . . corner . . .
Comply Highbury Corner . . .

EXT. STREET IN STEPNEY. NIGHT
CHRIS *and* JANET, *arms round each other's shoulders, walking
along.* JANET's *holding the list of runs.*
CHRIS: (*Straining to remember*) Comply Highbury Corner . . .
    sod it!
JANET: What?
CHRIS: That's it!
JANET: It isn't!
CHRIS: It is for me. I'm turning it in. It's bloody impossible.
JANET: *Other* fellers do it!
CHRIS: Yeah, well . . . other fellers have . . .
JANET: Haven't got *me*!
    (*They stop. He looks at her. They share a small, sad smile.*)
CHRIS: (*Suddenly*) Comply Highbury Corner, right Theberton
    Street, then right Gibson Square!! (*Looks at her numbly.*)
    Done it.
JANET: (*Delighted*) See!
CHRIS: Not that anyone ever goes from Manor House Station to
    Gibson Square.
JANET: You remembered it!
CHRIS: (*Shouting*) I know the way from Manor House Station
    to . . .
    (*He's forgotten.*)
JANET: (*Shouting it for him*) Gibson Square!!
    (PASSERSBY *look at them warily, and give them a wide berth.*)
CHRIS: (*Shouting*) I know the way from Manor House Station to
    Gibson Square!!
    (*He simmers down. They stand smiling at each other. Just as
    sadly as before.*)
    One down. Only four hundred and fifty-nine to go.

EXT. LONDON STREETS. DAY

CHRIS *driving along on his moped, looking at street names and buildings – and checking with his clipboard.*

CHRIS: (*Voice over*) In a way that's even worse than four hundred and sixty to go. I'd have packed the whole thing in, then and there, if it hadn't been for Janet's boot up my backside. *That* and knowing I wasn't on my tod. There's a *lot* of suffering in the world.

EXT. STREETS. DAY

GORDON's *agonized face – as he rides along in his oilskins and leggings. To his relief, he spots a transport café ahead. He screeches to it, and frantically dismounts and parks. Dying for a pee, he starts undoing his zips and dashes into the café. After a moment, the café door reopens and* GORDON *is hustled out by the* OWNER.

GORDON: I tell you I'm bloody *not*!

CAFÉ OWNER: Go on! On your way!

GORDON: I'm a *Knowledge* boy! Hell's Angels dress *different*.

    (*The* CAFÉ OWNER *slams the door in his face.*)

EXT. WEST END STREET. DAY

TED *is stopped against the kerb, astride his moped, pensively checking his A-to-Z map against the run written on his clipboard. Traffic speeds by. A* MAN *in Arab costume approaches him, solicitously.*

ARAB: You need some assistance?

    (TED *looks up at him, puzzled.*)

TED: No, thanks.

ARAB: Where do you wish to go to?

TED: I don't. I'm not lost. I'm trying to sort out the one-way system across Oxford Street.

    (*The* ARAB'S WIFE *joins them. She's laden with Marks and Spencer's carrier bags.*)

ARAB: You want Marks and Spencer's?

TED: You what?

ARAB: They're very good.

TED: (*Mesmerized*) You what?

ARAB: You want the one near Oxford Circus or the one near Marble Arch?

TED: I'm going to Grosvenor Square!
(*The* ARAB *looks at his* WIFE, *deeply puzzled, then back at* TED.)
ARAB: (*Gently, sympathetically*) There is *no* Marks and Spencers in Grosvenor Square.

EXT. SOUTH LONDON STREETS. EVENING
CHRIS *is riding along on his moped.*
CHRIS: (*Voice over*) Leave Clapham Junction Station, left by Prested Road, left St John's Hill, forward Lavender Hill, forward Wandsworth Road, right Lansdowne Way, left Clapham Road, forward Kennington Park Road –
(*As he crosses a minor junction, he glances automatically down the street to his left. He's puzzled by what he sees and brakes to a halt. Cut to* CHRIS's *point of view. We see* GORDON *riding his moped towards* CHRIS.)
You're *keen*, ent you?
(GORDON *stops.*)
GORDON: You what?
(*They both take their helmets off in order to hear – their hair will be plastered down with sweat.*)
CHRIS: (*Puzzled*) What you are *you* on, then?
GORDON: (*Evasively*) What are *you*?
CHRIS: Page 1, number 8. Clapham Junction to Lambeth Hospital.
GORDON: Same here. *I* am.
(*Puzzled,* CHRIS *looks down the street* GORDON's *just emerged from.*)
CHRIS: From down there?
GORDON: (*Evasively*) It's a longer way round, that's all.
CHRIS: (*Even more puzzled*) Well, if it's *longer*, why the hell are you – I mean you want Newington Butts, Dante Road, Brook Drive and –
(GORDON *is smiling at him, shaking his head, indulgently.*)
GORDON: Got more than the Knowledge to learn, haven't you, darling?
CHRIS: (*Blankly*) Eh?
(GORDON *grins, puts his helmet back on, and rides off.* CHRIS *stands watching, baffled.*)

EXT. STREET IN CLAPHAM. EVENING
GORDON *rides along, passes out of frame.* CHRIS, *unseen by* GORDON,
rides into shot . . . following him.

EXT. SECOND STREET IN CLAPHAM. EVENING
As preceding scene.

EXT. THIRD STREET IN CLAPHAM. EVENING
GORDON *brakes outside a house. Dismounts and parks his moped
against the kerb. He knocks on the door. Looks up and down the street,
warily. A* YOUNG WOMAN *opens the door. She grins.*
YOUNG WOMAN: You going off me or something? He left for work
    nearly ten minutes ago!
    (*They laugh and go in, closing the door behind them. Cut to*
    CHRIS, *astride his moped. A few yards down the street. Watching.
    The door opens again.* GORDON *pops his head out and calls to*
    CHRIS.)
GORDON: You're miles out of your way for Lambeth Hospital,
    darling!
CHRIS: You what?
    (GORDON *goes back in.*)
    (*Voice over*) *Now* I was learning.

EXT. LONDON STREET. DAY
TITANIC *is riding along, engrossed in the run pinned to his clipboard.
He veers his bike into the path of an oncoming, opulent car. Horrified,
the* DRIVER *manages to swerve the car out of* TITANIC'S *way.*
CAR DRIVER: (*Through window*) You tired of living, are you?
TITANIC: Sorry!
    (*The car zooms away.*)
    (*To himself*) 'Tired of living', he says. (*Calls after the quickly
    disappearing car*) I'm waiting to *start*, mate! I'm still waiting to
    start! (*Pause, then to himself again*) That told him . . . Couldn't
    answer *that* one . . .
    (*He resumes wobbling off down the street.*)

EXT. TAXI PULL-UP CARAVAN, STOREY'S GATE,
WESTMINSTER. EVENING
CABBIES *are in their parked cabs, reading newspapers. Others are*

leaning against their cabs, chatting, drinking tea. CHRIS *rides into shot, sees the* CABBIES – *and stops. He stands astride his clipboarded moped, staring at them as though they're gods.* THREE CABBIES, *chatting together, see him. They grin at each other.*

FIRST CABBY: Aye, aye. Another lost soul in torment. (*Calls*) Had your first Appearance yet?

CHRIS: You what?
 (*He takes his helmet off to hear.*)

SECOND CABBY: How you doing?

CHRIS: I haven't done fifty-six days yet.

FIRST CABBY: Thought not.

SECOND CABBY: Well, pray you don't get the Vampire when you have.

CHRIS: Who?

THIRD CABBY: When he's disguised as a human being, he's called Mr Burgess.

CHRIS: Oh, I know Mr Burgess.

FIRST CABBY: No one knows Mr Burgess, pal.

CHRIS: What's he do to you?

SECOND CABBY: You'll see. Take a crucifix and a pointed stick, you'll be all right.

CHRIS: What?

FIRST CABBY: Like some good advice, son?

CHRIS: Yes, please.

FIRST CABBY: Give it up and go back to ladies' hairdressing.
 (*Which, to* CHRIS, *is like a kick in the stomach.*)

CHRIS: (*Angrily*) Well, *you* made it, didn't you? *You* got your Green bleeding Badge!

FIRST CABBY: That's why I'm in a position to give you good advice, innit, you berk! This game's finished.

THIRD CABBY: Always has been.

SECOND CABBY: You're better off on the dole.
 (*The* CABBIES *resume their tea-drinking and chatting between themselves.* CHRIS *prepares to ride off again, despondently.*)

CHRIS: (*Voice over*) Terrific. That's all I needed, wasn't it? Know what I mean?

INT. THE MARGOLIESES' BEDROOM. NIGHT
TED *and* VAL *are in bed.* VAL *has a list of runs, checking* TED *as he*

recites the points perfectly.

TED: Forward Lombard Street, forward Bank, left by Mansion
House Street, foward Poultry, forward Cheapside, forward
Newgate Street – St Paul's tube station – forward Holborn
Viaduct. Williams National House on right, forward
Holborn Circus, Hatton Gardens on right –
(*He looks across at* VAL. *She's fallen fast asleep – the run still
in her hand. He smiles. Kisses her. Turns the light out. A
moment later, he turns it back on again. Takes the list of runs
from her hand, gets out of bed and starts pulling clothes on on
top of his pyjamas. He starts to creep from the room.* VAL
wakes.)

VAL: Ted. . . ?

TED: You get your head down, doll.

VAL: Where you going?

TED: Nowhere. One more run. It's a doddle this time of night.
Kings Avenue to Montpelier Square – something like that.
No traffic, nothing. I'll be home by three.

VAL: And what'll the next run be? St Thomas's Hospital? For
six months?

TED: What?

VAL: You're going to be ill, doll! You've to be up half-past six!

TED: All in a good cause, doll.

VAL: You didn't come in till eleven.

TED: Yeah, well I've been loafing since then, ent I?

VAL: I forgot to water Joanna.

TED: I'll do it.
(*He exits. She turns the light out and settles down to sleep.*)

INT. CHILD'S ROOM, MARGOLIESES' HOME. NIGHT
TED *enters, goes to child's bed and picks up his sleeping
three-year-old daughter in his arms.*

TED: Only Daddy, darling.
(*He sits her on a potty.*)

JOANNA: (*In her sleep*) Daddy doesn't live here any more. Daddy
lives on a moped.

INT. KNOWLEDGE BOYS' CAFE. DAY
One or two KNOWLEDGE BOYS *sitting about with cups of tea. They*

seem nervous, edgy. At another table is GORDON, *nonchalantly sitting back, reading a newspaper, whistling to himself. At another table is* TED – *the A-to-Z and list of detailed runs in front of him. He's doing last-minute revisions.* TITANIC *is collecting a cup of tea at the counter. He's very strained and nervous. He wanders to Ted's table.*

TITANIC: Anyone sitting here? Sort of, you know. Here. And that.

TED: Help yourself.

(TITANIC *sits down. Looks at the lists of runs, at the table, then at* TED.)

TITANIC: (*Uncertainly*) I met you, didn't I, at the . . .

TED: Margolies. Clapham.

TITANIC: That's it! I'm Mr –

TED: Walters. Kennington Oval.

TITANIC: (*Delighted*) That's it!

(*A pause. He sips his tea.* TED *resumes his swotting.* TITANIC *racks his brain for an excuse to continue the rare treat of having an actual conversation with someone.*)

Got a better memory than me, mate. I'll give you that – *free* of charge. No one ever remembers *my* name.

TED: (*Shrugs, smiles.*) Photographic, they say. Well, I say 'they'. The wife does.

TITANIC: What – for a living or what?

TED: (*Puzzled*) What?

TITANIC: 'S a good trade, by all accounts. Seasonal I should think.

TED: What is?

TITANIC: Eh?

(TED *cottons on to the misunderstanding.*)

TED: Oh, I see what you – no, no . . . I'm an Hoffman presser by trade. In a laundry.

TITANIC: (*Totally puzzled*) How d'you mean?

TED: No – it's all right.

TITANIC: The photographic's just an hobby, then, is that it?

TED: Yeah.

(*He returns to his swotting hastily. A pause.*)

TITANIC: I enjoyed that discussion. Don't often get the chance of a good discussion. Swapping points of view, pros and cons and that . . .

TED: (*A little warily*) No.

> (CHRIS *enters and makes his way to the counter. Like the others, he's wearing his best suit and new shirt and tie. He looks panic-stricken, almost shaking with nerves.*)

CHRIS: (*To the* PROPRIETOR) Cup of tea and a wodge of – (*Sees the clock on the wall.*) Christ, is that the time?

PROPRIETOR: Should be. It's a clock. That's what it specializes in.

CHRIS: I don't want no tea. Sorry!

> (*He starts to rush out. He passes* GORDON *turning the page of his newspaper.* GORDON *looks up, calmly.*)

GORDON: Appearance?

CHRIS: Ten thirty.

GORDON: Well?

CHRIS: What?

GORDON: It's only *twenty* past. You could bloody hop there in half a minute.

CHRIS: Yeah. Well. Still.

> (*He exits.* GORDON *laughs.* TED *grins.* TITANIC *tries to laugh. Since he's just as scared as* CHRIS *is, it's not very convincing.*)

TITANIC: (*Shaking with fear*) Poor sod. Bloody petrified, ent he? Still. Only young. (*Beat.*) Can't eat us, can they?

EXT. CARRIAGE OFFICE. DAY

Nearby is gathered a group of KNOWLEDGE BOYS, *carrying their crash helmets and sitting astride their mopeds. They all seem edgy. A man* (GINGER) *emerges from the office entrance. He looks pale. The others immediately surround him and bombard him with questions.*

KNOWLEDGE BOYS: Who did you have, mate?

GINGER: Wilson on a 56.

KNOWLEDGE BOYS: What came up?

GINGER: (*Despondently*) Could only answer one, couldn't I? Liberty's to Swiss Cottage. And I got *that* bastard wrong.

KNOWLEDGE BOYS: (*Variously, while writing down the run*) Cut up Regent Street/Portland Place/BBC on right/cut through the Park . . .

> (*During this,* CHRIS *approaches from the café, passes them and goes into the carriage office.*)

106

INT. WAITING ROOM, CARRIAGE OFFICE. DAY

All the Knowledge boys (and Knowledge girl) whom we met at the acceptance interview, are seated round the room. Groomed, in their best clothes, sitting in stiff silence. And frozen with fear. All except GORDON, *that is. He seems totally relaxed. He's surreptitiously smoking – with his cigarette cupped in his hand – blowing smoke through the slightly opened window.* MISS STAVELY *glances at* CHRIS *and half smiles. He looks away. During the above, we hear* BURGESS *questioning* O'REILLY *at his Appearance in the adjacent office.*

BURGESS: *(Out of vision)* Spitalfields Market to Brecknock Road.

(No answer.)

Spitalfields Market to Brecknock Road.

(No answer.)

All right. How about Spitalfields Market to Brecknock Road, then?

(No answer.)

Billingsgate Market to Newington Green?

(No answer.)

Fair enough, Spitalfields Market to Brecknock Road.

(With the exception of GORDON, *they all begin to reach terror stage. The door suddenly opens. They all jump.* O'REILLY *emerges, looking very shaken. He closes the door behind him. They all stare at him.)*

O'REILLY: *(Subdued)* He says Mr Weller next.

*(*GORDON *stubs his fag out and wafts the smoke away.)*

GORDON: Needless to say. *(Gets up.)* My luck. I don't get Mr Wilson, the Gentleman. I get the Vampire.

CHRIS: *(To* O'REILLY*)* What was he like? The Vampire?

O'REILLY: A bleeding blood-sucker.

(He exits. GORDON *rolls his shoulders, jauntily, and cockily goes into the office.)*

INT. APPEARANCE ROOM. DAY

BURGESS *is behind his desk. On it is a mound of folders and files. The one in front of him is Gordon's. The Interviewee's chair is some feet away.* GORDON *strides in, beaming.*

GORDON: Afternoon!

(*He takes the chair and starts moving it nearer to Burgess's desk.* BURGESS *watches him impassively.* GORDON *is about to sit down.*)

BURGESS: Pickford's?

GORDON: (*Stopping, puzzled*) Pardon?

BURGESS: Are you a furniture-removal man by trade?

GORDON: Eh?

BURGESS: Or a kleptomaniac?

GORDON: Um . . . Weller, G. Mr . . . Mr Gordon Weller.

BURGESS: Where it was, please. The chair.

GORDON: What chair? (*Realizes.*) Oh, I see.
(*He replaces the chair.*)

BURGESS: Thank you. Now sit on it.
(GORDON *sits.*)
Well done. (*Opens Gordon's file.*) Now, Mr Weller. Your first appearance.

GORDON: (*Cockiness evaporated*) Yes. Yes, it is. Spot on. Very first. That's correct.

BURGESS: How do you feel about the American fraternity, Mr Weller?

GORDON: Pardon?

BURGESS: Americans.
(GORDON *is utterly baffled about the relevance of the question.*)

GORDON: Film stars, you mean?

BURGESS: (*Puzzled*) What?

GORDON: *Which* Americans?

BURGESS: In general.

GORDON: What do I think of them?

BURGESS: What do you think of them.

GORDON: Sean Connery's very good. Why?

BURGESS: I ask the questions, Mr Weller. The Irish?

GORDON: Sorry?

BURGESS: Don't have me repeating every syllable, Mr Weller. I've had a long day ahead of me ever since I woke up, and it's getting longer. And I've *still* to go to Sainsbury's on my way home. What do you think of the Irish?

GORDON: Well, Sean Connery's one, isn't he? (*Beat.*) I've come for the Knowledge . . .
(BURGESS *gets up abruptly.* GORDON *jumps.* BURGESS *starts*

*wandering round the room, looking at pictures, rearranging some
wilted flowers in a vase, straightening office equipment.* GORDON
stares at him throughout – bemused.)

Is it something I've said?

(BURGESS *ignores him, and continues doing the above, throughout
the following.*)

BURGESS: I'm standing outside St Mary's Hospital. I want to go to
the Great Eastern Hotel.

(GORDON *stares at him, numbly. His mind an icy blank. A long
pause.*)

I'm standing outside St Mary's Hospital, Praed Street,
Edgware Road. I want to go to the Great Eastern Hotel,
Bishopsgate.

(GORDON *still stares at him as though he's speaking in a foreign
language.*)

And it's raining.

(*Still no answer. He sighs.*)

I'm standing outside Arding and Hobbs. I want to go to the
London Fire Brigade Headquarters.

(GORDON *is in total paralysis.*)

Arding and Hobbs, *Battersea Rise*, to London Fire Brigade,
Albert Embankment. (*Pause.*) To report a fire. (*Pause.*) In the
Bedding Department.

GORDON: Um . . . forward Lavender Hill . . . um . . .
Wandsworth Road . . . left, no right, no forward, no right,
Nine Elms Lane . . .

(BURGESS *sits at his desk, suddenly he picks up a mug which holds
a dozen or so pencils and pens. Deadpan, he ejects the pens and
pencils all over the floor in front of his desk.* GORDON *stares at
them. Then at* BURGESS. *Then back at the pens. A pause.*)

Excuse me . . . you . . . um . . . you appear to have thrown
your pencils on the floor, Mr Burgess.

BURGESS: (*Deadpan*) Never mind what *I'm* doing, Mr Weller.
Concentrate on what *you're* doing.

(GORDON *sits staring – convinced he's in a room with a madman.*)

INT. GORDON'S LIVING ROOM. DAY
BRENDA *is vacuuming the carpet. She looks worried. She glances at the
clock.*

BRENDA: Our Father which art in heaven, hallowed be thy name. Thy kingdom come, thy will be done, on earth as it is in heaven. Give us this day our daily bread . . .

INT. WAITING ROOM, CARRIAGE OFFICE. DAY
The others waiting as GORDON *emerges from the Appearance Room, white-faced.*
CHRIS: How was it?
GORDON: (*Deeply shaken*) Mr Margolies next.
(TED *straightens his tie, takes a deep breath and goes in.*)
CHRIS: (*To* GORDON) How was it?
(GORDON *exits as though in a trance.* CHRIS *swallows.*)

INT. APPEARANCE ROOM. DAY
TED MARGOLIES *is seated, trying to stop himself shaking, opposite* BURGESS.
BURGESS: How do you feel about the Jewish fraternity?
(TED *boggles at him.*)
TED: The what??
(BURGESS *glances down at Ted's file.*)
BURGESS: Oh, as you were! You're . . . er Mr Margolies, aren't you? Um, right then. (*Beat.*) How do you feel about Manchester United Football fans? (*Beat.*) *Drunk.*
TED: (*Grins.*) Depends whether they've beaten Crystal Palace or not, really. (*He laughs weakly.* BURGESS *remains stony-faced.*) (*Lamely*) Sir.
BURGESS: I'm at the northern approach to Tower Bridge. I want to go to BP House.
(TED *stares. His mind's gone blank.*)
Tower Bridge – which is at Tower Bridge – to BP House, which, as you no doubt know, but prefer to keep secret, is in Carlisle Place.
(TED *sits, petrified.* BURGESS *gets up, goes to the window and stands looking out into the Carriage Office car-park.*)
TED: Um . . . left Tower Hill, forward Byward Street, forward Lower Thames Street, forward Upper Thames Street, forward What's-it Underpass –
BURGESS: (*Still looking out of the window*) Where?
TED: *Blackfriars* Underpass.

BURGESS: What's-it or Blackfriars?
TED: Blackfriars.
BURGESS: Where?
TED: (*Now unsure*) Blackfriars . . . Underpass . . .
BURGESS: Where?
> (TED *sits, as though in a nightmare. He's certain it's Blackfriars Underpass – or is he?*)
TED: Um . . . Black . . . Blackfriars Under . . . um . . . Blackfriars . . . um
BURGESS: (*Shouting*) Where??
TED: (*Yelling back*) Blackfriars Underpass!!
> (BURGESS *turns slowly from the window and looks at him. A pause.*)
BURGESS: (*Calmly, quietly*) I'm not saying you're wrong. For all you know I may be a little hard of hearing. (*Bleak smile.*) Not very nice, is it? Losing your temper with unfortunate people who are hard of hearing. Of which there are regrettably many thousands. Continue.
> (*He returns to looking out of the window.*)
TED: (*Lost*) Um . . . um . . .
> (*He subsides into silence.*)
BURGESS: (*Still looking out of the window*) You'll never make it, son. You'll never make a cabby in five hundred years.
> (TED *stares at him, wounded. Tears start into his eyes.*)
TED: It's my first Appearance! I've learnt ten pages! A hundred and eighty runs! I know them backwards! And you say –
BURGESS: (*Turning with exaggerated innocence*) Not you. (*Nods towards window.*) Him down there. Taking his driving test.
> (*Shot, from his point of view, of cab-driving examination.*)
> (*Smiles bleakly at* TED.) Not putting you off at all, am I, Mr Margolies?
> (TED *boggles.*)

INT. TED'S AND VAL'S KITCHEN. DAY
VAL *is slicing vegetables for dinner. She cuts her finger.*
VAL: Ow!!

INT. APPEARANCE ROOM, CARRIAGE OFFICE. DAY
TITANIC *is in the chair facing* BURGESS – *who is once again seated at*

his desk. A long silence. TITANIC *is going through agonies.*

BURGESS: Would you like me to repeat the question?

TITANIC: Yes. Please. Sir.

BURGESS: What was it?

TITANIC: Marylebone Magistrates Court to Wilton Place.

BURGESS: Why do you want me to repeat it?

TITANIC: I don't know.

BURGESS: You don't know why – or you don't know the run.

TITANIC: I don't know.

BURGESS: Thank you, Mr Walters. Next Appearance – fifty-six
days.

(TITANIC *remains seated.*)

See the young lady at the Appointments Window.

(*He makes a note in Titanic's file.* TITANIC *still doesn't move.*)

Good afternoon, Mr Walters.

(TITANIC *remains seated.*)

Go through the door. That's the door. Walk out. With your
legs. Thank you.

TITANIC: Thank *you*, sir. Very nice.

(*He still remains seated.*)

INT. TITANIC'S LIVING ROOM. DAY

LILIAN *is talking to an ornament on the mantelpiece.*

LILIAN: So I said to her, 'Thirty-two p??' I said. Just like
that. 'Thirty-two p?? It was only twenty-nine last week.'
And she turned round and said, 'Well, chocolate's gone
up.' So I turned round and said, 'Why?' I said. Just like
that. 'Why?' And she said, 'Well, the world price of cocoa's
gone up.' And I said, 'I don't want cocoa, I want a bar of
bloody chocolate.' I was a lady, though. I didn't swear.
(*Very politely*) 'I don't want cocoa, miss,' I said, 'I want a
bar of chocolate.' (*Curtly*) 'Yes, well,' she said, 'chocolate's
made out of cocoa.' 'Oh, is it?' I said, 'Well *I'm* not made
out of *money*!' and walked out. (*Pause.*) So she didn't get no
profit out of *me*! That showed her. Couldn't answer that.
(*Pause.*) 'Course *I* didn't get no *chocolate* . . .
(*Which is only one of the good things in life she didn't get. And
never has. And never will. And knows it. And has now
forgotten even to wonder why.*)

INT. WAITING ROOM, CARRIAGE OFFICE. DAY
The others waiting, as before. TITANIC *emerges like a limp rag. They all look at him in dry-lipped apprehension.*

TITANIC: Which is Mr Matthews?

CHRIS: (*Heart thumping*) Me.

TITANIC: You're on.

> (*He exits.* CHRIS *stands up – and wants to die. Walks to Burgess's door. Knocks. Then starts being sick. He stuffs his hanky to his mouth and runs back through the waiting room and out.*)

BURGESS: (*Out of vision*) Come in!

EXT. STREET TELEPHONE KIOSK. DAY
Holding his hanky to his mouth with one hand, and the phone with the other, CHRIS *is waiting to be connected to the Appointments Clerk at the Carriage Office. He hears the Clerk's voice.*

CHRIS: (*Takes hanky away.*) Hello? Is that the Appointments Window? (*Pause.*) Er . . . this is a mate of Mr Matthews, he was supposed to come for an Appearance this morning, but what he's done, he's pulled his back out shifting some RSJs, so he couldn't come this morning, so he wondered if he could come another morning. Like, he's very sorry and that.

EXT. BALCONY OF HIGH-RISE FLATS. EVENING
JANET *and* CHRIS *are leaning on the rail looking at the panorama of London streets. A morose silence.*

CHRIS: Do you believe in God?

> (JANET *throws him a slightly scared and irritated glance. He continues to stare out over the bleak streets.*)

JANET: Look, if you want to go barmy, let's do it indoors, eh? They won't be back for twenty minutes yet.

CHRIS: (*Still staring, forlornly*) He must have one *hell* of a memory.

JANET: Who?

CHRIS: What's-'is-name. God. (*Looks down at the streets.*) And it's not just streets with him. Thousands and thousands of houses, millions of people. And that's only London. There's everywhere else in the world as well. Millions of places. Middlesborough. Hard to credit, innit?

JANET: Look, are you coming in or not? If not I'm putting a coat on.

CHRIS: (*Still staring*) We had two Mormons come to the door once. They said, 'Do you believe in God?' And my dad said, "Course, I'm just not all that sure *He* believes in *me*.' (*Pause.*) And that was *before* he turned nasty.

JANET: I don't know what you're talking about.

CHRIS: *I* don't.

JANET: And all this just because you did a rotten Appearance? He can't have been all *that* horrible to you! What happened in there? You went in – then what?

CHRIS: (*Guiltily*) Look, just bloody drop it, will you! Give it a rest! I'm sick of the bloody Knowledge.
(*He subsides into silence.*)

JANET: (*Sympathetically*) It's not the end of the world, Chris. It's your first one. Another fifty-six days it'll be different again.
(*A pause.*)

CHRIS: If I jack it in, you'll find someone else. Eddie Bloody Hairstyle in your Packing Department . . .

JANET: Who says!

CHRIS: *I* say!

JANET: Well, you talk cobblers, don't you! Where'd you learn English? The Chinese-bloody-take-away?
(*A pause.*)

CHRIS: You can't do the Knowledge like I'm doing it. Dun't work. If you do it, you do it.

JANET: (*Half to herself*) Eddie Hairstyle, he says . . .

CHRIS: You do full-time. *All* the time. You do nothing else. There *is* nothing else.

JANET: (*Exploding*) There's the rest of bloody life, Chris! What's the Knowledge? A few months ago we'd never even *heard* of it. There's other things in the world.

CHRIS: Is there?

JANET: There's *us*!

CHRIS: Same thing, innit? That's what I'm on about.
(*They look at each other – neither understanding the other.*)

EXT. LONDON STREETS. EVENING
CHRIS *is riding along on his moped.*
CHRIS: (*Voice over*) Page 9, run 9: East Street, Walworth, to the

Apothecaries' Hall. Run 10: West End Central Police
Station to Spa Road, SE16. Run 11: Custom House to
Victoria Park. Run 12: Mile End Hospital to North London
Magistrates' Court. Run 13: Beaver Hall to Drayton Park
Station. It's a big place London. It's so bloody big, you
forget how small it is.

(*He brakes to a halt on seeing Gordon's bike parked outside a
house (recognizably different from the house of his girlfriend in
Clapham). He looks at it, puzzled.* GORDON *comes out of the
house.*)

GORDON: (*To* WOMAN *seeing him out*) Yeah, next week. Be
good. Know what I mean?
(*He laughs. Closes the door. Turns, sees* CHRIS.)
Oh, hell. Kojak's with us again. Is my old lady paying you?
In bloody lollipops?

EXT. COFFEE STALL BEHIND STRAND PALACE HOTEL.
EVENING
CHRIS *and* GORDON, *seated astride their stationary mopeds, are
drinking tea.*
GORDON: Mind you, it's only Mondays and Thursdays I'm at it;
the other nights I *am* on the Knowledge. It's the finest alibi
in the entire history of how's-your-father, this caper.
CHRIS: What about your missus?
(GORDON *stares at him, blankly.*)
GORDON: Sorry, I don't understand the question.
CHRIS: Doesn't she mind?
(GORDON *stares at him as though he's bananas. For quite a
long time.*)
GORDON: Ignorance is bliss, Christopher – know what I mean?
(*Beat.*) My Brenda's highly blissful about the whole thing.
CHRIS: Oh, I see.
GORDON: I take it *you* haven't fixed yourself up with nothing,
then?
CHRIS: Me? I'm going steady.
GORDON: (*Exaggerated patience*) We're talking about on the *side*,
you berk!
CHRIS: (*Uncomfortably*) I appreciate that.
GORDON: Well, then!

115

CHRIS: I'm sort of engaged.

GORDON: *I'm* sort of bloody *married!* (*Responsible self-righteousness*) And very happily at that, I may add! (*Beat.*) There's too many decry marriage, these days. (*Beat.*) It only needs a bit of give and take.

INT. GORDON'S AND BRENDA'S BEDROOM. NIGHT

BRENDA *is sitting up in bed, reading. She doesn't look too pleased. We hear the front door open and close quietly. She listens, mouth hardening. We hear* GORDON *gingerly, creakingly, creeping upstairs,* BRENDA *turns the light out.* GORDON *creeps in.* BRENDA *turns the light on.*

BRENDA: Good morning.

GORDON: Oh! (*Smiles warmly; then, with exaggerated innocence*) It's not midnight yet, is it?

BRENDA: Twenty to one.

GORDON: You should be chuffed!

BRENDA: Should I?

GORDON: I did two runs instead of one. Shattered I am. You get your head down, eh?

BRENDA: 'S all right. I'm not sleepy.

GORDON: (*Apprehensively*) What do you mean?

BRENDA: Well, I haven't stayed up till twenty to one to do bloody call-overs with you, have I?

GORDON: Ah. (*Pause.*) If I just wasn't so *shattered* . . . I've been working my balls off.

BRENDA: I see.
(*A pause. He starts getting undressed. She watches him, beadily.*)

GORDON: What's wrong?

BRENDA: Gordon. I don't care who she is, and what you get up to together –

GORDON: (*Injured innocence*) Who? What?

BRENDA: What I *do* object to is – if you're spending all your time doing her when you should be doing the Knowledge –

GORDON: What the hell are you on about?

BRENDA: – you'll never get your Green Badge, you'll always be a cowboy and *I'll* always have tuppence in my purse!
(*She switches the light off.*)

GORDON: (*Innocently*) I don't even know what you're on about. You got a very suspicious mind, you know that, Brenda. You've hurt me now.

INT. APPEARANCE ROOM, CARRIAGE OFFICE. DAY

CHRIS (*in his best clothes*) *is seated opposite* BURGESS, *who's at his desk.* BURGESS *is inserting a nasal inhaler up his nose as he speaks.*

BURGESS: (*Loudly*) I am outside (*then very quietly*) The Fishmongers' Hall. (*Then loudly*) And I wish to go to (*very quietly*) the Salvation Army at Cambria House.

(*The nasal inhaler remains stuck up his nostril, throughout.* CHRIS *stares at it. A silence.*)

(*Strong Northern accent*) I haven't all day, Mr Matthews. If you carry on at this rate, I shall have to go by bus. And we'll *all* be out of a job.

CHRIS: (*Doubly thrown by inhaler and accent*) What?

BURGESS: (*Briskly, normal accent*) Come on, sonny.

CHRIS: (*With hand gestures*) Um . . . leave by left London Bridge, forward bear left King William Street, forward Lombard Street, forward Bank . . .

(*During this,* BURGESS *has risen from his seat, and stretched himself out on the carpet in front of Chris's chair.* CHRIS *boggles.*)

Um . . . left by Mansion House Street . . . forward Poultry . . .

(BURGESS *starts doing press-ups.* CHRIS *doesn't know whether to cry or send for a little yellow van. He tries to ignore him.*)

Um . . . forward Cheapside . . . forward Newgate Street . . .

(BURGESS *gets up and goes back to his seat.* CHRIS *sighs with relief.*)

. . . with St Paul's tube station on left . . . forward Holborn Viaduct . . .

(BURGESS *starts laughing.* CHRIS *stops. The laughter continues.* CHRIS *warily resumes.*)

. . . forward Holborn Circus, Hatton Gardens on right, forward Holborn . . .

(*By now* BURGESS *is laughing uproariously.* CHRIS *stops again. Smiles back at* BURGESS, *nervously.*)

. . . right Grays Inn Road, left Guilford Street . . .
(BURGESS *is still laughing.* CHRIS *warily, tentatively, joins in the laughter.* BURGESS *immediately stops.*)
BURGESS: (*Strong Midlands accent*) Is something amusing you, Mr Matthews?
CHRIS: (*Manically*) What?
BURGESS: (*Strong Scottish accent*) Please continue, Mr Matthews.
CHRIS: (*Wild-eyed*) What??
(BURGESS *takes another nasal inhaler and sticks it up his other nostril.* CHRIS *stares. A broken man.*)

EXT. TITANIC'S FLAT. SUNDAY AFTERNOON
TITANIC *emerges from his front door, wheeling his pushbike. He's dressed in his best and wears a bowler hat.*
TITANIC: (*Voice over*) Fair enough. I'd done my duty. I'd passed the invitation on to her. A nice run-out of a Sunday afternoon. Meet my new mates and their lady wives. And she doesn't want to know. Doesn't even answer.
(*He starts cycling down the street.*)
(*Voice over*) I mean, special occasion. You'd think she'd talk for a special occasion. High tea in Gunnersbury Park. How often has she had the chance of high tea in Gunnersbury Park? (*Pause.*) Well, sod her, I thought. She never speaks to *me*. I'll never speak to *her*. No more. Seventeen years. I've had enough. My lips is sealed.
(*He rides past the church. Its wayside pulpit now reads:* HE THAT HATH KNOWLEDGE SPARETH HIS WORDS (PROVERBS 17.27). *He falls off his bike.*

EXT. STREET IN STEPNEY. SUNDAY AFTERNOON
CHRIS *and* JANET *riding along on the moped.*
JANET: Where does he live then?
CHRIS: Commercial Road to City, West End, Kensington, on to A315 –
JANET: Just what part of London!! Wandsworth, Mayfair, the Isle of bloody Dogs!! I don't need a running commentary on every lamp-post!
CHRIS: Gunnersbury Park.

JANET: Thank you! (*Sighs.*) Like going steady with a bloody
    roadmap!
    (*They ride on for a moment. A* GIRL *passes, walking along the
    pavement.* CHRIS *turns his head slightly to watch her go by.*
    JANET *notices and a tiny frown crosses her face. She's never
    seen him do that before.*)
    Is it their own place – or rented?
CHRIS: Dunno.
JANET: Have they got kiddies?
CHRIS: Dunno.
JANET: Are they happy or what?
CHRIS: How do *I* know?
JANET: Don't you lot ever *talk* to each other?
CHRIS: 'Course we do.
JANET: What about?

INT. GORDON'S LIVING ROOM. SUNDAY AFTERNOON
GORDON, CHRIS, TITANIC *and* TED *are seated round a table –
which is covered with dog-eared Blue Books, street maps, question
papers, etc. They're arguing about the correct sequence of streets on a
particular run. Seated at the other side of the room, in silence, are*
BRENDA, VAL *and* JANET. *Half-drunk tea and half-eaten cake are
on a coffee table before them. They're bored stiff, feel deserted and
have exhausted their small talk. All they have in common is
Knowledge boys' widowhood. From time to time, they smile bleak,
half-hearted, sociable smiles at each other, then sink back into their
own little worlds again. Cut to the men.*
TED: So, seven o'clock in the morning I'm shlepping down
    Eastcheap, right?
CHRIS: Seven o'clock??
TED: Thought I'd get an hour in before I set off to work. I do
    most mornings.
    (CHRIS, GORDON *and* TITANIC *share a guilty glance.*)
    So there I am – forward into Cannon Street, forward Queen
    Victoria Street – and suddenly I'm only in a traffic jam, ent
    I! Traffic jam, seven o'clock in the morning! Never been
    known in the annals of Christendom!
CHRIS: (*Perturbed*) You were doing Eastcheap??
TED: Eastcheap to Oval Station. So I rationalizes, y'know, to

myself, 'How can there be a traffic jam at this time? I mean, this is it.' So there I am thinking of the points I should be clocking – Candlewick House on left, Cannon Street station, Bank of China, the London Stone on the Wall – and suddenly –

GORDON: (*As perturbed as* CHRIS) Eastcheap to *where*?

TED: Oval Station. This bloke in an Alfa Romeo [*pronounced as in* Romeo and Juliet] P registration, in the outside lane –

CHRIS: What run's that, then?

TED: What?

CHRIS: Eastcheap to Oval Station.

GORDON: Page bloody 15 if I know him!

TED: Page 20. First run on page 20, so anyway –

(CHRIS, GORDON *and* TITANIC *share a dead look*.)

– this bloke, chuckling away to himself there, says, 'Well, that's made my day, that has, mate!' And I says, 'What has?' And he says, 'I could do with her in our *office*: luncheon vouchers no object!' And I says, 'Who?' And he says, 'Didn't you see her?' And I says, 'Who?' And he says, 'She ran right past you at the lights.' (*Leans forward smiling confidentially, about to reveal all*.) Only a naked female, wasn't it? Stark nude. Jogging. Well, when I say stark nude, by all accounts she had tennis shoes on. In the middle of the bloody City. Jogging. In the altogether. No wonder the Stock Exchange want men only. And that's why there was a traffic jam. Seven in the morning, right? Everybody jumping on their brakes, clocking an eyeful. It's a wonder there wasn't a ten-mile pile-up. Now, the point is, there's Joe Soap here, and I didn't even *notice* her! All *I* bloody noticed was the Bank of China, London Stone, St Andrew by the Wardrobe, the Salvation Army HQ. You wouldn't credit it, would you?

(*Cut to* BRENDA. *She turns to* VAL, *wryly*.)

BRENDA: Well? *Would* you?

(VAL *smiles a small pinched smile*. TED *is laughing at his story. He looks at* CHRIS, GORDON *and* TITANIC – *who aren't laughing at all*.)

CHRIS: (*To* TED) You're on list 20, then?

TED: No, no . . .

(*The other men seemed relieved.*)
That was, oh, a week or two ago. I'm on 33 now.
(*The other men's relief evaporates.*)
(*Cut to* BRENDA, VAL *and* JANET. *They sit in silence.*)
VAL: Do you ever feel you want to scream?
BRENDA: All day. I just haven't the energy.
VAL: I sometimes cry. In the supermarket.
BRENDA: I haven't the energy.
    (*She suddenly screams – piercingly.* VAL *starts quietly sobbing.*
    The men turn to look at them, bewildered.)
CHRIS: What's wrong??
JANET: (*Yelling at him at the top of her voice*) We're here! We're
    here an' all! What bleeding list are we on!
    (CHRIS, TED *and* GORDON *go over to the women to comfort*
    them. TITANIC *sits alone at the table.*)
TITANIC: I never hear a wrong word from *my* missus. Never.

EXT. JANET'S BLOCK OF FLATS. EVENING
CHRIS *and* JANET, *on the moped, riding back from Gordon's party.*
They stop outside the flats. JANET *dismounts – expecting* CHRIS *to*
do the same. He doesn't. She looks at him, puzzled.
JANET: Is that it, then?
CHRIS: What?
JANET: We're all right for an hour or two. They won't be back
    till Max Bygraves, half eight.
CHRIS: Um . . . no, what it is . . . I think I'll have an early
    night . . .
JANET: Well?? Half eight! How early can you get??
CHRIS: Then I can make an early start in the morning . . .
JANET: (*Not pleased*) I see.
    (*A pause.*)
    You enjoyed it in there, didn't you? With your mates.
    Lapped it up.
CHRIS: What do you mean?
JANET: Talking. I don't think I've heard you talk since the
    night I met you. The Ilford Tiffany. (*Beat.*) Not to me,
    anyway.
CHRIS: (*Defensively*) What are you niggled about?
    (*She starts to go in.*)

JANET: See you lunchtime outside work.

CHRIS: Er . . . what, half twelve? I think I might be out Cricklewood way, half twelve-ish . . .

JANET: *After* work, then.

CHRIS: Er . . . well, half five-ish, I'll probably be . . .

JANET: I see. When then?

CHRIS: Dunno, really. Praps Wednesday.

JANET: 'Praps'?

CHRIS: Definite.

JANET: I always thought Tuesday came before Wednesday. Tuesdays been cancelled, have they?

CHRIS: Eh?

JANET: 'Night, then.

CHRIS: You're *niggled* about something, aren't you? (*She goes in.*)

EXT. ALBERT BRIDGE. DAY

CHRIS *drives across the bridge in long shot.*

CHRIS: (*Voice over*) It was round about then that I started getting these shooting pains in my shoulder. I went to the doctor. He said it was growing pains. Bloody barmy! I'd stopped growing years ago. (*Beat.*) Gordon thought it was a touch of lumbago from being on the moped in the rain. During List 9 – Bedford Square to Sussex Square, Porchester Square to Princes Gate, Berkeley Street to Battersea Dogs' Home, thy Kingdom come, thy will be done, on earth as it is in heaven.

EXT. PENTON STREET. DAY

CHRIS *walking towards the Carriage Office in his smartly groomed shabby best.*

CHRIS: (*Voice over*) Normal people know time's gone by from what's happening in the world. Like President Carter shouts the odds on something, or Elvis Presley dies or Liverpool win the European Cup . . . something like that. (*Beat.*) Or a bloke and a bird slip up one night, and then next thing she has a little nipper. Well, then she sort of knows it was nine months ago when it happened, right? (*Beat.*) With Knowledge boys it's different. Time goes by from when they start roadworks in Camden High Street to when they finish, or when they try a new one-way system in Seven Sisters Road then jack it in again . . . something like that. All you know about Elvis dying is they put a show on about him at the Astoria Theatre, Charing Cross Road – and what's the quickest way to get there from the Hilton Hotel.

INT. WAITING ROOM, CARRIAGE OFFICE. MIDDAY
A group (including CHRIS) *are waiting to be called for their Appearance – all as terror-stricken as usual.* MISS STAVELY *emerges from Burgess's room. She smiles at* CHRIS.
BURGESS: (*Out of vision*) Mr Matthews!
    (MISS STAVELY *smiles encouragingly at* CHRIS. *He almost . . . almost smiles back. Then goes tensely in.*)

INT. APPEARANCE ROOM, CARRIAGE OFFICE. DAY
CHRIS *is facing* BURGESS, *answering a run.*
CHRIS: Left by . . . um . . . what's it . . .
BURGESS: And what's 'what's-it'?
CHRIS: Um . . . where-d'you-call-it . . . Maltesers . . .
BURGESS: What?
CHRIS: Not Maltesers . . . Liquorice All-sorts . . .
    (BURGESS *stares at him.*)
BURGESS: What?
CHRIS: Liquorice All-sorts . . . Bassetts . . . Barretts . . . Barretts of Wimpole Street . . . That's it. Left Wimpole Street . . .
BURGESS: Liquorice All-sorts is Wimpole Street?
CHRIS: Word association. That's the way I remember it. To make it easier.
BURGESS: (*Flatly*) Easier.
CHRIS: To remember.
    (*A long pause.*)
BURGESS: I was eighteen numbers off winning a Premium Bond last week. Fifty thousand quid. I thought I'd blocked it from my mind . . . but I haven't.

EXT. CARRIAGE OFFICE ENTRANCE. MIDDAY
A group of KNOWLEDGE BOYS *are besieging* GORDON *noting the points he was asked at his Appearance.* CHRIS *emerges from the*

entrance. The KNOWLEDGE BOYS *immediately leave* GORDON *and besiege* CHRIS. CHRIS *fights his way through them to* GORDON.

CHRIS: How was it?

GORDON: Subject normal. *He* sits there saying Westminster Cathedral to St Paul's Cathedral, like a religious maniac or something. And *I* sit there like a bloody Toby Jug saying nothing. (*Beat.*) Next Appearance fifty-six days. As per bloody usual. Why the hell he doesn't ask me Piccadilly Circus to Piccadilly Circus and give me a break . . . How d'*you* get on?

CHRIS: Three right, three wrong. Next appearance twenty-eight days again. Can't be bad. Fancy a cup of tea?

GORDON: Why not? If you can't drown your sorrows, take the buggers for a paddle.

(*They start off towards the Penton Street café. As they do so,* TED *emerges from the Carriage Office building entrance. He's radiant with excitement. He sees them and yells after them.*)

TED: Chris! Gordon! Hey!!

(*They turn.* TED, *almost crying with happiness, races towards them – waving a Green Badge.* CHRIS *and* GORDON *look at each other, open-mouthed. Awe-struck.*)

CHRIS: He's done it!!

GORDON: Never! He *has*! He's got his Green sodding Badge!

(*They race over to meet him.* TED *starts dancing and kissing his badge.*)

CHRIS: Let's see it! Let's see it!

(TED *waves it in front of* CHRIS's *face.*)

In the flesh! In the flesh!

(TED *hands him the badge. The group of* KNOWLEDGE BOYS *at the entrance of the building stand watching, poker-faced.* CHRIS *examines the badge, in awe.* GORDON *takes it from him, looks at the reverse side.*)

GORDON: (*Pretending to read inscription*) 'Made in Hong Kong. Forward by Ping-Pong Street, left Chop Suey Street, right what's-it street – Prawn Balls . . .'

(CHRIS *grabs it back.*)

CHRIS: It's handsome, innit? Still warm.

TED: Well?? Somebody say mazeltov!

CHRIS: Mazeltov.

TED: Thank you.

CHRIS: I don't even know what it means . . .

GORDON: Who cares! Sod the tea! Come on, they're open!

TED: Who are?

GORDON: What do you mean, 'Who are?' (*To* CHRIS) What's Jewish for 'champagne'?

TED: I don't drink.

GORDON: (*Mock disbelief*) You stand there. A little feller with big ear-lobes. You pass the Knowledge in fourteen months . . .

TED: Thirteen and three-quarters.

GORDON: Thirteen and three-quarters – and you say you don't *drink*!!!

TED: (*Laughing*) Listen – what do you want – I'm a Yiddishe boy. Cards, yes. Women, certainly. Drinking? One small egg-flip at Christmas, tops.

(GORDON *ignores this and turns to* CHRIS.)

GORDON: How much have you got?

CHRIS: About three quid. I need it, though, for my –

GORDON: Hand it over.

(CHRIS *starts getting his wallet out.* GORDON *gets his and flicks through its contents.*)

Three you've got. Eleven I've got. (*To* TED) Fourteen quids' worth of champagne, all right?

TED: I don't drink!

GORDON: It's *Christmas!* (*Beat.*) *Cabby.*

INT. KNOWLEDGE BOYS' CAFÉ, PENTON STREET. EARLY AFTERNOON

TITANIC *sits at a table, alone, with a cup of tea. The* PROPRIETOR *is busy behind his counter.*

TITANIC: (*Calling to* PROPRIETOR) Ain't seen my mates, have you?

(*The* PROPRIETOR *ignores him.*)

Must still be doing their Appearances, I expect.

(PROPRIETOR *ignores him.*)

They said, 'You bag a table, we'll follow you on, have a cup of tea, bit of a chat . . .' (*Looks at his watch.*) Half an hour ago, that was. More. Unless they've forgotten. Hardly do

that, though, would they? Mates and that. (*Pause.*) They'd
have noticed I'm not with them. (*Pause.*) Sometimes people
don't notice me when I *am*. (*To* PROPRIETOR – *still busy*) I
said, 'Sometimes people don't notice me when I *am*.'
(*The* PROPRIETOR *continues working . . . still unaware of*
TITANIC's *existence.*)

EXT. PUB. MID-AFTERNOON
Sounds of singing. They grow louder. CHRIS, GORDON, *and* TED
*emerge. All a bit tipsy, and very happy. They each go to their
mopeds, which are parked in line. They bid each other 'So long', get
on their mopeds, and ride off, a little uncertainly in their different
directions.*

EXT. A STREET. MID-AFTERNOON
TED *is wobbling down the street on his moped, singing contentedly to
himself. He rides past a side street. A police car is parked in it. As*
TED *wobbles past, the car starts up and overtakes him. The*
POLICEMAN *inside waves him to a stop.* TED *stops.* TWO
POLICEMEN *get out of the car and walk towards him. One of them
carries a breathalyser.*
TED: We're *always* a bit wobbly on our bikes. Knowledge boys.
   It's traditional. I was a Knowledge boy till three hours
   ago . . .
FIRST POLICEMAN: Ought to have more sense, then, oughtn't
   you, sir?
TED: (*Beaming happily*) That's when I got my Green Badge.
   (*Looks at his watch.*) Well, two and a half hours, say. I'm a
   cabby now.
SECOND POLICEMAN: (*Flatly*) Want to bet?
   (TED *stares at him – heart pounding.*)
TED: What d'you mean?
FIRST POLICEMAN: I'd like you to blow into this bag, sir, if you
   don't mind.
   (TED *continues to stare at* SECOND POLICEMAN . . . *he then
   swallows . . . and turns to* FIRST POLICEMAN.)
TED: What did he mean? When he said that? (*To* SECOND
   POLICEMAN) What did you mean?

126

EXT. TITANIC'S STREET. MID-AFTERNOON

TITANIC *is riding angrily home on his pushbike. He passes the church. Its wayside pulpit now bears the message:* HE THAT INCREASETH KNOWLEDGE INCREASETH SORROW (ECCLESIASTES 1:18). *He falls off his bike.*

EXT. PATHWAY BESIDE CANAL AND RAILWAY LINE. DAY

CHRIS *and* JANET. CHRIS *is moody and morose.* JANET *is irritated.*

JANET: Look, are you in love with him or something? I mean, just say the word. He can have all my brochures – dining-room furniture, table lamps, music centre, the lot!

CHRIS: He started the day *I* did, Janet. How'd you feel if all *my* grafting was for nothing?

JANET: It *might* be yet.

(*A pause.*)

CHRIS: (*Hurt*) Thanks.

JANET: He's not dead, is he, for God's sake? Fair enough, so he's buggered up the Knowledge . . . he's still got a home, though, hasn't he? And a wife, and a kid. *And* a job.

CHRIS: (*Sharp look at her*) Thanks again.

JANET: Look, I can't help the word 'job' creeping into the conversation now and then. It's a *word*.

CHRIS: He's had it for a year now. The Carriage Office say they'll review his case in a year. (*Pause, then almost tearfully angry*) I mean, he'd *got* it! He'd got his licence. He had his Green Badge in his *hand*. (*Pause, then matter-of-factly*) He was a genius at the Knowledge was Ted Margolies. And no one'll ever know.

JANET: You didn't look all that heartbroken at *first* . . .

CHRIS: (*Defensively*) What do you mean?

JANET: When you heard he'd been nicked.

CHRIS: (*Stung*) I don't know what you're hinting! You mean I was chuffed or something??

JANET: (*Evasively*) Look, you're out with me now, all right? Once in a blue moon we're out together – and that's now! We're not calling over runs, we're not listing points, we're not spending all night in the loo because you've an Appearance tomorrow, we're doing *other things*, right!?

(*A pause.*)

CHRIS: I was bloody *choked* when I heard.

JANET: All right, forget it.

CHRIS: He was my mate!

JANET: Chris! I'm not going into mourning for Ted Margolies! So he's had it for another twelve months. He'll still be a cabby before *you* will!

(*A pause. She sighs . . . half relenting, half sick of the whole thing.*)

(*More tenderly*) It's only the Knowledge, Chris.

CHRIS: How do you mean?

JANET: It' not real life.

CHRIS: (*Shocked*) I don't know what you're saying!!

JANET: Chris, it's like a bloody illness with you. *Mental* illness. Streets and streets and streets and squares and roundabouts to comply and names and names . . . and what are you at the end of it? A cabby.

CHRIS: (*Vindicated*) Well, then!

(JANET *stares at his victoriously smiling face, bleakly.*)

JANET: What 'well, then'?

CHRIS: A cabby! I'll be a cabby!

JANET: (*Flatly*) That's right, Chris. Not a bank manager, you notice. Not a doctor. Architect or something. A bloody tuppenny-halfpenny cabby.

(*He stares at her as though he doesn't know her.*)

INT. APPEARANCE ROOM, CARRIAGE OFFICE. DAY

GORDON *is facing* BURGESS. *Their hatred for each other has now blossomed like a cactus.*

BURGESS: Well?

GORDON: I don't know.

(BURGESS *flicks through Gordon's file, wryly. He sighs.*)

BURGESS: You never *do* know, do you, Mr Weller?

GORDON: I know one thing, your Royal Highness –

BURGESS: Now be careful, Weller!!

GORDON: I know you've been getting up my nostril since the day I met you. As a consequence of which, your Majesty, any minute now, you're liable to get my *fist* up *yours*!

(BURGESS *snaps the file closed.*)

BURGESS: I think I'm safe in saying you're off the Knowledge officially as from *now*. Goodbye, Mr Weller.

GORDON: I come in here. Every two months. Yes, sahib. No, sahib. Who the hell do you think you are!! I'm a grown bloody *man* – at least I was before I started coming to this bloody torture chamber! Do you know something – I've shrunk three inches in height. Straight up, I've measured myself! I sit here like Red rotten Riding Hood, scared to open my mouth, while you're shouting an' bawling, needling, whispering, cracking on you're deaf, scratching your backside . . . You don't *want* us to pass! You do everything you can think of to *stop* us! You're driving me bloody cocoa, mate! I used to be a smart feller. Birds used to give me the eye in Selfridge's. Now I wake up in the middle of the night and my belly's shaking . . .

(*A pause.* BURGESS *sighs, wearily.*)

BURGESS: Mr Weller –

GORDON: (*Pointing a violent finger at him*) One more poncey insult and you go on a charter flight through the window, all right?

BURGESS: Mr Weller. Has it ever crossed your mind why?

GORDON: (*Thrown by his reasonable tone*) Why what?

BURGESS: There are two things a cabby has to know. One is the Knowledge. The other is people. Because it's people who ride in cabs. And people are a very peculiar form of life. Compared to people, the Knowledge is a piece of marzipan. They mumble. They can't hear you. They don't know where they want to go to. They get up *both* your nostrils. They treat you like rubbish. They spend their lives doing it to each other. In a cab they do it to *you*. And I have to find out if that bothers you at all. Because if it *does* – and you do it to *them*, you're no cabby.

(*A long pause.*)

GORDON: Well, I think you've got your answer, darling.

(BURGESS *picks up Gordon's file and hands it to him.*)

BURGESS: Do you want to tear it up or shall I?

GORDON: (*Happily*) Oh, I'll do that! That I *can* do!

(*He tears his file into little pieces, then puckers his lips and mouths a kiss at* BURGESS, *throws the pieces in the air and walks out.* BURGESS *calls after him.*)

BURGESS: Tell me something. Do they still call me the Vampire?

GORDON: The others do. *I* call you a part of the vampire's anatomy. A very small part.

(*He exits.*)

EXT. CINEMA ON DESERTED STREET. EVENING

JANET, *dressed up for a date, is waiting for* CHRIS. *She's not in the best of moods: she's been waiting for a long time.* CHRIS *comes chugging down the street on his moped, still dressed in his moped gear. She sees him. Her face hardens. He pulls up beside her.*

CHRIS: Sorry I'm late. Am I late?

JANET: Only three-quarters of an hour.

CHRIS: I was stuck on the North Circular.

JANET: You haven't been home to change.

CHRIS: I've just told you! Hanger Lane was solid.

JANET: Well, it's been terrific standing here freezing to death.

CHRIS: I've said I'm sorry!

JANET: Did you?

CHRIS: Yes, I bloody *did*!

JANET: Well, I wasn't bloody listening.

(*A pause.*)

CHRIS: I suppose the pictures have started . . .

JANET: We could go for a drink.

CHRIS: I get sick of tomato juice.

JANET: Well, you can forget my dad's garage. I'm not dressed for it.

CHRIS: You don't fancy a ride up the North Circular?

JANET: You've just *been* up the North Circular!

CHRIS: There's some fair pubs out that way.

JANET: Chris! I'm not going learning street names on our one night out!

CHRIS: Who said anything about . . . no one *mentioned* . . . I was just . . . Anyway, it's not our one night out! We go out Saturdays. (*Beat.*) Sometimes.

JANET: (*Sighs.*) We'll go to my dad's garage. You *know* all the streets from here to there.

(CHRIS *doesn't want to.* JANET *sees his reluctance in his face as she's about to climb on to the pillion.*)

What's wrong?

CHRIS: Nothing.

JANET: Don't tell me you don't *want* to??

CHRIS: 'Course I do.

> (*She gets on. They start to ride off, then the moped begins to slow down. Then stops.*)

JANET: Now what?

CHRIS: Run out of petrol, ent I?

EXT. FACTORY GATES. DAY

With growing impatience, JANET *is standing waiting for* CHRIS, *at the end of her day's work. Looks at her watch. She smiles pinched, bleak smiles at the last of her* WORKMATES *leaving the factory. One of them indicates a cool-looking young worker who's following them out of the factory.*

GIRL WORKER: Keep moving, Jan. Eddie Hairstyle's coming.

JANET: It'd take more than *him*.

> (*The other* GIRLS *laugh and go on their way.* EDDIE *strolls up to* JANET – *the laid-back King of Stepney.*)

EDDIE: Not turned up, then, hasn't he?

> (*She ignores him.*)

Fancy a lift home? Or somewhere?

> (*She ignores him.*)

Janet?

> (*She ignores him.*)

I've got my brother-in-law's van round the corner.

> (*She ignores him.*)

The back seat folds flat.

JANET: What makes you think *I* do?

EDDIE: Please yourself.

> (*He starts to walk away.* JANET *watches him – troubled, angry with* CHRIS, *angry with herself. She reaches a sudden decision.*)

JANET: Hang about!

> (EDDIE *turns. Combs his beloved hair. She walks up to him and links his arm.*)

I do wish you'd do something about your bloody *hair*.

> (*He grins. They walk off arm-in-arm.*)

INT. WAITING ROOM, CARRIAGE OFFICE. DAY

Most of the chairs are empty. In the others, CHRIS *and* TITANIC *sit side by side.* MISS STAVELY *sits well away from them. She smiles at* CHRIS. *He looks away – with rather more difficulty than usual. She smiles to herself all the more.*

CHRIS: (*Voice over*) He'd been right that very first day, Old Burgess Vampire. At the Acceptance Interview. He said seven out of the ten of us'd never make it. So far *none* of us had. But six had dropped out altogether. (*Beat.*) And Ted, of course, was still banned.

INT. TED'S AND VAL'S LIVING ROOM. NIGHT

CHRIS: (*Voice over*) On top of that, he got sacked from the laundry for going to that last Appearance without asking for time off. The one when he got his Badge. On top of that, his dad started saying Jewish Prayers for the Dead, cos he tried to get a job in a minicab office. Last I heard, him and Val was thinking of selling up and emigrating to Israel. (VAL, *from an English/Hebrew book, is asking* TED *test questions as she did when he was on the Knowledge. He answers the questions swiftly and correctly with his usual skill.*)

INT. WAITING ROOM, CARRIAGE OFFICE. DAY

As before except that TITANIC *is now in with* BURGESS, *and* CHRIS *and* MISS STAVELY *are alone.*

CHRIS: (*Voice over*) The last time I saw Gordon he was touting tickets to the queue for *Close Encounters of the Third Kind* at the Odeon. *I* wasn't in the queue. I was riding past clocking points on a run. Anyway, seems he'd landed on his feet since he was kicked off the Knowledge. He told me he'd now got a job with Lotus Cars as a test-driver.

EXT. SUBURBAN STREET. DAY

GORDON, *in milkman's uniform, is delivering milk to a house from his milk-float.*

CHRIS: (*Voice over*) And he said everything was OK with him and his missus now. He'd packed in chasing spare crumpet. Got more sense.

(*A* YOUNG HOUSEWIFE *opens the door.* GORDON *beams at*

her, eyes smouldering. She smiles back.)

INT. EDDIE HAIRSTYLE'S VAN. NIGHT
Somes weeks after we last saw them, EDDIE *and* JANET *are in a passionate embrace.*
CHRIS: (*Voice over*) 'Course it wasn't much fun for Janet, them days. Me being, you know, out on the Knowledge day and night. Still. She was very understanding. Didn't complain or nothing. Kept herself occupied an' that.
(EDDIE *whispers something to* JANET. *She shakes her head.*)
EDDIE: (*Niggled*) Why not?
JANET: I don't want to.
(*He promptly leans across her and violently jerks open the passenger door.*)
EDDIE: Goodnight. Good riddance.
(JANET *sits immobile, grim-faced. Torn.*)
JANET: I didn't say I wouldn't. I said I didn't want to. Doesn't mean to say I *won't*.
EDDIE: No one's forcing you, darling.
JANET: *I* am, darling.
(*A glance of mutual dislike between them, then they resume their hot embrace, coldly.*)

INT. WAITING ROOM, CARRIAGE OFFICE. DAY
Unoccupied apart from MISS STAVELY *in her chair.* CHRIS *is in Burgess's office answering runs.* MISS STAVELY *is listening carefully, nodding thoughtfully as* CHRIS *answers them correctly.*

INT. APPEARANCE ROOM, CARRIAGE OFFICE. DAY
CHRIS *and* BURGESS *facing each other across the desk.*
CHRIS: Left by Threadneedle Street, left Bartholomew Lane, right Throgmorton Street, left into Austin Friars. (*Beat.*) I think.
(BURGESS *is writing in Chris's file.*)
BURGESS: (*Without looking up*) Think or know?
CHRIS: Know.
BURGESS: (*Still writing*) And you know what that run *was*, out of interest?
CHRIS: (*Puzzled*) You *asked* me it! Ramillies Street to Austin Friars!

BURGESS: I'll tell you what it was, son. The last one I'll be
   asking you.
CHRIS: (*Puzzled*) What?
BURGESS: I'm giving you your Requ. Officially known as your
   Requisition. Officially meaning you've passed your
   Knowledge of London. So now I put you down for your
   driving test. If you can get a bit of practice driving a cab
   beforehand – so much the better. Saves you smashing ours
   against the canteen wall. Meanwhile start swotting up your
   Knowledge of the Suburbs. There's only sixty-odd of them.
   Got a list?
CHRIS: Yes, sir. Thank you, sir. I have, sir. Yes, sir.
BURGESS: I don't detect a note of doubt, do I?
CHRIS: (*Fervently*) No, sir!
BURGESS: (*Sighing*) That was a joke. I tell jokes. I have a very
   comical nature. (*Resumes.*) Your next Appearance is in
   fourteen days. You'll know most of the suburbs by then.
   Child's play. (*Beat.*) Now, wheel the next one in. Jugular
   vein first.
   (CHRIS *sits in a daze.*)
   Well, cheer up, laddie! You've passed your Knowledge.
   You're allowed to crack your face a little bit. What we in
   the Carriage Office refer to as Happiness.

EXT. THE BALCONY OF JANET'S FLAT. DAY
CHRIS *and* JANET *are leaning on the rail looking out over London.*
Both sad. Bewildered. Lost.
CHRIS: With Eddie Hairstyle. . . ?
JANET: What's it matter who it was with? Anyone. It just
   happened to be Eddie.
   (*A long pause.*)
CHRIS: I can't believe what you're saying.
JANET: Me neither. (*Beat.*) Yes, I can.
CHRIS: Yeah, I can, too. (*Pause.*) It was you that bought me the
   moped in the first place.
JANET: And your shirt and tie for your Appearances.
CHRIS: Yeah.
JANET: And half your sodding petrol.
CHRIS: I'll pay you back.

JANET: (*Sad smile.*) Just get that Green Badge – we'll call it straight. (*Pause.*) You don't want me, Chris. Not for a long time, you haven't. If ever. You just didn't know you didn't, that's all. (*Pause.*) And the same goes for me. With you. (*Pause.*) You know who comes into my mind sometimes . . . at work . . . when I'm bored out of my bloody skull? The little kid in the house where we went to buy the skateboard. Crying his little cross-eyes out 'cos we'd come for it. And his pig-ignorant father that was flogging it. Belting him across the head for crying. So all he did was cry all the more.

(*A pause.*)

CHRIS: We had some *good* times, though.

JANET: When?

(*They look at each other. The end of the road.*)

INT. CARRIAGE OFFICE: 'APPOINTMENTS AND
APPLICATIONS' WINDOW. DAY

CHRIS *is sitting on a bench waiting to receive his Green Badge.*
TWO MEN *are queuing for attention at the window.*

CHRIS: (*Voice over*) It all ended one Wednesday nine hundred and sixty-nine days after it all started. Two years, eight months and one week. I had my last Appearance with the Vampire. At the end of it, he said: 'You got your Inner London, your Suburban, your driving test, your Police identification, your references. Now go to the Appointments Window and get your Green Badge.' (*Pause.*) Just like that. No fanfare of trumpets. Nothing. I didn't bother shaking his hand. I *thought* about it. But then it'd have been just like him to be a secret judo expert and sling me into the filing cabinet.

(*A* RECEPTIONIST *appears at the window.*)

RECEPTIONIST: Yes?

FIRST MAN: Is this where I apply to go on the Knowledge?

RECEPTIONIST: Got your driving licence and birth certificate?

(*The* MAN *hands them to her. She hands him documents.*)
That's your application form. You fill that in. And that's your medical form – your doctor fills that in. And that's your slip for the photographer in Upper Street. For your photo. Six copies. Thank you. Next!

135

(FIRST MAN *wanders away with his papers.* SECOND MAN *approaches the window.*)

SECOND MAN: Excuse me . . . I want to apply to –
(*An* OFFICE GIRL *behind the window taps the* RECEPTIONIST *on her shoulder and hands her a badge and licence. The* RECEPTIONIST *glances at it.*)

RECEPTIONIST: (*To* SECOND MAN) Hang about. (*Calls to* CHRIS) Mr Matthews?
(CHRIS *jerks his eyes to her.*)
Your Green Badge.
(CHRIS *goes to her.*)
That'll be fifteen p, please.
(CHRIS *pays her, takes the badge and looks at it. The most significant moment in history and the world doesn't bat an eyelid.*)
(*To* SECOND MAN) The Knowledge is it?

SECOND MAN: 'S right.

RECEPTIONIST: That's your application form. You fill that in. And that's your medical form – your doctor fills that in. And that's your slip for the photographer in Upper Street. For your photo. Six copies. Thank you. Next!

EXT. FACTORY GATES, STEPNEY. DAY
JANET *comes out of work with her* FEMALE WORKMATES. EDDIE HAIRSTYLE *comes out of work with his* MALE WORKMATES.
JANET *and* EDDIE *then leave their* MATES *and walk along the street together. A car draws up beside them. It's embellished with coloured football streamers. The* DRIVER, *wearing a similarly coloured scarf, leans out of his window.*

DRIVER: West Ham?

JANET: You what?

DRIVER: West Ham Football Ground. Cup replay.

JANET: What about it?

DRIVER: How do I get there?

JANET: You're best bet is to try saying 'please'!

DRIVER: You what?

JANET: (*Pointing down street*) Forward to the main road, right at first set of traffic lights, filter left by second on left, right Alie Street. Forward Goodman's Stile into Commercial

Road – the Proof House of the City of London Gunmakers'
Company on right – the London College of Furniture on
left. Bishop of Stepney's House on right, forward East
India Dock Road – Blackwall Tunnel approach on left,
comply roundabout, leave by Barking Road, left into Green
Street, set down on right.

(*The* DRIVER *stares at her, bewildered.*)

DRIVER: Um . . . I go down the main road . . . then I what?

EXT. LONDON STREET. DAY

In the midst of the heavy traffic, we focus on a taxicab. Driving it is
CHRIS. *His badge borne proudly on his lapel. A* MAN *hails from the*
kerb. CHRIS *pulls over to him.*

MAN: Manor House Station, all right?

CHRIS: Right, guv.

(*The* MAN *gets in.*)

INT. CHRIS'S CAB – TRAVELLING. DAY

The MAN *calls through the interconnecting window.*

MAN: I'm picking someone up at Manor House. From there we
want Gibson Square.

(CHRIS *stares at him, incredulously.*)

CHRIS: Manor House to Gibson Square? You're joking!

MAN: Don't get awkward with me, son. I'll have your bloody
number!

(CHRIS *drives on.*)

EXT. TITANIC'S HOUSE. DAY

TITANIC *emerges from his flat, wheeling his bike. Strapped to it are*
old suitcases and rickety parcels containing his belongings.

CHRIS: (*Voice over*) The only other Knowledge boy that started
when I did – and got his Green Badge – was Titanic. The
following morning he went to pick up his cab. He also
packed all his bits and pieces and left home – for good.
According to him, his missus came to the door . . .

(*Titanic's wife,* LILIAN, *appears at the doorway, holding the*
ornament that she talks to.)

(*Voice over*) . . . and spoke to him for the first time in
seventeen years – pleading for him to stay . . .

LILIAN: Piss off, and don't come back!
> (*She storms back into the house.* TITANIC *gets on his bike and rides off.*)

EXT. TITANIC'S STREET. DAY
TITANIC *rides past the wayside pulpit, it now reads:* KNOWLEDGE IS POWER (FRANCIS BACON). *He looks as though he's about to fall off but – at the last moment – regains his balance, and rides serenely on.*

EXT. STREET IN CENTRAL LONDON. DAY
Chris's cab and another cab, both FOR HIRE, *are stopped at traffic lights. A* WOMAN *across the junction hails* CHRIS. *He nods acknowledgement. The lights change from red to green. The other cab races to get to the* WOMAN *before* CHRIS *can. The* WOMAN *gets in the first cab.* CHRIS *drives up and brakes to a halt alongside the first cab, fuming.*

CHRIS: (*Voice over*) I forgot to mention. There was another of our lot got a Green Badge. Not a Knowledge boy – a Knowledge girl.
> (*He turns and yells at the other* CABBY.)

Hey, buggerlugs, that was *my* –
> (*He stops. Cut to other* CABBY *from his point of view. It's* MISS STAVELY. CHRIS *smiles warmly.*)

Oh, hello . . .

MISS STAVELY: (*Brisk, businesslike*) See you, mate. Be lucky.

CHRIS: Hey, if you ever fancy, you know, a cup of coffee or something . . .
> (*But she's already driven off.* CHRIS *sits for a moment watching her go. Sighs philosophically.*)

(*Voice over*) Like I said . . . We live, we *never* bloody learn . . .
> (*A barrage of hooting from cars behind him shakes him out of it. He drives off into the traffic.*)

Ready When You Are, Mr McGill

CHARACTERS

JOE MCGILL
PHIL (Director)
DON (Cameraman)
TERRY (Floor Manager)
KENNETH (Sound Recordist)
GEOFF (Assistant Cameraman)
COLIN (Boom Swinger)
GAFFER
VALERIE (Production Assistant)
SHIRLEY (Make-up Girl)
JEAN (Wardrobe Girl)
DEIRDRE (Assistant Stage Manager)
BERNARD (Principal Actor)
BETTY (Principal Actress)
RONNIE SKIDMORE (Unit Manager)
CATERING WAGON PROPRIETOR
MRS LOMAX
MRS STEVENS
MRS PENNINGTON
MR CLEGG
MR DANBY
TWO GOSSIPING WOMEN
SCHOOLGIRL (DEBORAH)
CHILD
DECORATOR
NANCY
MILKMAN
Sparks, Grips, Props Men, Factory Workers, School-kids

Ready When You Are, Mr McGill was produced by Granada Television and first broadcast in January 1976. The principal members of the cast were as follows:

JOE MCGILL	Joe Black
PHIL	Jack Shepherd
DON	Stanley Lebor
TERRY	Mark Wing-Davey
KENNETH	Fred Feast
GEOFF	Jim Bywater
COLIN	Peter Russell
VALERIE	Diana Davies
SHIRLEY	Wendy Brown
JEAN	Eileen Davies
DEIRDRE	Joyce Kennedy
BERNARD	William Hoyland
BETTY	Marty Cruickshank
MRS LOMAX	Jill Summers
MRS STEVENS	Frances Goodall
MR CLEGG	James Lynch
MR DANBY	Frank Crompton
NANCY	Barbara Moore-Black

Crew	
Designer	M. Grimes
Producer	Michael Dunlop
Director	Mike Newell

INT. BEDROOM. MORNING

Very early morning and the room is in darkness. A middle-aged couple – JOE and NANCY – are in bed, seemingly fast asleep. NANCY snores gently. In the stillness, we eventually hear . . .

JOE: (*Quietly*) 'I've never seen the young lady in my life before. And I've lived here fifty years.'

(*Abruptly, the alarm clock starts to ring. JOE immediately switches on the light, then stops the alarm. NANCY begins to rouse slightly from her deep sleep.*)

NANCY: (*Muttering*) Joe. Six o'clock, Joe.

JOE: I'm up, love.

(*Still lying there, he picks up a script from his bedside table. It's open at a particular page. He reads aloud.*)

'I've never seen the young lady in my life before. And I've lived here fifty years.'

(*He lays the script aside and repeats the line again 'from memory'.*)

'I've never seen the young lady in my life before. And I've lived here fifty years.'

(*He gets out of bed. His clothes are arranged ready, hanging from a hanger on the outside of the wardrobe. He starts dressing.*)

You go back to sleep, then, Nancy. (*Calls gently.*)

Nancy . . .

NANCY: (*Waking*) Hmmm?

JOE: You go back to sleep.

NANCY: (*Closing her eyes again*) Good luck, then.

JOE: Thanks, I'll need it. (*Laughs.*) I say, 'Thanks, I'll need it.'

NANCY: (*Succumbing to sleep again*) You'll be very good.

JOE: (*Shrugs, smiles confidentially.*) You can only do your best. Would you like to test me again? On my words?

(*He picks up his script and offers it to her. But sees she's fast asleep again. He covers her up, solicitously.*)

'S all right. I think I've mastered it. Got it off perfect now.

EXT. TV STUDIOS' CAR-PARK. MORNING

The Cameraman and his Assistant (DON and GEOFF), the Sound Recordist and Boom Swinger (KENNETH and COLIN) are loading their equipment into the camera estate cars. The PROPS MEN are loading their wagon. The SPARKS and their GAFFER (wearing a hat) are connecting the genny and loading their lights. There's a dreamlike deadness over the whole scene. Everyone is more than half asleep, some of them still yawning – no one speaking. VALERIE, the PA, is threading her way through the silent activity towards the Director (PHIL) and Floor Manager (TERRY) who are studying papers on Terry's clipboard. She speaks as though to herself.

VAL: Anyone seen my stopwatch? I can't find my stopwatch . . .

GAFFER: (*Yawning*) Washed your neck this morning?

VAL: Eh?

> (*He nods towards her chest. She follows his glance. The stopwatch is in its usual place, strung around her neck. She makes a yawned acknowledgement to the GAFFER and walks on towards PHIL and TERRY. PHIL gives a colossal yawn.*)

TERRY: (*Sleepily*) What?

PHIL: What?

TERRY: All right?

PHIL: (*Dead with the accumulation of two weeks' fatigue*) Fine. Great. (*Pause.*) I was stretching my mouth.

INT. JOE'S HALL. MORNING

On the walls are old theatre posters, bearing Joe's name some way down the bill. JOE comes down the stairs, muttering his lines to himself. He continues towards the front door.

EXT. JOE'S HOUSE. MORNING

A milkfloat parks outside. A MILKMAN disembarks. He takes a bottle of milk towards the house. JOE emerges from his front door, wearing his best suit and carrying his script.

JOE: (*Brightly*) Morning!

> (*The MILKMAN looks at him, surprised at him being out and about so early.*)

MILKMAN: By hell. After *my* job, are you?

JOE: (*Confident smile*) Got one of my own today, thanks all the same. (*Taps his script.*) A drama. TV play.

MILKMAN: (*Continuing towards the doorstep*) Has it got a beginning, a middle and an end?

JOE: I speak in this one.

MILKMAN: Never bloody do have, do they?

JOE: Character part. I've got lines and everything.

MILKMAN: (*Not interested*) By hell.

JOE: (*As the* MILKMAN *returns to his float*) I'll let you know when it's on.

MILKMAN: (*Totally uninterested*) Don't forget.
(*They separate and go their different ways.*)

EXT. TV STUDIOS' CAR-PARK. MORNING
A few minutes later. Crossing from the building, towards TERRY, *who's still studying his clipboard, come* SHIRLEY (*Make-up Girl*) *carrying her make-up case,* JEAN (*the Wardrobe Girl*) *carrying costumes over her arm,* BERNARD (*the Principal Actor*) *in soldier's uniform,* BETTY (*the Principal Actress*) *in tennis clothes. Both* BERNARD *and* BETTY *carry copies of the* Guardian.

SHIRLEY: (*Yawning weakly*) If I never *see* another Campari and soda, it'll be too soon.

BETTY: I once worked with a director in Portugal. He has Guinness in his porridge at breakfast.

SHIRLEY: (*Confused*) This was Campari.

BETTY: And always had one hand in his trouser pocket.
(*They approach* TERRY. *They all exchange a desultory barrage of 'good mornings' with him.*)

BERNARD: Morning.

TERRY: Morning.

BETTY: Morning.

TERRY: Morning.

SHIRLEY: Morning.

TERRY: Morning. (*Turns to* JEAN, *sympathetically.*) All right this morning, Jean?
(JEAN *nods, sullenly. They all start getting into Terry's car –* SHIRLEY *and* JEAN *first.* BERNARD *suddenly notices Betty's paper.*)

BERNARD: (*Concerned*) Hey! We've both got the *Guardian*!

BETTY: (*Looking from her paper to his*) Oh, buggeration!

TERRY: Crossword?

145

BERNARD: Yeah.

TERRY: (*To* BETTY) I'll swap you my *Telegraph*.

BETTY: (*Delighted*) Boo–boom!

> (*As* TERRY *gets into the driving seat, he calls to* DEIRDRE, *the ASM, who's passing.*)

TERRY: Deirdre!

> (*He takes a sheet of paper from his clipboard and waves it at her.*) Extras!

DEIRDRE: (*Taking it as she passes*) Ta.

INT. TRAVELLING BUS. MORNING

The seats are occupied by FACTORY WORKERS (*male and female*) *on their way to work. All have the freshly washed, sleep-filled faces of early risers. And all are still cocooned in their own little worlds of silence.* JOE *is seated next to one of them. He has his script opened on his knee and is muttering his line of dialogue to himself, occasionally checking it with the script. The* FACTORY WORKER *looks at him puzzled at what he's muttering at* (*as* JOE *hoped he would*).

JOE: Sorry! Rehearsing.

> (*He taps his script by way of explanation. The* FACTORY WORKER *returns to his daydreaming. A pause.* JOE *taps his script again.*)
>
> TV play I'm in. For my sins.
>
> (*The* FACTORY WORKER *neither understands nor is interested. He gets his* Daily Mirror *out and starts reading.*)
>
> (*Glancing at his watch*) Crack of dawn, eh? (*Laughs.*) Who'd be an actor! Must be barmy!
>
> (*The* FACTORY WORKER *looks at him deadpan. He's been getting up at the crack of dawn for forty years, day in, day out and not to spend the day poncing about being an actor. After his long look, he dismisses the whole affair and returns to his* Daily Mirror. JOE *realizes his* faux pas.)
>
> Sorry – I didn't mean . . . what I meant . . . was . . .
>
> (*But the* FACTORY WORKER *is now busy being convulsed in a smoker's violent coughing spasm.*)

EXT. SUBURBAN STREET: FILMING LOCATION. MORNING

The location consists of a church hall standing some distance away in its grounds. The action of the scene to be filmed takes place on the pavement

outside the gates to the grounds. The film unit is positioned in the
road. To one side are parked the camera cars, props wagon, lighting
wagon, genny and a couple of private cars. The SPARKS *are setting*
up their lights; GEOFF *is checking and setting up the camera with the*
GRIPS; COLIN *is checking and positioning his sound equipment.* VAL
is standing to one side – almost asleep on her feet. PHIL *and* DON *are*
standing together. KENNETH *is slightly behind them.* PHIL *is*
outlining the first set-up of the day – very tentatively, hoping neither
DON *nor* KENNETH *will think his ideas pedestrian or impracticable.*
All three are very, very weary: PHIL *most of all.*

DON: And you don't want me to zoom?

PHIL: No, thanks.

KENNETH: It'd give *me* a few grey hairs if you did.

PHIL: I don't.

KENNETH: I mean, I'm not Uri Geller . . . If you wanted to
    zoom right down to –

PHIL: I don't.

KENNETH: No, I'm saying, if you did –

PHIL: No, well, I *don't* . . . Jesus!
    (*A pause.*)

DON: We haven't *got* the zoom till Thursday.

PHIL: What day is it today?

KENNETH: Wednesday, all day.

PHIL: Right. OK. Fair enough. No panic.
    (DON, PHIL *and* KENNETH *stand waiting. They're cold, tired,*
    fed-up, and only by now on speaking terms because they're paid
    to be. They ran out of sociable conversation over a week ago. A
    pause.)

KENNETH: You take my point, though?
    (*A pause.*)

DON: Went to see *Murder on the Orient Express* last night.

KENNETH: Good?

DON: Some bloody comedian nicked my fishing rod out of the
    boot of my car.
    (*A pause.*)

PHIL: (*To no one in particular*) The trick is to *think* yourself
    warm. I.e., it is a warm day; I am consequently extremely
    warm. (*Pause; shivers.*) God, it's cold . . .

INT. EXTRAS' MINIBUS (PARKED IN TV STUDIOS'
CAR-PARK). MORNING
DEIRDRE *is standing beside the driver's seat with Terry's list of
extras. Several* EXTRAS *are already seated – dotted about the
minibus.*

DEIRDRE: Sheila Lomax?

MRS LOMAX: Here.

DEIRDRE: Freda Pennington?

MRS PENNINGTON: Yes, chuck.

DEIRDRE: Brian Clegg?

MR CLEGG: As ever, sunshine.

DEIRDRE: Mabel Stevens?

MRS STEVENS: Here.

MRS LOMAX: Mabel, are you down for Second Gossiping
     Housewife?

MRS STEVENS: No one said.

MRS LOMAX: I should imagine I'm down for First Gossiping
     Housewife. In all probability.

DEIRDRE: All parts will be allocated on arrival at the location.

MRS LOMAX: I happen to know what I auditioned for, dear.
     (*She pulls a 'that showed that snooty bugger where to get off'
     face at* MRS STEVENS. JOE *clambers aboard.*)

DEIRDRE: Harold Danby?

JOE: Joseph McGill. Joe.

MR DANBY: Here. Harold Danby.
     (JOE *realizes his error.*)

JOE: Sorry! (*Smiles at* DEIRDRE.) Sorry.
     (*She smiles 'good morning' at the other* EXTRAS *as he finds a
     seat. They ignore him. He sits down, glances round, finding it
     hard to restrain his excitement at the day ahead.* MR CLEGG
     leans forward and taps him on the shoulder.)

MR CLEGG: *Leeds United*?

JOE: Pardon?

MR CLEGG: Were you on *Leeds United*? Play for Today?

JOE: No. I had lumbago.

MR CLEGG: Ah. Confusing you with some other party.
     (*He sits back, having now lost interest. After a moment,* JOE
     turns round to him.)

JOE: I was *asked*. I had lumbago.

EXT. SUBURBAN STREET: THE LOCATION. MORNING
PHIL, DON *and* KENNETH *stand studying the script.*
PHIL: What do you reckon? Feasible?
DON: Up to you.
PHIL: Kenneth?
KENNETH: What?
PHIL: (*Decisively*) We'll do it your way, then. (*Not so decisively*)
    Yes?
DON: I've just *said.*
PHIL: I know. I know.
    (*He looks around and calls to* TERRY, *who's some distance
    away with* SHIRLEY, JEAN, BERNARD *and* BETTY.)
    Terry!
    (TERRY, BERNARD *and* BETTY *pick their way through
    technicians moving equipment, to* PHIL. *Cut to* SHIRLEY *and*
    JEAN, *gathering their gear for the move.*)
SHIRLEY: My own fault, mind you. I should've stayed on
    Bacardi and Babycham. (*Looks at her sympathetically.*) You
    OK?
    (JEAN *nods miserably. Bites her lip, fights back a tear.*)
    (*Sympathetically*) Still feeling. . . ?
    (JEAN *nods.*)
    Is it because of. . . ?
    (JEAN *shakes her head and bursts into tears. She gathers up her
    gear and goes off towards* PHIL's *group.*)

EXT. STREET: ADJACENT TO LOCATION. MORNING
The extras' minibus arrives and pulls to a halt. Two or three
EXTRAS, *led by* MRS LOMAX, *at once disembark, followed by*
DEIRDRE, *trying to stop them, in some agitation.*
DEIRDRE: Will you all stay on the coach, please! Till as and
    when required!
MRS LOMAX: Sorry, pet.
    (*The others go back in.* MRS LOMAX *hovers.*)
DEIRDRE: Everyone, please. Mrs Lomax!
MRS LOMAX: (*Confidentially, now that she's got her alone*) If it
    saves you a job, dear . . . having to choose . . . Mrs Stevens
    and I are excellent as First and Second Gossiping
    Housewives. We did it in *Country Matters.* Five times.

EXT. SUBURBAN STREET: SET-UP LOCATION. MORNING
TERRY *stands with* BERNARD *and* BETTY *who are studying the script.* PHIL *stands to one side with* DON, KENNETH *slightly behind. All three dead, numb, cold and tired. They speak with no real attempt at communication.*

PHIL: Like winter, isn't it . . .

DON: It *is* winter.

PHIL: (*Remembering*) Oh, yeah.
(*A pause.*)
I fell asleep putting my pants on this morning. Sat on the bed to pull on my pants, and the next thing I knew I was . . . (*Yawns; pause.*) Was it any cop?

DON: What?

PHIL: *Murder on the Orient Express.*

DON: Cost me over thirty quid, that fishing tackle.

PHIL: You can claim.

DON: Oh, I'll *claim.*
(*Which appears to be the end of the conversation, possibly the end of life. A silence.*)

TERRY: Ready, Phil.

PHIL: Right. Quick run-through for Don.

KENNETH: And me.

PHIL: (*A politely irritated glance at* KENNETH) And him. So it's Bernard dropping Betty off at the door and the extra walking past.

TERRY: 'Old Man in Street'.

PHIL: Is he here?

TERRY: (*Calling towards minibus*) Deirdre! 'Old Man in Street'.

INT. MINIBUS. MORNING
The EXTRAS *are chatting quietly among themselves.* JOE, *script in hand, is learning his line.* DEIRDRE, *at the door, turns inside.*

DEIRDRE: Mr McGill, please. You're on.

JOE: (*Startled*) Now??

DEIRDRE: Please.
(JOE *glances at the others with barely restrained excitement.*)

JOE: In at the deep end, eh? Splash.
(*He gets up, clutching his script, and clambers off the coach*

after DEIRDRE. MRS STEVENS *watches him go, then turns to* MRS LOMAX.)

MRS STEVENS: (*Impressed*) He's a *speaking* extra. He's got sixteen words.

MRS LOMAX: (*Totally unimpressed*) Mmm. I was with him on *Family at War*. We both had to shout 'Hear! Hear!' He was only average.

EXT. STREET: WALL OF A HOUSE. MORNING
A DECORATOR, *carrying ladders, paint, brushes, snap-tin and morning paper wanders past the unit, watching their preparations with a blank-faced fascination. He starts to organize himself, preparing for his own day's work – painting the entire wall of the house.*

EXT. SUBURBAN STREET: SET-UP LOCATION. MORNING
BERNARD *and* BETTY *are now seated in a small, pre-war convertible car. They're being given last minute attention by* SHIRLEY *and* JEAN. PHIL, DON, KENNETH, TERRY *and* VAL (*juggling with her stopwatch and continuity sheets*) *are watching them.*

PHIL: (*To* BERNARD *and* JEAN) So we're just on you two saying blah, blah, blah . . .

BETTY: Do you want us to go through it?

KENNETH: Be good for *me*.

PHIL: Well, terrific! We're only three days behind; we'll only finish up on the dole. (*Turns back to* BETTY.) Yes, please, Betty. Action.

BETTY: (*In character*) 'Well, thanks for the lift.'

BERNARD: (*In character, smiling*) 'Thank you.'

BETTY: (*In character*) 'What for?'

BERNARD: (*In character, winks.*) 'See you Saturday.'
(*They kiss very briefly. She gets out of the car and goes into the church hall.* JOE *has meanwhile arrived and stands to one side, watching.*)

DON: (*To* PHIL) Is that it?

PHIL: That's it. Another little gem.

TERRY: 'Old Man in Street'.

PHIL: (*Remembering*) Oh, hell! Sorry, yeah. (*To* DON *and*

KENNETH) Sorry, there's more. Old Man in Street comes towards . . . (*To* TERRY) Where is the old fart?

TERRY: (*Calling to minibus*) Deirdre! We're waiting.

JOE: Here. Me. Excuse me.

TERRY: (*Turning*) Oh. (*To* PHIL) Here, Phil.

PHIL: Right. Stand over there.

JOE: McGill. Joe McGill.

PHIL: Right, Joe. You start from over there and –

JOE: Good morning.

PHIL: Morning. You come from over there and walk towards –

JOE: Pleasure to have the pleasure of working with you.

PHIL: Thank you. And walk towards the car. As soon as she goes in you do your dialogue with Bernard, right?

JOE: Yes, Mr Shaw.

PHIL: Go on, then.

JOE: Pardon?

PHIL: Walk. Walk towards the car. (*To* BETTY) In you go, sweetheart. Action.

(BETTY *goes into the church hall.*)

JOE: Are the cameras going?

TERRY: It's a rehearsal.

JOE: Fair enough. (*To* BERNARD) Morning to *you*, sir.

BERNARD: (*Not interested*) Morning.

JOE: Pleasure to have the privilege of –

PHIL: And action!

(*He impatiently waves* JOE *to start walking towards the car.* JOE *does so.*)

JOE: (*To* BERNARD, *in character*) 'I've never seen the young lady in my life before. And I've – '

BERNARD: (*To* PHIL) I speak first, don't I?

PHIL: Mmm? Right, yeah, sorry. (*To* JOE) After *he* speaks, compré?

JOE: Sorry.

PHIL: Again, then. Action.

BERNARD: (*In character to* JOE) 'Prettiest girl in the village, eh, grandad?'

JOE: 'I've never seen the . . .' (*Reads the rest from his script.*) '. . . young lady in my life before. And I've lived here fifty years.' (*To* PHIL) Was that right for interpretation? A bit

152

wooden, perhaps? Next time I'll get more –

PHIL: (*To* DON) Then he sods off. (*To* JOE) Walk past.

(JOE *does so.* PHIL *returns to* DON.)

And we tighten on Bernard for his reaction. OK?

DON: OK.

KENNETH: OK.

PHIL: Pardon?

KENNETH: OK with me, too.

PHIL: Oh. Good. (*To* TERRY, *wearily*) Right, mate, we're doing it. Let joy be unconfined.

TERRY: (*Calling to the entire unit*) OK, girls, chop, chop. This is it.

(*An immediate chaos of bustle and noise as everyone starts setting up for the shot: camera, sound, props, sparks, make-up, costume, etc.* JOE *stands, at a bit of a loss, in the middle. He tries to attract the attention of* TERRY, *then* JEAN, *then* VALERIE . . . *but they're all bustling about, too busy to listen.*)

EXT. STREET CORNER. MORNING

TWO WOMEN, *carrying shopping bags, are standing on the corner in mute, puzzled fascination at all the activity. Nearby is a young* SCHOOLGIRL *holding a small* CHILD *by the hand. They're also watching. All of them are virtually frozen in the walking position they were in when they first caught sight of the unit a few moments previously.*

FIRST WOMAN: What *sort* of play?

SECOND WOMAN: For the telly.

FIRST WOMAN: Is it what-d'you-call-it?

SECOND WOMAN: *Upstairs, Downstairs?*

FIRST WOMAN: Yes.

SECOND WOMAN: No.

SCHOOLGIRL: (*To the* CHILD) Stand *still.*

CHILD: I want to wee-wee.

SECOND WOMAN: (*To the* CHILD) We can't have everything we want in life!

FIRST WOMAN: (*Peering at* BERNARD) I've seen *him* before. He's been in something.

SECOND WOMAN: According to the *TV Times*, his pet hates are Man's Inhumanity to Man and gardening.

(*They watch the seeming chaos of the unit setting up for the shot. Both very impressed.*)

153

Every man to his trade, eh?

FIRST WOMAN: Better than *working* for a living.

    (*Another pause.* FIRST WOMAN *watches* PHIL, *who's looking cold, tired and worried.*)

SECOND WOMAN: See that half-dead one? He's in charge.

FIRST WOMAN: Fancies himself, does he?

SECOND WOMAN: Oh, he thinks he's God.

EXT. SUBURBAN STREET: SET-UP LOCATION. MORNING

PHIL: (*Calling to the* SPARKS) OK, let there be light!

    (*Cut to* WOMEN's *reaction. The* SPARKS *switch on. Everyone is now in position, ready to shoot.* PHIL *yawns helplessly.*)

    Right, here we go. Nice and . . . (*yawns*) . . . nice and bright, everyone!

TERRY: Absolute quiet, everywhere, please!

    (*Cut to the* TWO WOMEN.)

FIRST WOMAN: I think I read in the paper that she's got a new nose. I hate to think what her *first* one looked like.

TERRY: (*To the* WOMEN) Please, ladies! Very quiet!

FIRST WOMAN: (*Giggling fatuously to* SECOND WOMAN) Oops, it was me, that!

TERRY: (*To* FIRST WOMAN) Sssshhhh!

PHIL: OK. Turn over.

    (*Throughout the following, intercut between Joe's point of view and* JOE, *tensing more and more as his big moment nears.*)

KENNETH: Sound.

PHIL: Don?

DON: Yep?

PHIL: Mark it.

DON: Hang about! You're just in, Colin!

    (COLIN *shuffles back a pace and readjusts his boom.*)

COLIN: OK?

DON: Wonderful.

PHIL: Mark it.

DON: Hang about! There's a foreign body on Bernard's knee.

SHIRLEY: I should be so lucky.

TERRY: Bernard. What's on your knee?

BERNARD: Just the *Guardian*.

    (TERRY *runs to the car, takes* BERNARD Guardian *and runs back to position.* JOE *wets his lips tensely.*)

KENNETH: Still running.

PHIL: Don?

DON: Yep.

(GEOFF, *after his two false starts so far, runs into position with his clapperboard.*)

GEOFF: 241, take 1.

PHIL: OK, Don?

DON: Never better.

PHIL: Action!

BETTY: 'Well, thanks for the lift.'

BERNARD: 'Thank you.'

BETTY: 'What for?'

BERNARD: 'See you Saturday.'

(*They kiss briefly. As* BETTY *starts to walk towards the church hall,* PHIL *waves wildly to* JOE *to start walking.* JOE *takes a deep breath and sets off.*)

BERNARD: 'Prettiest girl in the village, eh, grandad?'

(JOE *opens his mouth to say his line.*)

PHIL: Cut! Cut it!

(*Various random murmurings of 'What's wrong?'* TECHNICIANS *give their colleagues or assistants instructions for making the next take better.*)

(*To* JOE) 'Jimmy', is it?

JOE: Sorry?

PHIL: 'Jimmy'?

JOE: Joe. Joe McGill. 'Old Man in Street'.

PHIL: Joe. I had a very unhappy childhood. I'd now like it to end. Where the hell are you going!! A Buckingham Palace garden party??

JOE: (*Baffled at the outburst*) No. Just from there (*pointing*) to here.

PHIL: Terry, why has he come as a Fortnum and Mason Christmas Cake?

(TERRY *looks at* JOE. *Grimaces at the mistake that's been made.*)

TERRY: Damn.

PHIL: Exactly.

TERRY: (*Calling*) Jean!

(*Cut to* JEAN – *whose lip at once begins to quiver. She comes*

PHIL: (*Holding his script for* JEAN *to read*) Act 1, scene 1, page 1, line 1 – 'A village street in 1940'. *Not*, you notice, Carnaby Street in 1975!

(JEAN *at once starts crying*.)

Oh, Jesus . . . 'S all right, love. Not important. An old jacket and cloth cap'd do.

(JEAN *just stands there crying*.)

TERRY: (*To* PHIL) I'll get them. I'll get them. I like to keep sodding busy.

(TERRY *runs to where* JEAN'*s left her costumes.* JEAN *follows, reluctantly, still weeping*.)

JOE: (*Upset, to a passing* TECHNICIAN) No one said about clothes. I wasn't notified re clothing apparel.

(TERRY *scoops up a jacket and cap and dresses* JOE *in them. The jacket's a bit too big*.)

PHIL: (*Calling*) All right, we're going again, then. Stand by.

TERRY: Absolute quiet, now, please! (*To* FIRST *and* SECOND WOMAN) Thank you, ladies!

FIRST WOMAN: (*Offended, to* SECOND WOMAN) I never opened my mouth! I get enough of that at *home*.

TERRY: (*To* FIRST WOMAN) Ssshhh! (*To* KENNETH) Turn over.

KENNETH: Sound.

TERRY: Camera.

DON: OK.

TERRY: Mark it.

(GEOFF *races in with the clapperboard*.)

GEOFF: 241, take 2.

PHIL: Action!

BETTY: 'Well, thanks for the lift.'

BERNARD: 'Thank you.'

(*Cut to* KENNETH, *grimacing worriedly at what he can hear in his headphones. He looks up at the empty sky.* BETTY *and* BERNARD *meanwhile continue their dialogue. Just as* JOE *is about to say his line,* KENNETH *removes his headphones emphatically*.)

KENNETH: Cut it, Phil.

PHIL: (*Wheeling round, horrified*) What's wrong???

(KENNETH *nods towards the empty skies.* PHIL *follows his eyes*.)

Well?

KENNETH: Listen.

PHIL: What to??

KENNETH: Aircraft.

PHIL: (*Peering hard at the sky*) Where???

DON: Have we cut or what?

PHIL: What do you mean – 'aircraft'??

KENNETH: Like big iron bird from great land in sky. An *aircraft*!!

PHIL: (*To* DON) Cut. Sorry, pal.

TERRY: (*Calling*) Relax, everyone.

PHIL: (*Still searching the sky*) *What* bloody aircraft!!!

KENNETH: Ssshh . . .

> (*Everyone stands stockstill and listens . . . the* UNIT, ACTORS, JOE, *the* TWO WOMEN *and* SCHOOLGIRL *on the corner, the* DECORATOR *up his ladder. After a moment,* PHIL *shakes his head.*)

PHIL: Well, I know I'm clogged up with catarrh . . .

KENNETH: Listen.

PHIL: What the hell *to*?

> (*We hear a faint aircraft noise in the distance . . . gradually growing louder.*)

OK, stand by to go again as soon as it's passed.

KENNETH: (*Vindicated, self-righteous*) Boeing 707.

PHIL: (*Niggled*) Pan Am or Aer Lingus?

KENNETH: (*Equally niggled*) Lufthansa!

PHIL: (*Sharply*) All right, mate . . .

KENNETH: (*Equally sharply*) Yeah, well, I'm only doing my job!

> (*An explosive situation is quickly building up between them.*)

PHIL: Fine. OK, I was only joking.

KENNETH: (*Grimly*) *I* was.

PHIL: (*Grimly*) OK, then.

KENNETH: (*Grimly*) OK.

> (*The explosiveness peters away.* KENNETH *puts his headphones back on.*)

PHIL: (*Cold, weary*) Again, Terry.

JOE: (*To* BERNARD) All in fun, really. No bones broken. Relieves the tension.

TERRY: (*Shouting tensely*) Going for a take! Stand by! Quiet, everywhere!

SECOND WOMAN: (*To* FIRST WOMAN) He doesn't mean us this time.

TERRY: (*Shouting at her*) Quiet!!
(*She flinches. He then speaks quietly.*)
Turn over.

KENNETH: Sound.

TERRY: Don?

DON: Yep. Hang on. Yep.

TERRY: Mark it.
(GEOFF *races into position with his clapperboard.*)

GEOFF: 241, take 3.

PHIL: Action!

DON: Hang on. Out too quick, Geoff. Give it me again.

BETTY: Are we still running?

PHIL: One second, sweetheart.

BETTY: Have we cut?

PHIL: One *second*!! No.

GEOFF: 241, take 3.

PHIL: Action!
(JOE *swallows and tenses.*)

BETTY: 'Well, thanks for the lift.'

BERNARD: 'Thank you.'

DON: (*Looking away from viewfinder*) Sorry, Phil.

PHIL: What??

DON: No good.

PHIL: Cut?

DON: There's a cable in shot, my hand slipped and she got the line wrong.

PHIL: She got the line *right*.

DON: Well, there was a cable in shot and my hand slipped.

PHIL: Cut!! Cut everyone! Cut it! Cut! Bloody cut! Cut! Jesus.
(*He stands rigid as* SPARKS *move the cable.*)
OK, settle down, everyone. We're doing terrific. OK, Don?

DON: (*In position again*) Yep.

PHIL: (*Sighing*) Terry.

TERRY: Stand by. Quiet, everywhere.

SHIRLEY: (*Tentatively*) Phil, can I just see to Betty's hairpiece? There a curl keeps falling down.

PHIL: (*Not interested*) It's nice. I like it falling down. It's all the rage. Turn over.

KENNETH: Sound.

DON: Camera.

TERRY: Mark it. Hold on!

> (*He touches* PHIL's *arm for him to look behind them.*
> KENNETH *is pressing his headphones to his ears . . . puzzled.*)

KENNETH: Are we *expecting* a hovercraft?

> (*He looks round, as does* PHIL. *Cut to the catering wagon driving up nearby, from their point of view.*)

PHIL: It can't be breakfast time!

TERRY: (*Looking at his watch*) Dead on.

PHIL: It'll wait two minutes.

TERRY: *They* won't.

> (*Cut to see the* GAFFER *and one or two of the* PROPS MEN *already* en route *to the wagon.*)

They haven't had a decent strike for nearly a *fortnight*.

PHIL: (*Sighs.*) Great.

TERRY: (*Calling to everyone*) Breakfast everyone! Ten minutes absolute maximum. Nine at the most. Everyone back here with indigestion in eight minutes exactly. (*Wearily*) Doesn't time fly when you're having fun?

EXT. STREET: CATERING WAGON SITE. MORNING

The PROPRIETOR'S WIFE *is inside having a good cough over the breakfasts she's cooking. The* PROPRIETOR *is at the hatch serving the* GAFFER. *Ready on the counter is a fried-egg bap on a plate, an egg-and-bacon bap on another plate and a hamburger bap on a third plate. Open on the food.*

PROPRIETOR: Egg bap, egg-and-bacon bap or hamburger bap?

GAFFER: Yes, please.

> (*The* GAFFER *piles all three baps on to one plate, all for himself.*)

PROPRIETOR: Tomato sauce, brown sauce or onions?

GAFFER: Yes, please.

> (*He starts pouring all three on to his three baps.*)

PROPRIETOR: Tea or coffee?

GAFFER: Either. They *both* taste like bloody cocoa.

EXT. SUBURBAN STREET: SET-UP LOCATION. MORNING

DON, GEOFF, KENNETH *and* COLIN, *grumbling to themselves, are slowly bringing up the rear of everyone else's mass exodus to the catering wagon.* PHIL *has stopped a little way behind, deep in thought, harrassed by a million problems, pencilling notes on his script.* JOE *lengthens his stride to catch up with him. As soon as he's level, he acts, not very convincingly, as though his catching up was in no way deliberate.*

JOE: One of the hazards of the job, eh, Phil. Mr Shaw?

PHIL: (*Preoccupied, turning*) Mmm?

JOE: Technical hitches . . . aeroplanes and so forth . . .

PHIL: (*Uncomprehending and irritated*) What about it?

JOE: (*Weakly*) No, just saying. One of the hazards of the job, really . . . *Profession.*

(PHIL, *who's already stopped listening before* JOE's *hardly started replying, remembers something he has to talk to* TERRY *about and trots off after him, leaving* JOE *to wander along on his own towards the end of the queue.*)

EXT. STREET: CATERING WAGON SITE. MORNING

EXTRAS, TECHNICIANS, *etc., are queuing for breakfast. We move along the queue to where* MRS LOMAX *and* MRS STEVENS *stand whispering conspiratorially.*

MRS LOMAX: He'll be more amenable after breakfast. I'll tell him we've been playing First and Second Gossiping Housewives ever since *Z-Cars.*

MRS STEVENS: Ever since *Z-Cars.*

MRS LOMAX: I'll tell him.

(*We move along the queue.* DEIRDRE *is sneezing into her latest Kleenex.* VAL, *eyes closed, is asleep on her feet. We move on to* SHIRLEY *and* JEAN.)

SHIRLEY: I couldn't so much as look a fried egg in the face.

(*She looks with deep sympathy at* JEAN, *who's downcast and near to tears.*)

Is it anything to do with. . . ?

(JEAN *shakes her head, miserably.*)

Or is it. . . ?

(JEAN *shakes her head, fighting back tears.*)

Still, you're a lot more cheerful than yesterday, aren't you?

(JEAN *dissolves into helpless weeping. We move along the queue* to BERNARD *and* BETTY, *both standing doing their respective crosswords.*)

BETTY: 'Provides a tour of the Globe Theatre, question mark.' Two words.

BERNARD: How many letters?

BETTY: Four and five.

BERNARD: (*Immediately*) Round House.

BETTY: 'Round House'??

BERNARD: Tour. Globe. Round globe. Theatre.

BETTY: (*Delighted*) Round House! Boo–boom!

EXT. STREET: WALL. MORNING

The DECORATOR *painting the wall . . . and making very good progress.*

EXT. SUBURBAN STREET: SET-UP LOCATION. MORNING

Everyone is once again in position to shoot the next take of the scene.

PHIL: Away we go, then. Fast as we can.

(DON *grimaces at the sky and at his meter.*)

DON: The light's getting dodgy.

PHIL: (*To* TERRY) Even faster, then.

TERRY: Quiet, everywhere! Dead quiet and – turn over!

KENNETH: Sound.

TERRY: Don?

DON: Getting darker.

TERRY: Mark it.

(GEOFF *races into position with his clapperboard.*)

GEOFF: 241, take 4.

PHIL: And action!

(*Cut to* JOE *hastily stuffing the last of his breakfast into his mouth. He at once starts a coughing fit.* PHIL *stares at him, then at* KENNETH – *who's pressing his headphones harder to his head, puzzled at the sound of coughing. He looks at* JOE. *So does everyone else.* JOE's *coughing fit subsides. The whole incident has lasted only a few seconds.*)

(*With another glance at* JOE) And action!

BETTY: 'Well, thanks for the lift.'

(DON *steps away from his camera, decisively.* PHIL *looks at him, then at the sky then back at* DON.)

PHIL: It's not that bad, Don.

DON: I refuse to shoot it. I just refuse. I'm sorry, I refuse.

PHIL: Cut!

TERRY: Cut!

(*Everyone relaxes and stares up at the sky.*)

PHIL: (*To* VAL) What do you think of the story so far?

(*Everyone stands, at a loss.* PHIL *feels tireder, colder and older than ever before.*)

DON: Be lovely for fishing.

(*Cut to* JOE. *He calls softly across to* BERNARD *and* BETTY.)

JOE: 'Bad light stopped play,' eh? Decent pun, that. 'Play' signifying TV play. Be good in your crossword.

BETTY: (*To* BERNARD, *slightly annoyed*) 'Round House' was wrong. It's supposed to be 4 letters and 5. That's 5 and 5.

BERNARD: (*Blank aggression*) Boo–boom.

(*Cut back to* PHIL, DON *and* TERRY *in a huddle, discussing the situation.*)

PHIL: Agreed then. Elbow. We'll do the church interior instead.

TERRY: (*Calling to everyone*) Everyone that's needed for scene 23, church interior! That's unit, artistes and miscellaneous congregation! Fast as we can!

(*The unit starts gathering up all the equipment, to move off to the church.* JOE *stands, suddenly apprehensive, in the midst of the chaos. As* PHIL *hurries past him . . .*)

JOE: (*Trying to attract his attention*) Mr Shaw!

PHIL: (*Calling*) Donald!

(*He hurries towards* DON. JOE, *disappointed, picks his way past* TECHNICIANS *and their equipment to* TERRY.)

JOE: We'll do my scene once the weather bucks up, I expect. . . ?

(TERRY *has already moved out of earshot.*)

(*To himself*) That'll be it.

(DEIRDRE, *sneezing into a Kleenex, leads her band of* EXTRAS *past* JOE *towards the church.*)

Is it in order if I come and watch, Miss? Seeing I'm not in it.

DEIRDRE: Sorry. We'll be like sardines in tomato.

JOE: Fair enough.

(Everyone – except JOE *– is now massing towards the church entrance.* JOE *wanders along the deserted street towards the catering wagon. The* PROPRIETOR *is outside it, clearing up the mess.)*

Is there a cup of tea going, Colonel, milk no sugar?

PROPRIETOR: Just locking up.

JOE: Fair enough.

EXT. CHURCH HALL ENTRANCE. MORNING

Members of the UNIT, *with their equipment, are making their way inside.* PHIL, TERRY, DON *and* KENNETH *are a little to one side, walking slowly.*

PHIL: Hang on!

(He stops and stamps his foot on the ground once or twice.)

DON: *(Not really interested)* Are you having a tantrum?

PHIL: Pins and needles.

KENNETH: Circulation.

PHIL: I've got *chilblains* on the *other* bugger.

KENNETH: Circulation.

*(*KENNETH *and* DON *go into the church.* PHIL *suddenly stops and grabs* TERRY *by the arm. He's caught sight of the* TWO WOMEN *who were on the corner watching the filming. They're still there – now watching the change of set-up.)*

PHIL: *(The last frustrated straw)* Terry! *They're* not right at *all!!!*

TERRY: *(Following* PHIL's *gaze, blankly)* Who?

PHIL: First Gossiping Housewife and Second Gossiping Housewife! They're not *real* enough!

TERRY: *(Blankly)* Who?

PHIL: They look too much like extras.

TERRY: *(Baffled)* They're not *them.* They're two housewives who happen to be gossiping.

PHIL: Eh?

TERRY: *They're* the extras.

(He points. Cut to MRS LOMAX, MRS STEVENS, MRS PENNINGTON, MR DANBY *and* MR CLEGG *following* DEIRDRE, *like passengers behind an air-hostess.)*

PHIL: *(Defeated, but having to extricate himself)* Yes. Well. As long a they look *real.*

TERRY: Which two do you want?

163

(MRS LOMAX *beams at them, seductively.*)

PHIL: Any. The two at the front.

(*He goes into the church.*)

TERRY: (*Calling*) Deirdre! The two at the front. First and
Second Gossiping Housewives. Official.

(*The front two are* MRS STEVENS *and* MRS PENNINGTON.
DEIRDRE *ushers them towards* TERRY. MRS LOMAX's *smile
fades in bitter disbelief.*)

EXT. STREET. MORNING

JOE, *now virtually alone, is seated on the car bumper, rehearsing his
line of dialogue to himself from his script. The young* SCHOOLGIRL
approaches.

SCHOOLGIRL: Excuse me. Can I have your autograph, please?

JOE: (*Delighted*) By golly! First today.

(*She gives him an exercise book and pen from her satchel.*)
Now, 'To Phyllis'? 'To Sylvia'?

SCHOOLGIRL: 'Deborah'.

JOE: (*Writing*) 'To Deborah, sincere best wishes, the show must
go on, Joe McGill.'

SCHOOLGIRL: (*Simply*) Joe Who?

JOE: You're lucky catching me today, really. It's my only day on
this particular epic.

SCHOOLGIRL: Sort of a guest star, like?

JOE: That sort of thing. (*Smiles happily.*) Big day for both of us,
Deborah.

(*He gives her the exercise book back.*)

SCHOOLGIRL: Thanks. Ta, ra.

JOE: All the best, love.

(*She runs off.* JOE *watches her go, smiling to himself. Feeling
happier, more appreciated. A little more important.*)

(*To himself*) 'Old Man in Street' was played by Joe McGill.
Joe McGill is a National Theatre Player. Joe McGill is a
member of the Royal Shakespeare Company. Joe McGill
appears by kind permission of the English Stage Company.
Joe McGill is now appearing in *Sleuth* at the Fortune
Theatre, London. (*Intones in character but more confidently
and strongly than hitherto.*) 'I've never seen that young lady
in my life before, and . . .'

(He breaks off suddenly, realizing he's still holding Deborah's pen; he calls after her.)

Deborah! Your biro! Deborah! Ooo–ooh! Your pen, love!

(Cut to TERRY *at the church hall door, racing from inside angrily.)*

TERRY: *(Calling to* JOE*)* Well, thanks a bloody bundle, mate! We were in the middle of a take! You've ruined a take!

(He disappears inside again. Cut to DECORATOR, *peering to see what all the noise is about. He resumes work.* JOE *stands, upset, guilty. He swallows. Then, in a weaker, more subdued voice . . .)*

JOE: '. . . in my life before, and I've lived here fifty years.'

(Dissolve to . . .)

EXT. STREET: WALL. MIDDAY

Three hours later. About half the wall has now been painted. The DECORATOR *is squatted against the wall, eating lunch from his snap-tin and reading a morning paper.*

INT. PHONE KIOSK ON SUBURBAN STREET. MIDDAY

JOE, *part way through his lunch, balances his plate (bearing what's left of his meal) on the pay box, dials a number and puts the coins in. He forks a little food into his mouth during the dialling tone.*

JOE: *(Brightly, into phone)* Hello, Nancy! *(Pause.)* Me. *(Pause.)* Yes, lunch break. *(Pause.)* Steak and kidney pie, runner beans and mashed. *(Pause.)* Not bad. Bit stingey with the pie. *(Pause, then very enthusiastically)* Oh, very well indeed! It's going to be a cracking little scene when we've done it! *(Pause.)* No, not yet. Technical hitches beyond our control.

MONTAGE. SUBURBAN STREET: SET-UP LOCATION. MIDDAY

(a) BERNARD *and* BETTY *in the props car, eating their lunches while solemnly doing their respective crosswords.*

(b) DON *and* GEOFF, *in the camera car eating their lunches.* DON *is reading an angling magazine;* GEOFF *a pin-up magazine.*

(c) PHIL, *seated on the genny tailboard, huddled in his anorak, script on his knee, half-heartedly eating an apple and almost dropping off to sleep. He then abruptly falls asleep, his jaw hanging open. His half-eaten apple falls to the ground. His script slithers off his knee.*

(d) KENNETH, *standing at the catering wagon. He's standing finishing his main course while queuing in line behind a* TECHNICIAN, *waiting for his dessert.*

PROPRIETOR: One Manchester tart.

  (*He hands the tart to the* TECHNICIAN.)

KENNETH: *And* me.

PROPRIETOR: (*Ignoring him; to* TECHNICIAN) Last one, that.

KENNETH: What about *me*??

(e) EXT. PUB ON STREET

The GAFFER *is making his way to the door.*

(f) INT. PUB

The GAFFER *enters. The rest of the film crew are relaxing with a drink or playing darts, etc.* DEIRDRE *has her hand on* COLIN's *knee, surreptitiously under the table. He keeps pushing it away. Their faces deadpan.*

(g) INT. LADIES' TOILET IN PUB

SHIRLEY *is just finishing being violently sick in a washbasin.* VALERIE *is holding her by the shoulders.* SHIRLEY *straightens up,* VALERIE *mops her face with a Kleenex.*

VAL: Better now?

SHIRLEY: (*Groaning*) If I never see another fried egg, it'll be too soon!

VAL: *Or* steak and kidney pie, you pinhead!

  (SHIRLEY *blows and shivers.*)

SHIRLEY: Or steak and kidney pie.

  (*We hear the helpless sobbing coming from one of the cubicles.* VAL *turns towards the cubicle.*)

VAL: (*Calling*) You all right, Jean?

(h) INT. EXTRAS' MINIBUS

All the EXTRAS *eating their lunch from trays on their knees.* MRS STEVENS *and* MRS PENNINGTON *are now sitting together, matily.* MRS LOMAX, *seated opposite, sits giving them extremely bitter, hostile looks behind polite, pinched smiles.*

Cut back to the phone kiosk. JOE *still speaking into the phone.*
TERRY *is outside, banging on the windows.*

JOE: (*Into phone*) Hang on, Nancy. I think I'm wanted.
(*Opens the door.*) Yes, Colonel?

TERRY: Finger out, please. I've to ring the office urgently.

JOE: Fair enough. (*Returns to the phone.*) I have to go now,
love. For my close-ups. (*Pause.*) Oh, several, I expect.
See you tonight. (*Hangs up and exits.*) Sorry about that.
Business call. BBC.

TERRY: (*Drily*) Oh, goody.
(*He rushes past him into the kiosk.*)

EXT. CAMERA CAR. MIDDAY
DON *glances lethargically from his magazine out of the window, then
up at the sky. He puts his panglass to his eye and peers again at the
sky.*

DON: (*Calling*) Phil!
(*Cut to* PHIL, *jolted out of his sleep leaning against the
tailboard of the genny. He quickly grabs his script and pretends
to be engrossed in it.*)
Phil!

PHIL: Sorry. Just thinking.

DON: It's getting lighter. We can polish off shot 241.
(PHIL *looks up at the sky.*)

PHIL: Yes. That's what I was *thinking*.

EXT. STREET: WALL OF HOUSE. MIDDAY
The DECORATOR *neatly folds up his morning paper, puts his used
greaseproof paper back in his snap-tin and puts them in his
haversack. Stands up, stretches and prepares to start his afternoon's
work. Dissolve to . . .*

EXT. SUBURBAN STREET: SET-UP LOCATION. AFTERNOON
Wide-shot establishing the UNIT *setting up again to shoot shot 241.
Everyone is in, or taking up position. A car comes driving up and
screeches to a halt near to where* JOE *is standing on his mark.*

EXT. SUBURBAN STREET: SET-UP LOCATION. AFTERNOON
RONNIE SKIDMORE, *the Unit Manager, gets out of his car. He's*

dressed, incongruously by comparison with the rest of the crew, in suit, collar and tie.

JOE: (*Self-important*) Excuse me, young man. No parking here. Verboten. We're busy filming.

RONNIE: (*Brushing past him*) Thank God for that.

(*Go with* RONNIE *to* PHIL, *who's standing with* TERRY, *while everyone sets up around them.* PHIL's *heart sinks on seeing him.*)

PHIL: Morning.

RONNIE: Evening. Finished? (*Looks at his watch.*) *Must* have done.

PHIL: We've done the church interior.

RONNIE: And *this*?

PHIL: Not yet.

RONNIE: (*Incredulously*) *None* of it??

PHIL: Not yet.

RONNIE: You've done the master shot?

PHIL: (*To* TERRY) Tell him, 'Not yet.' I can't say it again. My brain's chapped.

RONNIE: Well, what the hell have you been doing??

PHIL: Sunbathing.

TERRY: We've had problems.

RONNIE: (*Sighing heavily*) Phil, you've only six days left. You'll never finish it.

PHIL: (*Worriedly*) We'll finish it. We'll finish it.

RONNIE: (*Looks at his watch.*) Anyway, see you. (*Starts to move off.*) I only came to give you encouragement.

TERRY: Aren't you staying a bit?

RONNIE: Sorry. *My* holidays aren't till *August*.

(*He gets in his car and drives off at screaming speed.* JOE *watches him.*)

JOE: (*To* BERNARD) Is he anyone I should know?

BERNARD: Unit manager. Ronnie Skidmore.

JOE: Ah. He said, 'Hello, Joe', when he got out of his car. Must've remembered me from a previous production.

(*Cut to* PHIL *and* TERRY. PHIL *watches the car go, bitterly.*)

TERRY: (*To mollify*) He's got problems.

PHIL: (*Mock sympathy*) Aaahhh. (*Sighs, then calls to everyone.*) Right, everyone! I want this scene doing so fast your backside'll be a blur. Sorry, Betty.

BETTY: (*Puzzled*) What for?

TERRY: (*Calling*) Settle down, everyone! We're doing it this time. Straight through. No messing. No mistakes, no booms in shot, no Boeings. Absolute quiet – and turn over.

KENNETH: Sound.

TERRY: Don?

DON: Yep.

TERRY: Mark it.

(GEOFF *races into position with clapperboard*.)

GEOFF: 241, take . . . take . . .

VAL: 5.

GEOFF: 241, take 5.

PHIL: And action!

(*The scene goes like clockwork, smooth, speedy, and absolutely correct. The perfect take*.)

BETTY: 'Well, thanks for the lift.'

BERNARD: 'Thank you.'

BETTY: 'What for?'

BERNARD: (*Winking*) 'See you Saturday.'

(*They kiss. She goes into the church hall.* PHIL *cues* JOE. *He walks towards the car*.)

'Prettiest girl in the village, eh, grandad?'

JOE: 'I've never seen that young lady in my life before. And I've lived here fifty years.'

(*He passes out of frame*.)

PHIL: (*In an orgasm of delight*) And cut! Terrific! *Great*! Well done, everyone! (*Turns to* DON, *happily*.) Good one, Don?

DON: Checking the gate.

PHIL: Really great! OK, on to the close-ups! On, on, on.

KENNETH: It was good for me.

PHIL: (*Turning*) Eh?

KENNETH: It was good for sound.

PHIL: (*Couldn't care less*) Oh. Fine. (*Sighs hugely in relief*.) Three choruses of Hallelujah, everyone. And a gross of Mars bars.

(*Cut to* JOE *beaming, slapping his fist into his hand in delight. His big day. His big moment. And he's done it. Fulfilment*.)

DON: (*Quietly*) Hang on.

(PHIL *turns to him, his smile already faltering*.)

(*A tiny sigh, then matter-of-factly*) Well, that's life, isn't it?

PHIL: (*Apprehensively*) What is?

DON: Hair.

PHIL: Where?

GEOFF: Hair in the gate.

PHIL: (*Horrified*) Hair in the gate?!

DON: Hair in the gate.

(*The entire* UNIT *slumps in weariness.*)

BERNARD: Oh, hell!

BETTY: Hell's bells!

JOE: (*To* BERNARD) Well, that's show business.

(BERNARD *would like to kill him.*)

The shot's no good, you see, not with a hair in the gate . . .
Like a hair or a bit of fluff behind the camera lens . . .
that's what it means.

BERNARD: I know what it means.

JOE: Still, we've done it perfect once. We can do it again. Are
we down-hearted?

(*Instead of enthusiastic cries of 'No!', he gets tired, hostile looks
from anyone who's in earshot.*)

TERRY: Stand by, everyone. It was no good. We're going again.
Ready, Phil?

(PHIL *is staring blankly, dully, into the middle distance.*)
Phil?

(PHIL *jerks back to consciousness.*)

PHIL: Action! (*Looks round.*) Sorry . . . er . . . sorry, my mind
went blank. (*Sighs brokenly.*) We'd got it. We'd bloody *got*
it! I thought that time . . .

DON: (*Matter-of-factly*) You want to try fishing, pal.

TERRY: Quiet, everyone. Turn over.

KENNETH: Sound.

TERRY: Don?

DON: Yep.

TERRY: Mark it.

(GEOFF *races into position with his clapperboard.*)

GEOFF: 241, take 6.

(PHIL *stands, sunk in his anorak, staring unseeingly ahead.*
TERRY *looks at him, as do* DON, KENNETH, BERNARD,
BETTY *and* JOE – *all waiting for him to shout 'Action'.* PHIL

suddenly notices them.)

PHIL: Sorry! My mind . . . um . . . cut! No, sorry, action! No, sorry; yes, that's right; action!

BETTY: 'Well, thanks for the lift.'

BERNARD: 'Thank you.'

(*Before* BETTY *can say the next line, we hear a lowly rumbling, babbling noise coming nearer and nearer.* KENNETH *grimaces – pressing his headphones closer to his head.* PHIL *swivels round to look at him, baffled as to what the noise can be.* KENNETH *looks back at him, equally baffled. The noise gets louder.*)

PHIL: Cut! (*To* KENNETH) What the hell is it? An earthquake? The end of the world?

(*Cut to the street corner. Around it spills a boisterous rabble of scruffy* SCHOOLKIDS, *who've raced there all the way from school, to watch the filming. Among them is* DEBORAH, *the* SCHOOLGIRL. *They're actually very intrigued and excited by the filming, but cloak it in an outward show of blasé cheekiness. Virtually everyone in the crew groans at the sight of them – every crew's worst enemy.*)

(*Frantically*) Terry! What the hell are they doing out of school at this time! You said they shouldn't be out till –

TERRY: (*Calling to stage hands*) Arthur! Graham! Get them back! Barricade us off at the corner!

(ARTHUR *and* GRAHAM *jog over towards the kids.*)

FIRST KID: (*Calling to the* UNIT *as a whole*) What are you filming? *Coronation Street*? Where's Ena?

SECOND KID: Who *are* you? BBC or ITV?

JOE: (*Helpfully*) ITV.

SECOND KID: (*Yelling raucously*) BBC forever! BBC forever! BBC! BBC! BBC!

(*The rest of the* KIDS *take up the chant, with* BERNARD, BETTY, PHIL, GEOFF, COLIN, ARTHUR *and* GRAHAM *yelling at them to shut up and clear off.*)

TERRY: (*Reasonably*) Now, lads. We've a lot of work to do. So, please. May I ask you to kindly –

FIRST KID: Is it *Mission Impossible*?

TERRY: No.

PHIL: (*To himself*) Yes.

TERRY: Would you all kindly –
  (*His voice is drowned by the* KIDS, *chanting, yelling, giving cheek, fighting among themselves . . .*)
  Please. Now, please. (*Finally, in frustration*) Bugger off! Go on, sod off, the lot of you!
DEBORAH: (*To the other kids, proudly*) That's him!
  (*She points at* JOE. *The* KIDS *all dash towards him, dragging bits of paper from their pockets or satchels, and pens or pencils from their pockets, yelling 'Give us your autograph, Mister!' etc.* JOE *stands, confused and embarrassed, not knowing whether to refuse or not . . . surrounded by a swarm of clamouring kids. He looks at* PHIL, *helplessly.* PHIL – *and the others – stare back. Equally helpless, dumbfounded, and angry. Dissolve to . . .*)

INT. EXTRAS' MINIBUS. AFTERNOON
Later. MR CLEGG *and* MR DANBY *in conversation. The others are dozing, knitting, reading, etc.*
MR CLEGG: So consequently, I had to have short hair for *Crossroads* on the Wednesday –
MR DANBY: I haven't done a *Crossroads* yet. Don't know why.
MR CLEGG: – long hair for a commercial on the Thursday –
MR DANBY: I've been up for *three* commercials. Didn't get them, though.
MR CLEGG: – and bald for the Beeb on the Friday! *Leeds United* that was. I had to shout, 'Give us the bob!'
MR DANBY: I've never worked for the BBC. Don't know what I've done to offend them.
  (*Dissolve to . . .*)

EXT. STREET: WALL OF HOUSE. AFTERNOON
Later. The DECORATOR *at work. Much of the wall has now been completed. Dissolve to . . .*

EXT. STREET: WALL OF HOUSE. AFTERNOON
Later. More of the wall now painted. The DECORATOR *hard at work. Dissolve to . . .*

EXT. STREET: WALL OF HOUSE. AFTERNOON
Later. The DECORATOR *progressing still further with his work.*
Dissolve to . . .

EXT. SUBURBAN STREET: SET-UP LOCATION. AFTERNOON
A long, establishing moment – to see that a thick blanket of
despondency has now descended over the entire UNIT. *Everyone is*
now very, very, weary indeed. All at their lowest ebb. When anyone
speaks, it's dully, very quietly, mechanically.
TERRY: Quiet, everywhere, please. Turn over.
KENNETH: Sound.
TERRY: Don?
DON: Yep.
TERRY: Mark it.
   (GEOFF *lethargically drags himself into position with the*
   clapperboard.)
GEOFF: 241, take 12.
VAL: 13.
GEOFF: Sorry. 13. 241, take 13.
PHIL: (*Weariest of all*) Action.
   (*Nothing happens.*)
   Action, Betty.
BETTY: (*Dully*) I'm sorry, I can't remember my line. Silly, isn't
   it? I can't –
VAL: 'Well, thanks for the lift.'
BETTY: (*Remembering*) Oh, yes. I knew it was *something* –
PHIL: And action.
BETTY: 'Well, thanks for the lift.'
BERNARD: 'Thank *you*.'
BETTY: 'What for?'
BERNARD: (*Winks.*) 'See you Saturday.'
   (*Now that the take is under way, it's going well.* BETTY *gets*
   out of the car, kisses BERNARD *and goes into the church hall.*
   PHIL, *beginning to liven up, thinking at last they may be*
   getting it right, cues JOE *to start walking.* JOE *does*
   so.)
   'Prettiest girl in the village, eh, grandad?'
JOE: 'I've never seen the *young* lady in my life before and – '
PHIL: (*Interjecting*) Again, Jimmy! Say it again. Don't stress the

word 'young'. (*To the* CREW) Keep running. (*To* JOE) Go
on, Jimmy.

JOE: 'I've never seen the *young* lady in my – '

PHIL: Don't stress 'young'! It sounds as though you *have* seen
the old lady before. And there isn't one! (*To the* CREW)
Keep running.

JOE: 'I've never seen the . . . I've never seen the . . . I've never
seen the *young* lady in my life before – '

PHIL: 'I've never seen the young lady in my *life* before.'

JOE: 'I've never seen the young *lady* in my life before – '

PHIL: '*Life* before.' Emphasize 'life'.

JOE: (*Now in a terrible state of tiredness and confusion*) 'I've never
seen the young lady in *my* life before – '

PHIL: Again!

JOE: 'I've never seen the young lady *in* my life before – '

PHIL: No! Not '*in*'! 'In my *life* before.' Again! (*To the* CREW)
Keep running.

(*The words have now become totally meaningless to* JOE.
*Everyone's staring at him, as they have ever since he began to
get it wrong. He's suffering tortures of stagefright, nerves, fear,
embarrassment, humiliation . . .*)

JOE: 'I've never seen the *young* lady in my life before . . . I've
never seen . . . never seen . . . I've never in my lady seen
before . . . No, never lady I've seen young . . . No –
(*Everyone, except* PHIL, *now finds* JOE's *total disintegration too
embarrassing and intolerable to watch.*)

TERRY: (*To* PHIL, *nervously*) Cut?

PHIL: (*Grimly staring at* JOE) Again!
(*Very slowly and deliberately,* JOE *makes a tremendous effort to
get the words in the right order. He succeeds . . . but his
performance is rigid, parrot-like and utterly appalling.*)

JOE: 'I've never seen. The young lady. *In my life* before. And
I've lived *here* fifty years.'

PHIL: (*Very quietly*) And cut.
(*A long, prickly, total silence. Everyone looks at* PHIL *for his
reaction.* JOE *waits in an agony of apprehension.* PHIL *begins
to sing, very gently, with Ophelia-like insanity, to himself.*)
'Big men don't cry . . . Big men don't cry . . .' (*Suddenly
screeches.*) Jesus!

(*He hurls his script on to the ground, and stands there numbly, hands in his anorak pockets.*)

God, I'm cold.

(VAL *picks up his script, nervously, and slips it through the crook of his arm.*)

TERRY: (*Quietly*) Was it OK for camera, Don?

DON: (*Checking camera*) Fine for me.

KENNETH: And me.

TERRY: (*Uncertainly, a little scared of* PHIL'*s mood of simmering hysteria*) We've done it, then, Phil. In the can. Set up for Bernard's close-up, shall we?

VAL: (*Sharing* TERRY'*s nervousness, to* PHIL) We're printing it, then, are we? Take 13?

(PHIL *still stands rooted, staring ahead. He turns, almost casually, to* JOE.)

PHIL: (*Calmly*) The most crucial scene in the play. (*To* JOE) What was your name again?

JOE: Joe. Joe McGill.

PHIL: (*Calmly, reasonably*) That, Mr McGill, was the most terrible, appalling, disgusting performance in the annals of acting history. Congratulations.

JOE: (*Trying, vainly, to hide his agony*) Yes . . . I wasn't entirely satisfied with my delivery, really . . .

PHIL: (*Calmly*) Weren't you?

JOE: Not entirely. A bit wooden.

PHIL: (*Exploding*) It was wooden, incomprehensible and the worst bloody mess I've ever seen in my bloody life! And I feel as though *I've* lived here fifty sodding years!!

TERRY: (*Tentatively*) Do you want to do it again?

PHIL: *Never* again.

TERRY: We'll do Bernard's close-ups, then, shall we?

PHIL: Another day.

TERRY: We're virtually set up . . . We could do it in two minutes . . .

PHIL: Tomorrow. (*Consults his script.*) We'll do Interior Hallway of House. Bernard calling for Betty on the Saturday.

TERRY: (*Calling*) OK, everyone! Scene 55. Interior Vestibule of Church Hall! That's a change of costume for Bernard and Betty! Fast as we can then. If you don't break a leg, you're not trying!

(*The* UNIT *starts gathering up the equipment – ready to move off to the new set-up. Much bustle, noise and activity releasing the tension of the last few minutes.* BERNARD *and* BETTY *move off to be attended to by* SHIRLEY *and* JEAN. *Everyone begins to leave the set-up.* PHIL *begins to walk away, in conference with* DON, *arm around his shoulder.* JOE *stands where he is. Dead inside. His big day in ruins.*)

JOE: (*Calling quietly*) Phil? Mr Shaw, sir?

(PHIL *turns.*)

Excuse me for interrupting you.

PHIL: Yes, Mr McGill?

(*Everyone stops work, in mid-movement, to watch what's happening.*)

JOE: Couldn't we give it another go? I've read the play. It's a scene of prime importance to the understanding of it.

PHIL: Why didn't you get it right, then?

JOE: (*Floundering*) We've had to do it over and over, hours and hours . . .

PHIL: That's what you're paid for.

JOE: We're not machines . . . We're not cameras and . . . and . . .

PHIL: You had one line to do, Mr McGill. *One*. And you couldn't.

JOE: It was the thirteenth take!

PHIL: All the more reason.

JOE: I did the others all right! One or two of them were *your* . . . well, not *your* . . .

PHIL: Do you know *why* you couldn't, Mr McGill? Because you're no good. And that's why you're an extra. Because you're a lousy bloody extra. A stupid lousy extra! Stupid old bugger!

(JOE *stands. Quiet. Peaceful. He speaks very simply.*)

JOE: You don't know me. You know nothing about me. You don't know if I'm stupid. Or no good. Or anything. You've only really met me today. (*Pause.*) I've been going for a lot of days before this one. Hell of a lot. I might be very good for all you know. I might be a very interesting person. I

might have been acting since before you were born. I might
have been on the landing at D-Day when I was your age. I
might have done all sorts of *really* important things . . . like
bringing up a family. Like –

PHIL: (*Subdued, very quiet*) Mr McGill. You'd one important
thing to do. And you couldn't.

JOE: (*Erupting, wildly, exploding*) That's not *real* life, lad! It's
pretend! It's *all* pretend! *You're* pretending! The damn-fool
play's pretending!
(*A long, long pause.*)

PHIL: (*Quietly, almost regretfully*) Real life is how *well* you
pretend, isn't it, sir? You, me. Everybody in the world.
(*A pause.* JOE's *mind shuts off. The thought's too painful too
dwell on.*)
(*Gently*) We'll perhaps try and find the decent bits from
what you did. And glue them together. No one'll know.
It'll be all right on the night.
(*He returns to* DON. *They start to walk off in consultation over
the next set-up. Everyone else resumes moving their equipment
and going about their various jobs.* JOE *stands for a moment,
then takes off his cap and jacket, collects his own from the back
of the props car (or wherever handy), puts them on, his old
smart, groomed self. Dissolve to . . .*)

EXT. STREET: WALL OF HOUSE. AFTERNOON
Later. The DECORATOR *busy painting. Very little of the wall now
remains to be done. Dissolve to . . .*

EXT. CHURCH HALL DOORWAY. AFTERNOON
The SPARKS *are organizing lighting for the interior vestibule scene.*
KENNETH (*inserting a new tape into his tape recorder*) *is standing to
one side with* DON. *They speak dully and mechanically, as ever.*

KENNETH: So what did you reckon to it, then?

DON: To what?

KENNETH: *Murder on the Orient Express.*

DON: Have you seen it?

KENNETH: Not yet.

DON: I went last night.
(*Which hardly answers Kenneth's question. Cut to* GEOFF *and*

        COLIN *watching* BETTY *being made up by*
        SHIRLEY.)
GEOFF: Fanciable, isn't she?
COLIN: Yeah. (*Pause.*) Who?
GEOFF: Betty Talbot.
COLIN: I thought so on the first day of shooting. I don't now.
GEOFF: I didn't fancy her at *all* on the first day.
        (*A long pause.*)
COLIN: Funny, that, isn't it?

EXT. EXTRAS' MINIBUS. AFTERNOON
DEIRDRE *is on the step, calling across the street.*
DEIRDRE: Ready when you are, Mr McGill!

EXT. STREET. AFTERNOON
JOE, *who is standing watching the* DECORATOR *at work, turns on
hearing his name. Intercut between* JOE *and* DEIRDRE.
JOE: Fair enough, love.
        (*He turns and hurries off to the new set-up.*)

EXT. CHURCH HALL DOORWAY. AFTERNOON
SHIRLEY *and* JEAN (*who is still sullen and sniffing*) *are attending to
Bernard's and Betty's make-up and costume. At the same time,*
BERNARD *and* BETTY *are engrossed in their crosswords.*
BETTY: (*Suddenly*) It can't be a two-letter word beginning with
        X. There's no such thing.
BERNARD: Are you sure the X is right?
BETTY: No.
        (JOE *approaches.*)
JOE: Just come to say cheerio, everyone!
SHIRLEY: (*Brightly*) Bye, bye, Mr McGill.
JOE: A great pleasure working with you all.
        (*He suddenly grasps* BERNARD'*s hand in an emotional
        handshake.*)
        An experience.
        (JOE *kisses* BETTY *on the cheek. She smiles a pinched,
        fractional smile back at him. He turns and goes off towards*
        TERRY, KENNETH, COLIN *and* VAL, *who are preparing for
        the new set-up now being organized in the hallway.*)

Excuse me! Just come to say goodbye and good luck,
then . . .
(*They turn, smiling and muttering embarrassed responses.*)
(*Wishing for the impossible*) Perhaps it won't look quite so bad
as we thought . . . you know . . . when it's all put
together . . .

TERRY: (*Lying*) No, no, it'll look all right.

VAL: (*Lying*) Not too bad at all, I shouldn't think.

KENNETH: It was OK for me.

JOE: Pardon?

KENNETH: It was good for sound.

JOE: (*Heart leaping*) Oh, really? Oh, good! Well, that's half the
battle, isn't it?
(KENNETH *is similarly affected by what is just about the first
unsolicited appreciation of the importance of his job that he's ever
had.*)

KENNETH: Well, yes . . . I suppose it is . . .

JOE: If not more!

KENNETH: If not more.
(*A pause.* JOE *gathers a little more confidence.*)

JOE: I'll just bid a fond farewell to Phil. Phil and Don.
(*He's about to make his way to the door.*)

TERRY: It's a bit cramped in there. They're setting up.

JOE: Ah. (*Stops.*) I just wanted to thank him for his . . . Not to
worry. I'll drop him a line. (*Pause.*) Will you tell him good
luck with the rest of the filming from me?

TERRY: Sure.

JOE: Right.
(*He still stands there, as though he'd like to say much more to try to
justify take 13 . . . But knows there is nothing more to say.*)
Fair enough. See you.

TERRY/KENNETH/COLIN/VAL: See you.
(*He stands a moment longer, then smiles a last farewell and walks
off.*)

EXT. SUBURBAN STREET. AFTERNOON
The GAFFER *and one or two others are working on the genny.* JOE
approaches on his way towards the minibus.

JOE: I'll say so long then.

179

GAFFER: Oh, yes?

JOE: And thank you for all your courtesy and efficiency.

GAFFER: Oh, yes?

JOE: I think it may turn out passable in the end.

GAFFER: The weather?

JOE: Shot 241.

GAFFER: (*Couldn't care less*) Oh, it'll turn out passable. They always do.

JOE: (*Grinning, happily*) Oh, well, then . . . Thanks again to you and your colleagues.

GAFFER: My who?

    (JOE *walks on.*)

INT. EXTRAS' MINIBUS. AFTERNOON

JOE *sits down, adjacent to the* DRIVER. *All the other* EXTRAS *are already seated.*

DRIVER: (*To* JOE, *as he switches the engine on*) Best part of the day, eh? When the bugger's over!

    (JOE *laughs politely by way of reply.*)

    Go all right, did it?

JOE: Mmm. Not bad. Very passable by all accounts.

    (*The minibus drives off. Dissolve to . . .*)

INT. CHURCH HALL VESTIBULE. AFTERNOON

Later. Everyone is in position for shooting scene 55 – PHIL, DON, TERRY, VAL, GEOFF, COLIN, BERNARD, BETTY *– all very cramped and squashed up in the tiny space.*

TERRY: (*Subdued*) Stand by. And quiet. And turn over.

KENNETH: Sound.

TERRY: Don?

DON: Yep.

TERRY: Mark it.

    (GEOFF *squeezes the clapperboard into shot.*)

GEOFF: 242, take 1.

PHIL: And action!

    (*Dissolve to . . .*)

INT. MINIBUS – TRAVELLING. EARLY EVENING

The EXTRAS, *nodding off, or knitting or chatting quietly. General weariness.* JOE, *very, very drained, is staring expressionlessly ahead at the road.* MR CLEGG *gets up and heaves himself down the aisle to sit behind* JOE.

MR CLEGG: It went pretty good, the scene in the church, this morning.

JOE: (*Turning*) Oh. (*Pause.*) All right, then, was it?

MR CLEGG: I had to sneeze in it. For added naturalism. (*Laughs.*) Not easy, sneezing when you don't want to!

JOE: *My* scene went very well . . .

MR CLEGG: Anyway, I did it. I get another few quid for that.

JOE: We had a little technical trouble. But it was a little cracker in the end.

MR CLEGG: It's deemed 'individual characterization', is sneezing. According to Equity Ruling.

JOE: Or it *will* be a little cracker. When they've tarted it up in the editing. Amazing what they can do. I think they'll be highly pleased with it, when it's, you know, tarted up.

MR CLEGG: It was my sneezing début. (*Pause; then, reasonably*) I once had to scratch my earhole in *Barlow at Large*.
(*Dissolve to . . .*)

INT. CHURCH HALL VESTIBULE. EARLY EVENING
The set-up as before.

PHIL: And cut!
(*Everyone relaxes. He turns to* TERRY, *dubiously.*)
A bit under-the-arm, was it?

KENNETH: It was for me.

PHIL: (*Too tired to care; to* VAL) Print it.
(*He's now absolutely dropping with fatigue.*)
Thanks, everyone. Smashing.

TERRY: (*Calling*) All right, it's a wrap! Home time. Another day tomorrow. Unit turn over.
(*Everyone starts packing up their gear. Much noise and bustle.*)

EXT. STREET: WALL. EARLY EVENING
The DECORATOR *stands back to appraise his day's work. The entire wall is now painted. Satisfied, he collects his snap-tin, paint, brushes, ladder, etc., lights a cigarette stub and walks off.*

EXT. STREET. EVENING
Much activity of everyone packing up their equipment.
SHIRLEY: (*To* VAL) Fancy a Campari and soda when we get
    back?
    (*She calls across to* DEIRDRE *who's watching* COLIN *starting
    his car.*)
    Coming back with *us*, Deirdre?
DEIRDRE: I think Colin's giving me a lift. (*Hopefully*) I think he
    intends making a dishonest woman of me.
    (COLIN *drives off past the waiting* DEIRDRE *and away.*
    DEIRDRE *watches the car go, sighs, and calls back to*
    SHIRLEY.*)
    Yes, OK, then.

INT. JOE'S LIVING ROOM. EVENING
NANCY *is watching TV. The table is set for tea. We hear the front
door open, then close.* NANCY *gets up with an anticipatory smile.*
JOE *enters, pleased to be home.*
JOE: Do I smell kippers?
NANCY: You do.
JOE: Good girl. Lovely and warm in here.
NANCY: How did it go?
JOE: (*Smiling*) Three guesses.
    (JOE *flops into an easy chair, to put on his slippers.*)
NANCY: I *am* pleased.
JOE: So were *they*.
    (NANCY *takes his tattered script. Still folded at the important
    page, from his coat pocket.*)
    We had a touch of double-double-toil-and-trouble, but we
    got it in the end. Spot on. 'I've never seen the young lady in
    my life before. And I've lived here fifty years.' Bingo.
    (NANCY *looks at him, shaking her head, admiringly.*)
NANCY: I don't know how you do it.
JOE: You just *do*.

INT. CAR ON SUBURBAN LOCATION STREET. EVENING
TERRY's *at the wheel.* BERNARD *beside him, doing his crossword.*
BETTY, *doing her crossword, is on the backseat with* SHIRLEY *and*
JEAN. *All exhausted.*

BERNARD: Did you ever get 14 across?

BETTY: No. I think it's an anagram.

> (TERRY *starts the engine, and* JEAN *starts crying.* TERRY *hears her, and swivels round, apprehensively*.)

TERRY: What's happened?

SHIRLEY: (*Drily*) Nothing.

> (*The car drives off,* JEAN *sobbing her heart out*.)

INT. JOE'S LIVING ROOM. EVENING

JOE *and* NANCY *are seated at the table, finishing their kippers.*

NANCY: You had a nice day out, then?

JOE: Well, it's a feller's *life*, isn't it? His job? (*Pause.*) Nice to be home, mind you.

> (*He sits sipping his tea, contentedly, confidently. He's now completely convinced himself that his scene was perfectly done.*)

I'll have to find out when it's on. We'll go round to our Gordon's. Watch it in colour.

INT. CAMERA CAR ON SUBURBAN LOCATION STREET. EVENING

DON *and* GEOFF *get in* (DON *at the wheel*). PHIL *is already hunched up on the back seat, fighting imminent, overwhelming sleep.*

PHIL: I'm going to cut the Old Man in Street completely. Scrub it altogether.

GEOFF: (*Puzzled*) I thought you said it was crucial?

PHIL: (*Very, very sleepy*) We'll put the same information in another scene. In reported speech. No Old Man in Street.

GEOFF: But isn't it the writer's intention to – ?

PHIL: (*Opening one eye*) *Whose* intention?

GEOFF: (*Sorry he's ever started*) The writer's . . .

PHIL: What's it got to do with the writer?

GEOFF: (*Very sorry he's ever started*) Um . . . well, he *wrote* it.

PHIL: (*To* DON) Is that heater working?

> (DON *starts the engine*.)

DON: (*Wearily*) I may go and see *The Sting* on Saturday.

GEOFF: I thought you were going fishing?

DON: I get sick of fishing.

> (*The car drives off*.)

EXT. CAMERA CAR. EVENING

As it drives away from us . . .

PHIL: (*Voice over*) There's nothing at the end of it all, anyway, is there?

DON: (*Voice over*) Not a lot.

(*Slight pause.*)

GEOFF: (*Voice over, confused*) At the end of *what*?

(*We stay on the newly painted wall, as the car drives off out of frame. After a moment, a stray dog comes sniffing along, stops at the wall and and sniffs the fresh paintwork. It cocks its leg — and pees on it.*)